O

Jovian smile... ...to kiss her full on the lips. She was ha... ...are of the storm that now began to rage overhead. All she knew was that his kiss thrilled through her like a charge, as if her body had absorbed the lightning. His lips moved slowly and luxuriously over hers in the skilled kiss of a man of experience, but at the same time it was innocent too, as if this was the first kiss that had ever mattered to him. Every heartbeat, every fraction of breath, every caress came from the soul, and there was no room left for doubting his motives. Love was what urged him, what urged them both. . . .

"We flew, my darling, we flew," he averred softly, and bent his head to kiss her again.

"Will we fly again?" she asked as the kiss ended.

"Oh, yes," he breathed. "I promise you."

Lavender Blue

Sandra Heath

A SIGNET BOOK

SIGNET
Published by New American Library, a division of
Penguin Putnam Inc., 375 Hudson Street,
New York, New York 10014, U.S.A.
Penguin Books Ltd, 80 Strand,
London WC2R 0RL, England
Penguin Books Australia Ltd, 250 Camberwell Road,
Camberwell, Victoria 3124, Australia
Penguin Books Canada Ltd, 10 Alcorn Avenue,
Toronto, Ontario, Canada M4V 3B2
Penguin Books (N.Z.) Ltd, Cnr Rosedale and Airborne Roads,
Albany, Auckland 1310, New Zealand

Penguin Books Ltd, Registered Offices:
Harmondsworth, Middlesex, England

First published by Signet, an imprint of New American Library,
a division of Penguin Putnam Inc.

First Printing, April 2003
10   9   8   7   6   5   4   3   2   1

For my dear friend Kelly Ferjutz

One

"*I* cannot believe it! Papa has remarried without so much as a word to us! Oh, Aunt Letty, how could he do such a thing?"

Lady Anthea Wintour stared dumbfoundedly at the letter that had just arrived from Ireland. Her father, the Earl of Daneway, was staying in County Fermanagh with Lord Lisnerne, an old friend from Oxford days, and Anthea had opened the letter in the full expectation of finding more rambling reminiscences of their riotous youth. Instead there was the astonishing news that she had acquired a stepmother.

All sound seemed suddenly deadened outside the second-floor window of Daneway House. It was the end of October 1813, and sunny Berkeley Square was bright with the hues of autumn, with no hint yet of the bitterly cold winter that was to come.

The absent earl's unmarried sister, Lady Letitia Wintour, was so shocked by the announcement that the heavy volume of Culpeper's *Complete Herbal* slid from her lap and landed with a thud on the drawing room floor. She was in her favorite armchair, and her face was rosy from the fire. "Don't tease so, Anthea, for you know my heart is weak!" she exclaimed.

"I'm not teasing, Aunt Letty. He writes that a month ago he married a Mrs. Pranton."

Lady Letitia was thunderstruck. "But who is she?" she asked; then a dread possibility struck. "A lady, I trust?"

"Well . . ." Anthea hesitated. "To be honest, I have no idea. All the letter says is that she was governess to the children of Lord Lisnerne's neighbors."

"A *governess*?" Appalled, Lady Letitia got up from her chair. She was a short, rather dumpy woman of fifty, with kindly light blue eyes, and salt-and-pepper hair that was tucked up beneath a lacy day bonnet. A bright pink-and-cream paisley shawl rested around the shoulders of her indigo merino gown, and there was a pair of spectacles perched on the end of her snub nose. She had always been far too absorbed in the delights of botany to surrender her precious time to matters matrimonial. At least that was what she said, but Anthea strongly suspected a great love affair that had long been a deeply buried secret.

Lady Letitia went to the window to look down into the Mayfair square. Elegant carriages were drawn up beneath the plane trees opposite Gunter's, the exclusive confectioner whose premises were only two doors away from Daneway House. The mildness of the autumn had prolonged the fashion for ladies to sample iced creams brought out to them by attentive gentlemen. A Union Jack fluttered from Thomas's Hotel in the northeastern corner of the square, and a military band played on nearby Berkeley Street. There was an air of excitement in the capital because the French star was now waning after years of warmongering throughout Europe. Napoleon had clearly lost his touch, for only a week ago word had reached England that he had lost the protracted battle of Leipzig. At long last there was a chance of enduring peace.

But right now, such things took second place in Lady Letitia's thoughts. "One can only hope that the old cradle will not have to be brought down from the attic embarrassingly soon after the nuptials," she murmured.

"Oh, surely not, Aunt Letty!" Anthea was aghast.

"Well, it has to be considered, my dear. Men will always

be men, and governesses will, I fear, always be eager to sink their claws into wealth and titles." Lady Letitia pursed her lips. "One wonders what Lisnerne thinks about it all."

"From what Papa writes, it seems he approves."

"Really?" Lady Letitia's mind turned to something else. "You know, Anthea, the more I think of it, the more familiar the name Pranton seems, yet, for the life of me, I cannot think where I have heard it before."

"It means nothing to me," Anthea replied.

"I'm sure I will recall in due course." Lady Letitia continued to look down into the square, where several people strolled the gravel walks in the central garden. An ugly lead equestrian statue of King George dressed as Marcus Aurelius presided in the middle. No one liked the statue, including a little white terrier that was being taken out for an airing by a footman in maroon-and-gold livery. The terrier was no respecter of royalty, for it cocked its leg against His Majesty's plinth, leaving a clearly discernible puddle. Being guilty of such an insult was of no concern to the little dog as it trotted on, pulling impatiently at the lead.

A roll of thunder suddenly rumbled improbably overhead. How could that possibly be when the skies were blue and cloudless? Puzzled, Lady Letitia craned her neck to look up, for such a flawless heaven was not at all what one associated with thunder. How very, very odd.

Anthea heard it too. "Good heavens, was that thunder?"

"So it would seem, my dear, although how and why I really do not know. The weather is perfect." Lady Letitia sighed. "Ah, well, no doubt stranger things have happened at sea."

"No doubt."

Lady Letitia's attention returned to the central garden as something in the far corner so excited the terrier that it began to yap furiously and strain at the lead. She screwed her eyes up shortsightedly to see what was there and perceived a brown animal on the grass in front of a privet hedge. It did not seem like another dog, or indeed like a cat, but at that particular size, Lady Letitia could not think what else it could be. Suddenly it pricked up its ears . . . such long ears that it looked more like a hare than anything else. Oh, that was ridiculous. *Lepus capensis* was a country creature through and through and was simply not found in the middle of Mayfair.

As she watched, the terrier broke free of the footman's grasp and hurtled toward the brown creature, which leapt up in the air with an audible shriek and fled behind the hedge with the diminutive dog in hot pursuit. There was no mistaking the long-legged gait and bobbing white scut of *lepus capensis,* Lady Letitia thought in astonishment. A commotion erupted beyond the close-clipped privet. Had the terrier actually managed to catch the hare? But no—suddenly a woman in pale chestnut silk clothes appeared from behind the hedge and hurried out of the garden for all she was worth, with the terrier in hot pursuit.

Where the woman had come from, Lady Letitia could not imagine, for there hadn't been anyone there a few moments before. Now, however, the unfortunate woman had to hold on to her velvet bonnet and pick up all the speed she could in order to elude her four-legged pursuer. The footman ran after them both, and the comical chase soon disappeared beyond Thomas's Hotel, cheered on by an impudent group of street boys idling on the corner.

Lady Letitia was quite bemused for a few moments, but then remembered the astounding news from Fermanagh. She glanced back at her niece. "Read the letter to me, there's a good girl," she said.

Anthea cleared her throat.

> *Castle Lisnerne, County Fermanagh.*
> *September the twenty-ninth, eighteen thirteen.*
> *My dearest daughter, I have something to tell you that makes me happier than you can imagine, and that I hope will make you happy too. It is this,*

*pure and simple: I am married again. The lady's
name is Mrs. Pranton, and she is English but has
lived here in Ireland for a long time now. Her
husband was a naval officer, but sadly he passed
away in 1795 within days of their marriage. She
was left in dire pecuniary circumstances and was
obliged to take employment as a governess. Her
name is Chloe—yes, my darling child, by a strange
coincidence she bears your second name, which is
doubly precious to me now.*

*We met a few months ago when her then
employers, Lisnerne's neighbors and friends Sir
Montague and Lady Fisher, visited the castle. They
brought their children, who were in the care of their
governess. Chloe captivated me from the outset.
Believe me when I say that she is the most
delightful person, with no artfulness or secret
designs, and that Lisnerne is more than glad to
accept her as Lady Daneway.*

*Darling daughter, please know that this new
marriage makes no difference to the regard and
enduring love I will always have for your dear
mother, for whom I have grieved ever since the
influenza took her back in '04. Ten years is a long
time to be on one's own, and I knew from the
moment I met my golden-haired, green-eyed
governess that I would be lonely no more. She is the
perfect wife for me, and I will, as I trust, be the
perfect husband to her. We intend to return to
London in the New Year. Be happy for us. Your
loving father.*

Lady Letitia was silent. If she had hoped for misapprehension on Anthea's part, the hope was now dashed.

Anthea folded the letter. "There is a postscript informing

me that I now have an eighteen-year-old stepsister called Corinna."

"Anthea, Chloe, Corinna? How very classical and Greek, to be sure."

"Mm? Yes, I suppose you're right, except these new ladies and I are very definitely English."

"Mrs. Pranton may be English, but if she was forced to become a governess, she is unlikely to be from a good family. Good families look after their own." Disapproval was evident in Lady Letitia's tone.

"Well, even good families can have their bad sides, Aunt Letty, and it is possible for anyone to fall on hard times. Besides, whatever she was before, she is Lady Daneway now, not Mrs. Pranton." *And she has very definitely married into money and a family that is good in every way.* Anthea was immediately ashamed of such arrogant and superior sentiments. Her father was not a fool and would not be taken in by an adventuress. At least, his only daughter did not think he would.

Lady Letitia pursed her lips. "Regarding my remark about the cradle, let us consider the possibility of a baby. If Mrs. Pranton has a daughter of eighteen, I imagine she must be in her middle to late thirties. At that age she is certainly not beyond more children. Not that I am seriously suggesting she was with child when she uttered her vows."

"You think Papa desires a son and heir?" Anthea looked at her.

"He has never said so to me, but it has to be faced that when he dies the Daneway title dies too."

"I'm sure that if he felt that way, he would have married before now. But there is no point in wondering anything at the moment, for all will be revealed when they return to London." Anthea got up to cross the elegant lemon, white, and gold drawing room to look at her father's portrait in the alcove by the gilded harpsichord. It had been painted some twenty-five years ago, not long after her birth, and was of a dark-haired young man leaning nonchalantly against a tree with a black-

and-white spaniel at his feet and a shooting gun over his arm. In the background was the fine Palladian facade and gracious park of Daneway Park, the family's country seat in Yorkshire.

Lady Letitia watched her only niece fondly. Anthea was slender and willowy in a long-sleeved lavender merino gown that had a golden belt around the high waist. She was a true Wintour, thought her aunt, with a pale complexion, thick black curls, and wide set blue eyes that were almost the same shade of lavender as her gown. How very perplexing that such a highborn, good-looking heiress remained stubbornly unmarried. A lack of offers was not the problem; it was just that foolish Anthea had turned them all down.

It did not occur to Lady Letitia that there was a certain irony about her judgment of her niece, for a middle-aged lady who had steadfastly refused to consider marriage herself was hardly in a position to approve or disapprove of her niece's similar decision. Yet disapprove Lady Letitia did, for in her opinion, Anthea was meant to be married. Only a year ago the ideal husband had been eagerly at hand, but unfortunately his suitability had been suddenly called into serious question.

Lady Letitia lowered her eyes sadly. Jovian Cathness, twelfth Duke of Chavanage, who happened to be Lord Lisnerne's nephew, had not long ago been the most attractive and eligible aristocrat in Society, with charm, wit, character, and poise enough to coax the very birds from the trees. Now, he had sunk into such a haze of alcohol that he was seldom sober. Heaven alone knew what had overtaken him this past twelvemonth, for he was a shadow of his former self, and the inexplicable decline had seemed to happen overnight. As had the breaking of Anthea's heart.

It wasn't as if a sudden bereavement had driven him to drown unbearable sorrows, or even that he had always been a drinker and simply succumbed completely to his lurking demon. There seemed no discernible reason why he suddenly chose to be unpleasantly bosky all the time. And it *was* choice, Lady Letitia thought tartly, for no one forced the glass to his unwilling lips.

She felt a stab of guilt for judging him so harshly; after all she had once liked him so very much that no one could have pleased her more as Anthea's husband. But he was a different man now. It had to be said that there had always been something otherworldly and intensely intuitive about him, so much so that he was the only person in the world she would swear possessed a sixth sense.

In the last year, some highly improbable stories had begun to circulate about him as well, such as that one night, while particularly intoxicated, he had been seen to *fly* to the upper windows of his town house near St. James's Palace. On another occasion, he was credited with the power to make a wine bottle slide across the table to his waiting hand. It was all nonsense of course. . . . "Yes, of course it is, Letty Wintour," she muttered, afraid of being supposed away with the fairies herself for even considering such whispers.

Anthea left her father's portrait and went to sit at the harpsichord. She began to play the old song "Lavender Blue," and Lady Letitia smiled. "Why, I haven't heard that tune in a long, long time, my dear; yet, it is such a pretty little tune." She sang some of the words.

> *"Lavender blue, dilly, dilly,*
> *Lavender green.*
> *When I am king, dilly, dilly,*
> *You shall be queen."*

Anthea finished playing, then clasped her hands in her lap. "I suddenly had the urge to play that. Heaven knows why it came into my head."

The fragrance of lavender seemed to drift into the room, as fresh and vital as if it were June, not October.

Two

*D*ecember was very cold indeed, with a constant frost and plunging temperatures that made any excursion out of doors an ordeal. Nevertheless on Christmas Eve afternoon Anthea braved the weather for a walk around the square. Icicles hung from eaves and from the plane trees, and every twig and blade of grass in the central garden was encrusted with white, but although it looked very beautiful, the bitter chill soon seeped through her several layers of clothing. A freezing fog seemed about to close in, and the harsh grip of this atrocious winter was already so deeply entrenched that Anthea was sure it would not relent before spring.

She pulled her crimson, fur-lined cloak more tightly around her, thinking she must have been mad to take a constitutional on a day like this. How much more sensible to have remained in the drawing room with Aunt Letty and the delicious hot chocolate that was always served about now. But the need to stretch her legs and feel fresh air in her lungs had been overwhelming after being indoors for days because of the cold.

A carriage passed her and drew up before a nearby house. Two half-frozen footmen climbed down from the back of the vehicle and rubbed their numb hands before opening the carriage door for a lady and her three excited children to alight after a final shopping expedition. As mother and offspring hurried into the bright warmth of the house, the footmen, complaining under their silvery breaths, began to unload the many festive purchases.

The afternoon light was beginning to fade, and the windows of the house were brightly lit, revealing lavish Christmas greenery and other decorations inside. There was a handsome kissing bough from which Anthea had to look quickly away because of the painful memories it aroused, for the last kiss she and Jovian had shared had been beneath just such a ball of mistletoe and red ribbons. Looking away from the house meant that she looked at the central garden instead, and in particular at the vilified statue of King George in the guise of Roman emperor. Oh, it was such an *ugly* object, a true eyesore in the heart of an otherwise gracious and beautiful square.

Then something blue caught her attention on the gravel at the base of the plinth. It was a ribbon tied around what looked like a bouquet of lavender. Not dried but fresh blue flowers with peppermint green stems and spiky leaves. Anthea was astonished to see such an incongruous reminder of summer on a winter day like this. And why was such a lovely bouquet simply lying there on the ground?

Intrigued, she went across to take a closer look. The lavender was the same color as her eyes, and she felt an odd affinity with the seemingly abandoned flowers. Slowly she bent to pick them up and breathed deeply of the invigorating scent. The pretty ribbon brushed her cheeks, like the loving touch of invisible fingers; like Jovian's fingers . . . As the thought occurred to her, his voice suddenly sang softly from the other side of the statue.

> *"Lavender blue, dilly, dilly,*
> *Lavender green.*
> *When I am king, dilly, dilly,*
> *You shall be queen."*

Then she heard steps, as he came around to where she stood. He was elegantly dressed in an ankle-length indigo woolen greatcoat over a sky coat and white pantaloons, and his expressive gray eyes were penetrating in the encroaching haze of fading winter light. He was thirty years old, tall, blond, and well made, with a ruggedly handsome face that had been described as the epitome of truly masculine beauty. It was also a strong face, from the dimple in his chin and smile, to the firm set of his mouth and the arresting quality of his eyes. Everything about him was enviably attractive, and he would still have been the most perfect of men were it not for his inability to resist alcohol.

He removed his top hat and bowed, his thick fair hair falling forward in that slightly unruly way she had always liked so much. "Good afternoon, Anthea," he said softly, his breath white in the incredible cold. Then his smile once again worked its magic on her foolish heart.

"Good afternoon, Duke," she said stiffly, afraid that he might see through her guard to the vulnerable creature within. She also feared he would sense the aching desire that continued in spite of his odiousness when drunk.

He raised an eyebrow. "Such formality? Am I no longer to be Jovian?"

"I hardly think it is appropriate, do you?"

"Why not? I still feel the same way about you."

She drew back. "Well, such sentiments are not mutual, especially at Christmas."

He had the grace to look remorseful. "I know I hurt you that Christmas, Anthea, but—"

"You were a monster, as every holly garland and every carol remind me."

"So you will not accept my posy of *lavendula vera*?" He sought to change the mood by teasing her with Lady Letitia's penchant for Latin names.

"*Your* posy?"

"Yes." ·

"But—"

"But what?" he inquired.

"Where did you get it?"

"A lavender field at Cathness, of course."

She stared at him, then at the lavender. "A *field*? Oh, come now!" she said incredulously, not realizing until then that deep down she imagined the shrub had been grown under glass.

"A field is where it came from, and I picked it only yesterday."

Annoyance now began to crease her brow. "That is nonsense, and you know it."

He seemed amused. "As you wish," he murmured.

"Besides, lavender field or not, I was under the impression you had been in London since the middle of November."

He glanced away. "Perchance the ribbon tied itself, and the posy flew of its own accord."

Anthea studied his matchless profile. "From all accounts the only thing that flies of its own accord is you, sir."

"Don't tell me you believe such tales?" There was mockery in his tone as he looked at her again.

She didn't answer, for unlike Aunt Letty she could not entirely discount the rumors. How could she, when to be with him was occasionally to suspect the closeness of another world, a place of magic and the supernatural, of spells and wonderful powers?

"Tut, tut, Anthea." He wagged a gloved finger sternly. "How can you, one of the most sensible and practical young ladies in London, actually admit to thinking I can fly? I leave that to gentlemen who imbibe far too much after-dinner port."

His words almost made her start, as for the first time she realized he was quite sober. There was no alcohol on his breath or slow mumble in his voice. But even so, she could not help her next words. "Too much after-dinner port? Well, you would know all about that."

"Is that what you think?"

"It's what I know, and the fact that for once you appear to be unfuddled by drink makes no difference. So if you are intent upon humbugging me that you now eschew all things alcoholic, please do not insult my intelligence."

His eyes arrested hers. "Anthea, I have never voluntarily taken more than a drink or two."

Her anger ignited. "A drink or two? Jovian, it's a miracle you are apparently sober today!"

"Well, at least I am Jovian again, if only so that you may insult me more. And to think that I was gallantly intent not only upon presenting you with lavender but also congratulating you."

"Congratulating me?"

"Upon your new stepmother."

She stared. "How did you—? Oh, of course—I was forgetting that Lord Lisnerne is your uncle. Your mother's brother, I believe."

"Indeed so, and he is very fond of me, whether or not I am pickled." He gave a light, infectious laugh that brought tears to her eyes.

"Why did you have to change so?" she whispered. "Why did you have to become so despicable most of the time that I cannot even respect you now, let alone love you?"

His laughter died away, and he reached out toward her. "Oh, Anthea, my dearest, darling—" He broke off as thunder rattled overhead.

Startled, Anthea looked up. Thunder? On a December day that would surely be acceptable at the North Pole?

Jovian glanced urgently all around the garden, clearly expecting to see something, and then his gaze fixed upon the low box hedge where a hare crouched on the frost white winter grass. It was watching them, as if eavesdropping. "Damn you," Jovian breathed, his gray eyes almost as cold as the winter as he regarded the wild creature.

"Jovian, it's only a hare!" Anthea said, puzzled by his reaction. But then, to her utter amazement, the hare stood up on its hind legs, drew its mouth back, and bared its teeth as if laughing at Jovian, who hurled a handful of gravel at it. After shaking its scut in a very insulting manner, the hare loped away behind the hedge, leaving paw prints in the frost.

As Anthea was doubting the evidence of her own eyes, it occurred to her that it was unusual to have seen a hare in the capital at all, even in the garden of spacious Berkeley Square. She turned to Jovian, but he spoke first. "Beware, Anthea, for things might soon happen that are far, far beyond your experience."

"What do you mean?" she asked a little fearfully, for there was a note in his voice that commanded belief.

"I pray that you need never know," he said, then looked suddenly past her, as if seeing something there. She turned instinctively to look, but all she saw was the gray half tones of the gathering fog. When she looked at Jovian again, he had gone.

A pang of deep unease chilled her heart, for she had not heard his steps upon the gravel; indeed, there had been no sound at all to signal his sudden departure. What was she to think? That he had . . . flown away?

She called his name, but there was no response. Suddenly the garden seemed a very strange place, especially as the fog had now closed in sufficiently to veil the surrounding houses. Her unease increased sharply, and with a shiver that was not only due to the cold, she hurried from the garden. On reaching the pavement her footsteps echoed through the chilling vapor, but she was sure other footsteps were following. Jovian? She halted hopefully by the wrought iron railings that fronted all the houses in the square.

"Jovian? Is that you?" But no one replied, and as the fog eddied, the following footsteps continued to draw closer.

Fearful of footpads, Anthea drew beneath the lantern arch of the houses, then pressed back by the door and kept very still as the footsteps grew louder. She held her breath as a figure emerged from the fog. To her relief it wasn't a footpad but a brown-cloaked woman of about forty. Relief quickly yielded to puzzled surprise as the woman, whom she did not know at all, directed at her an unmistakably hostile glance, then disappeared into the fog toward Berkeley Street.

Anthea was confounded. She did not know the woman at all yet had been subjected to a look of such antagonism that they might as well have been sworn enemies. The woman must have taken her for someone else. Yes, that had to be the explanation.

Gathering up her cloak, Anthea hurried on to Daneway House, where Aunt Letty had become so anxious about her that footmen were about to be dispatched to search.

Three

January 1814 found Napoleon in retreat and most of Britain and Europe still in the relentless grip of the worst winter in living memory, putting to shame even 1795, which was referred to as the famine year. Deep snow had now fallen too, and the Thames was covered with ice so thick that it supported a makeshift fair to which thousands of people had resorted.

At first Jovian's enigmatic warning by the statue had remained in Anthea's head, but as the days passed and nothing happened, she began to believe him to have been in drink after all that day, just concealing it well. She did not see him again, and by the time the lavender in the vase in her bedroom was past its best, she had all but forgotten what he'd said, although occasionally his words would cross her mind. *"Beware, Anthea, for things might soon happen that are far, far beyond your experience."*

One particularly cold afternoon, she and her aunt were once again seated in the warm drawing room when another letter arrived from Ireland. Anthea's heart sank as she saw that it was black edged. Oh, no! Papa?

Lady Letitia saw, too, and sat forward in dismay, but then Anthea saw that the letter was in her father's hand. "Be easy, Aunt Letty; it cannot be Papa for he has written it."

Lady Letitia had gone quite pale but now breathed out a

sigh of relief. "Oh, thank heaven, thank heaven!" Then her brows drew together. "Then it must be Lisnerne, I suppose."

Anthea thought the same as she broke the seal, but when she read the brief lines, she found it was not Jovian's uncle either. "Mrs. Pranton has passed away," she said haltingly. "At least—I mean—Papa's new wife . . . er, Lady Daneway, has passed away."

Lady Letitia's hand crept to her throat. "Lord preserve us," she whispered. "What happened?"

"She died unexpectedly in her sleep."

Lady Letitia stared. "She must have been very ill."

"Not that it was realized at the time, but the doctor now supposes it to have been a frail heart."

"Oh, my poor dear brother . . . Is he coming home?"

"No. He is so distressed that Lord Lisnerne has persuaded him that the only possible diversion is a long-discussed expedition to Brazil. Up the Amazon, to be precise. They plan to leave in April, and Papa will not return here beforehand."

Lady Letitia stared at her. "The Amazon? Well, I daresay it will give them both something else to think about. Such as caimans, flesh-eating fish, and boa restrictors."

"Boa constrictors," Anthea corrected gently.

"Mm? Well, whatever one calls them, delightful feather fashion accessories they are not. I would much prefer him to simply come home, instead of wandering off across the world. But grief takes us all in different ways, I suppose. When I—" Lady Letitia didn't finish, and busied herself quickly with the notes she was making from Culpeper.

Anthea looked quizzically at her. "When you what, Aunt Letty?"

"It doesn't matter, my dear."

Anthea did not pry further, but was once again prompted to suspect a sad love affair. Had Aunt Letty's sweetheart died? It would seem so from the tears that were now being blinked away.

Lady Letitia dabbed her eyes in a way she imagined was

surreptitious enough not to be noticed, then spoke again. "Your father has always wanted to explore the Amazon river. As a boy he was quite home loving, but from the moment he was sent on his Grand Tour he became a veritable Egyptian."

"Egyptian?" Anthea was perplexed.

"Gypsy," Lady Letty rephrased herself. "Does the letter say anything else?"

"Well, the most important thing as far as you and I are concerned is that my new stepsister, Corinna, is to come here to be with us."

"Oh. Well, I daresay the Amazon is hardly the place for young slips of things. If she is to be with us, I suppose we will have to wear mourning, even though we never met her mother."

Anthea nodded. "Full black, I should imagine. Well, for a time anyway." She glanced at the letter again, and for the first time noticed another sentence written in haste at the very bottom. "Oh, one moment, Papa mentions mourning here. He says we are not to wear black, or even gray. It seems the late countess loathed mourning, and Corinna has not worn so much as a black ribbon, so we must not, either."

"I have to say I agree about mourning, which is becoming a most onerous custom." Lady Letitia sat back in her chair. "That is that, then. Now we will never know what Mrs. Pranton was like."

"Lady Daneway," Anthea corrected automatically.

"Oh, yes. Lady Daneway," her aunt murmured sadly. "Still, we *will* meet Corinna."

"Yes." Anthea lowered her eyes sadly. "Poor Papa, he is destined to remain lonely after all."

In sunny late April, with the ferocious winter over at last and the defeated tyrant Napoleon on his way to exile on Elba, eighteen-year-old Corinna Pranton walked across the park at Castle Lisnerne toward island-dotted Lough Erne as it sparkled beneath the cloudless County Fermanagh sky. Tomorrow her new stepfather would leave for far-off Brazil with Lord Lisnerne, and later today, under the protection of her mother's former employer, Lady Fisher, she would commence her journey to England. It was the country of her birth, although she could not remember it at all.

Anthea's new stepsister was golden haired and beautiful, with green eyes to match the emerald countryside around her. Corinna turned heads wherever she went, but in her innocence hardly noticed anyone. She was being as brave as she could without her mother, whose sudden demise had left her quite bereft. Death had come from nowhere, for there had seemed nothing wrong the evening before, but come the next morning, she was cold in the bed beside her adoring new husband. The earl's grief had matched Corinna's, and he had gladly seized upon Lord Lisnerne's suggestion of Brazil. There was no such escape for Corinna, who now had to confront two ladies who might not feel at all like welcoming her into their household.

It had not seemed possible that the Earl of Daneway could in so short a time have made Corinna feel he really cared about her, but he had, and she loved him for it. She wished he would first come to London with her, instead of going so far away, but so intense was his anguish over the loss of her mother that he could not quit these shores fast enough.

On a day like today, however, with daffodils and creamy narcissi nodding among silver birches along the lake shore, Corinna found it a little easier to face her new future. She hummed "Lavender Blue" to herself as she walked. Her mother had often sung it to her when she was small, and it had remained a favorite ever since.

Corinna enjoyed the warmth of the spring sun on her face, and the scent of the flowers was so enticing that she bent to pick a particularly fine double-headed narcissus. But an Englishman's voice made her straighten guiltily.

"What's this? A fair flower thief?"

On a track nearby she saw a dashing gentleman in a yellow

phaeton that was drawn by black horses. He was dressed in the finest that London tailoring could provide and was tall and handsome, with dark hair, flashing eyes, and the sort of roguish smile that banished her embarrassment. How could he have driven up without her hearing? Was he a friend of Lord Lisnerne's?

He jumped lightly down from the phaeton, made the reins fast to a birch branch, then came over. Bending, he picked the narcissus for her. "It may not be lavender, and I may not be a king, but if I were, you would certainly be my queen," he said engagingly, as he held the flower out to her. "Take it. Allow me to be the despoiler of this beautiful corner of nature's garden."

Corinna gazed shyly into his eyes and unwisely accepted the bloom, even though she knew it was wrong to have anything to do with a stranger. A fragrant narcissus was what she perceived; yet in reality it was a sprig of mistletoe. The darkhaired, dark-eyed stranger had given her the mystical golden bough that marked the beginning of her beguilement, and from that moment, she was in the utmost peril.

Four

June came, and as London gave joyful thanks for peace, Britain's allies, Czar Alexander of Russia and King Frederick William of Prussia, paid state visits that gave considerable extra prestige to the festivities.

Corinna was now in residence at Berkeley Square, and she and Anthea were tentatively feeling their way toward a sisterly relationship. It was not easy for either of them, but their shared love for the absent earl ensured their best efforts. Not that Anthea found it difficult to warm to Corinna; indeed, within a week of that young lady's arrival at Berkeley Square, Anthea decided that if she was anything like her mother, it was easy to understand why the governess had become Countess of Daneway.

On first coming to Berkeley Square, Corinna had been so nervous she spoke only in monosyllables, but gradually, as Anthea strove to make her feel welcome, the new addition to the family began to relax and be herself. The loss of her much loved mother still lay heavily over her, but as the days passed and spring changed to summer, she began to come to terms with what had happened.

Lady Letitia approved greatly of her new charge, who had been very well brought up. Whatever the late countess's background, she had certainly seen to it that her daughter was given every possible advantage. Corinna could speak French,

was adequate in Latin, played nimbly and prettily on the
piano, and was talented at drawing and painting. In short, she
was most unlikely indeed ever to prove an embarrassment,
and her beauty inclined Lady Letitia to hope she might make
a very good match.

Her ladyship's eye soon settled upon sandy-haired, hazel-
eyed Viscount Heversham, who, although not the most handsome or prominent fellow in London, was certainly wealthy
and in need of just such a wife as Corinna. A match would be
the making of both of them, Anthea's aunt decided, her
matchmaking urges moving effortlessly from trot to canter.
Lady Letitia was in her element when it came to plotting other
people's romances. Anthea had proved a grave disappoint-
ment to her in that respect, so Corinna was an unexpected but
very welcome boon.

Corinna received a few social invitations from those of
Lady Letitia's friends who knew of her existence, but it was
decided she would not accept any of them this Season. Lady
Letitia considered it best that she should use her first summer
to settle into her new and very different life, and then come out
formally the following year. The only time Corinna met members of Society was when Lady Letitia gave a private dinner
party at Daneway House, to which young Viscount Heversham
was occasionally invited, of course. It was a gentle and sensitive introduction to the high society of which Corinna was
now bound to become a part, and Lady Letitia was gratified to
see several shy smiles secretly exchanged between the two
young persons she had decided were an ideal bride and groom.

So Corinna drove out with Anthea and Lady Letitia and
went shopping with them. She visited art galleries, attended
the theater in their private box, and accompanied Anthea on
long walks around Mayfair and in Hyde Park, but her name
did not figure among the guests at any grand balls or other
such occasions. Lady Letitia noted with some satisfaction that
she often mentioned Viscount Heversham. It boded well.

Anthea and Corinna talked a lot, especially during their

lengthy perambulations, but when the subject of Corinna's background was raised, there was very little she could actually tell. She did not know her father at all, for he had died before she was born, and her mother had refused to discuss any other family that might still be here in England, except to say she had had a twin sister who had died. It seemed Chloe Pranton came originally from the West Country, but for some reason she had fled to Ireland taking her newborn baby with her. Talk of a father who died before his daughter's birth and a mother's unexplained flight from England led Anthea to wonder if there was a scandal attached to the tale. Maybe Chloe had not been married at all and had gone to Ireland to escape gossip and start again. Not that such a possibility was put to Corinna, of course, or indeed to Lady Letitia. Anthea kept her thoughts strictly to herself.

Corinna admitted to wanting to know more about her roots but did not know how to go about it. "The West Country" was generally accepted to mean the area from the farthermost tip of Cornwall to the eastern boundary of Devon, and then north as far as Gloucestershire. That was a large tract, with many cities and towns, countless villages and hamlets, and myriad farms and cottages. There were also a vast number of country seats, whose masters were certainly not out of the question as Corinna's antecedents, given that Chloe had been able to instruct and educate her daughter to such a high standard.

But family secrets were the last thing on Anthea's and Corinna's minds as they sat on Corinna's bed one fine June morning. The rose-and-white bedroom faced over the square and was elegantly furnished in the Grecian style. It was a handsome chamber that ought to have been Anthea's, but she had always preferred to be at the back of the house, where there was a view over Lady Letitia's beautiful garden of flowers and shrubs, widely noted for their fragrance.

This particular morning Anthea was wearing bluebell-and-white sprigged muslin that went particularly well with her splendid lavender eyes, while Corinna was in ice green lawn. They sprawled undecorously on their elbows on the bed examining a ladies' journal for the latest fashion illustrations. One picture caused particular mirth, because — as Anthea observed — the expression on the lady's face suggested a forced drink of vinegar.

"What a very horrid thought," Corinna laughed.

"Well, if she dined at Lord and Lady Farnborough's, no doubt she would indeed have drunk vinegar, for I have it on the most reliable authority that their wine is little better."

Corinna's green eyes bore a doubting expression. "Is that the truth? Or are you teasing me?"

"It is the truth." Anthea gave her a sly look. "Ask Viscount Heversham next time you see him."

Corinna blushed. "I don't see him any more often than you do."

"No, but his name trips from your lips with much more frequency than it does from mine. Seriously, though, do you really like him, Corinna?"

The blush deepened. "Yes, I do. He's so kind and gentle."

"Yes, he is."

"But if my pulse is supposed to race when he is near, I fear mine doesn't quicken at all." Corinna heaved a long sigh. "I wish it did, because he is *so* agreeable."

Anthea knew all about racing pulses, for Jovian managed to make hers do precisely that even now, after he had ruined everything. But no matter what the situation, Anthea imagined a racing pulse was a prerequisite for a happy match. "Corinna, you do know Aunt Letty has her sights upon a match between you and the viscount, don't you?"

"I could hardly not notice," Corinna replied.

"Would such a match dismay you? Because if so, you ought to warn Aunt Letty now, before her eagerness to matchmake induces her to make an overture to him."

"Well, I like him very much, truly I do, but if I am honest,

I would have to say that he is virtually the only young gentleman I have met since I came here."

"That's true." Anthea broke off, thinking, then added, "Perhaps it would be wise to mention the true state of your feelings anyway. Just to be safe."

"If that's what you think, then of course I will."

Anthea smiled. "Right. Now, what was it we were discussing?"

"Lord and Lady Farnborough's vinegar," Corinna answered.

"Ah, yes. I was about to say that the only person who drinks it without grimacing is the Duke of Chavanage."

"And I suppose he is an elderly, gouty fellow who falls asleep before the desserts?"

Anthea glanced away. "No. As it happens he is young and extraordinarily handsome."

"Really? Oh, do tell." Corinna rolled over onto her back and looked quizzically at her.

"There is nothing to tell."

"Yes, there is. I can tell by your face. Are you in love with him?"

"No, certainly not! His Grace of Chavanage is constantly inebriated, and only a fool would continue to love him." Anthea got up from the bed, wishing her cheeks hadn't suddenly flushed even more than Corinna's.

"Continue to love him? So you did love him once?"

Anthea went to the fireplace, where a bowl of honeysuckle stood among the garniture of blue-and-white Chinese vases. Lady Letitia had picked the blooms especially for Corinna, who had greatly impressed her by knowing the plant's Latin name, *lonicera periclymenum*. Anthea ran a hand along the mantel, her fingertips stroking the carved white marble as she considered her answer. "Yes, I loved Jovian with all my heart, but then he commenced his drinking. There is nothing more disgusting than a drunkard, whether he be a common man or the highest in the land."

"Why did he change? Did some great tragedy ruin his life?"

Anthea smiled again, her glance moving to the beautifully bound volume of *Sense and Sensibility* that lay on the little table beside Corinna's bed. "You read too many novels, Miss Pranton," she chided fondly.

"And you do not read enough, Lady Anthea," came the prompt reply.

Noticing something between the pages, Anthea opened the book to see what it was. To her surprise, she found a pressed sprig of mistletoe inside. "Is this yours?" she asked, taking it out.

"I—I think it must be, although I don't recall picking a narcissus."

"A what? Corinna, this isn't a narcissus; it's mistletoe."

Corinna stared at her. "Mistletoe? Don't be silly. I know mistletoe when I see it, and that is most certainly *not* mistletoe."

Anthea did not want to provoke an argument, so she replaced the sprig in the book and said nothing more, but privately she was quite staggered. Corinna was intelligent and well educated, even to the extent of knowing the Latin name for honeysuckle; yet, she mistook mistletoe for a narcissus? It was a mystery.

Corinna sat up a little selfconsciously. "Anthea, I'm rather worried that I can't remember picking or pressing it. Don't you think I am a little young to have such lapses?"

"Papa may have put it there before he and Lord Lisnerne left for Brazil. It is the sort of thing he would do, you know," Anthea replied soothingly, although such an explanation still did not account for Corinna's belief that it was a narcissus.

"I had not thought of that." Corinna's eyes brightened; then she changed the subject. "What shall we do this afternoon? Drive in Hyde Park?"

"I don't think Aunt Letty will allow it. The crowds will be dreadful because of the visiting monarchs."

"Can we drive out to Marylebone then? We could take a glass of lemonade at that pleasure garden Lady Letitia took us to last week."

"Yes, I suppose we could do that."

Corinna smiled and then lay back again with her hands clasped behind her head. She began to hum to herself, and the tune was "Lavender Blue."

Anthea looked at her. "You like that song, don't you?"

"Mm? Yes, I do. My mother used to sing it to me when I was a baby."

"Mine did, too. I hadn't thought of it for ages, but it came back into my head last autumn and seems to have remained there ever since. Sometimes I even wake up with it going through my mind."

The sound of horses came from the square, and Corinna's head turned immediately. She got up and went to look from the window, then smiled over her shoulder at Anthea. "There are two gentlemen riders outside Gunter's who are almost too handsome for words."

Anthea joined her, but her heart sank almost immediately as she saw that one was Jovian. "Well, speak of the devil," she murmured.

"What do you mean?"

"The gentleman on the dappled gray thoroughbred is the Duke of Chavanage."

"Really?" Corinna gazed down at him. "Oh, he *is* good-looking," she breathed.

"Yes, and he is also drunk again, judging by the way he's swaying in the saddle," Anthea remarked in disgust.

Jovian was perfectly turned out in a pine green riding coat, mustard waistcoat, and white breeches. His gleaming boots rivaled many a mirror, and the nonchalant tilt of his top hat was just so. On seeing the two faces peering from the Daneway House window, he doffed his hat to bow to them. It might have been a graceful gesture, had he not been obliged to keep his balance by grabbing the pommel.

Anthea could have wept for him. *Oh, Jovian, Jovian, what has become of you . . . ?*

Five

Corinna pursed her lips as she looked down at the undoubtedly intoxicated Duke of Chavanage. "Hmm. I see what you mean. He *is* in his cups, isn't he?"

"Almost unfailingly," Anthea replied sadly, "and has been this past year or more. Before then . . ."

"Yes?"

"Before then he was incomparable."

Corinna looked thoughtfully at her, then out the window again. "Oh, who is his friend?" she asked with quick attention, as the other gentleman removed his hat and ran his tan-gloved hand through his raven hair.

He was a stranger to Anthea, who knew little of Jovian's more recent circle of friends. A boon companion, she decided disapprovingly, although she had to concede that he seemed as sober as a judge. He was about the same age as Jovian and very good-looking—hence Corinna's surge of interest—and his immaculately tailored riding clothes were the obligatory pine green coat and cream breeches of all gentlemen of the *ton*. Whoever he was, he could not lack a fortune, Anthea thought, for his black Arabian horse must have cost him a good few guineas.

As Anthea gazed down, he suddenly glanced up. She had expected him to notice Corinna's golden-haired loveliness, but to her surprise, she herself was the recipient of his admiring smile.

Corinna was a little stung. "Well, he appears to be your conquest, Anthea. It's not fair, for I do find him attractive. Much more so than—"

"Than Viscount Heversham?"

"Yes." Corinna lowered her eyes a little guiltily. "I feel I ought to have eyes only for the viscount, but when I look at this stranger . . ."

"So, miss, the unfortunate viscount is not the apple of your eye?" Lady Letitia's voice right behind them made them both jump. She had entered the room unnoticed and was standing on tiptoe to peer over their shoulders into the square. "As it happens, I know the name of that particular gentleman. He is Sir Erebus Lethe, a baronet who has been the duke's neighbor this past twelvemonths or so. He bought Wycke Hall, an estate that adjoins Cathness Castle. At least, that is my understanding."

"How do you know him, Aunt Letty?" Anthea asked.

"He sat next to me at dinner last week. Now, where was it? Ah, yes, the Farnboroughs. He is a most charming and entertaining fellow, whose company took my mind off the dreadful wine."

"He is Scottish, I presume?" Anthea said then.

Her aunt looked at her. "What makes you think that?"

"Well, his surname is Leith, and I—"

"Oh, he doesn't spell his name *that* way. It's *L-e-t-h-e*, as in the River of Forgetfulness, and he's definitely English."

Anthea was surprised by such a name. "How very odd to be called after the brother of Chaos and the River of Forgetfulness," she murmured.

Lady Letitia smiled. "I mentioned that to him, and the name Erebus seems a corruption of some ancient German version of Herbert. *Herebeorht*, I believe. He thinks Lethe may indeed have originally been Leith, although he does not know of any connection north of the border."

Corinna sighed. "Whatever his name, he has eyes only for Anthea, not for me."

"I doubt that very much," Anthea replied, a little embarrassed.

"I'm not imagining how he looks at you. Am I, Lady Letitia?"

"You certainly are not, my dear, although much good may it do him when Jovian is at his side."

Anthea's face became hot, and she looked away.

Lady Letitia's face assumed a thoughtful expression as she continued to regard Sir Erebus. "Hmm, I believe I shall send him an invitation to dinner," she said. "If Viscount Heversham is not the one for you, Corinna, mayhap Sir Erebus will soon forget Anthea when confronted by you."

Anthea was offended. "Thank you very much, Aunt Letty. It is pleasing to know that Corinna is Miss Goldilocks, while I am one of the three bears!"

"That is not what I meant, and you know it. You have virtually withdrawn from the Marriage Stakes, Anthea, but Corinna has yet to be guilty of such folly. Sir Erebus is all that is charming and eligible, so I will do my best to see that she meets him properly."

The remarks stung Anthea a little more. "Methinks the pot is calling the kettle black; after all, did you not also withdraw from the Marriage Stakes?"

"You do not know anything about it, miss," Lady Letitia replied tartly.

"I am not a fool, Aunt Letty, and know sufficient to make an informed guess that you were once deeply in love but for some reason could not marry the man concerned. Am I right?"

Now it was Lady Letitia's turn to go red. "That is enough, Anthea."

"My sentiments exactly, when it comes to your pronouncements upon my unmarried state."

Lady Letitia had the grace to look contrite. "Very well, my dear, I promise never to mention it again."

"Then I shall promise likewise," Anthea replied, a little huffily, and turned on her heel to leave the room.

Corinna gazed after her in astonishment. "I had no idea Anthea was so sensitive about the subject of marriage," she murmured.

Lady Letitia nodded down at Jovian. "And there, seated so drunkenly upon that gray horse, you have the reason. You mark my words, Corinna, the headiness of a true love match can be followed by sentiments that are very painful indeed. I know, for my heart was once broken, as Anthea's is now, although for a very different reason. You may gaze upon Sir Erebus and think him all that is exciting and desirable, and maybe he is, but sometimes it is best to settle for someone gentle and steady, like Viscount Heversham. Still, you are not yet quite nineteen, and there is ample time to reflect."

Corinna was nineteen on the last day of July, Lammas Eve. The following day, Lammas itself, was the ancient harvest festival, and it was set to be one such as London had seldom seen before. With the European monarchs gone, the British nation's own peace festivities were to commence, with fireworks, fairs, and all manner of delights in the parks. It was also one hundred years since the House of Hanover had acceded to the throne, so there was much to celebrate, and it was all to take place on the first of August. With so much to look forward to, it was decided that Corinna's birthday should not be too eventful and strenuous.

The warm, cloudless afternoon was spent sailing on the Thames with Lady Letitia's old friend, the Bishop of Fairwells, who hailed from a naval family and prided himself on his skills on a river. He was short, rotund, bald as a coot, and inclined to utter the occasional very unholy oath, in which failing he was matched by the other gentleman in the party, Lord Henley, another of Lady Letitia's many friends. His lordship was tall and thin, with a head of wispy white hair, and thus the very opposite of the bishop, although it wasn't just in appearance that they differed. Lord Henley was a radical Whig, while the bishop was a staunch Tory, and they argued politics whenever they met.

The wrangling commenced from the moment the hired sailing boat left Whitehall Stairs and continued for most of the day thereafter. Nevertheless, the three ladies enjoyed their cruise and the leisurely picnic beneath the willows upstream of the capital. When they made their way home at nightfall the two gentlemen were still at loggerheads. Lady Letitia explained to Corinna that they had always been the same and would probably never change. They throve on continuous conflict and would have hated to be denied the pleasure.

As the last minutes of July ticked slowly away, Corinna lay awake in her bed thinking about the unexpectedly happy birthday she had just enjoyed—the first since her mother's death. She felt a little guilty, yet knew her mother would have wanted her to be happy. Only one thing had spoiled it, and that had been the sight of Viscount Heversham rowing a lovely redheaded lady in a little boat near Vauxhall. He hadn't even glanced at the passing sailing boat and seemed to have eyes only for his beautiful companion, who languished in the stern of the little craft, a vision in yellow muslin twirling a blue parasol.

For Corinna it had been a salutary experience, forcing her to realize that the viscount was not her slave after all. It made her view him in a very different light, but although she tried to picture him now in her mind, all she could see was darkly handsome Sir Erebus Lethe.

The night was hot, and the window had been raised, so the curtains moved gently in the breeze that played across Berkeley Square. A carriage drove past, rattling on the cobbles, and she heard an owl in the plane trees. All seemed peaceful and ordinary, when suddenly she was conscious of a sound that was much nearer to hand—at her bedroom door, to be precise. Puzzled, she leaned up on an elbow and pushed her loose golden hair back from her face. The clock on the mantel began to chime midnight, and at the first stroke the door opened softly. The gentleman she had met by Lough Erne entered. Until that moment she had no memory of him at all, but as he smiled at her now, she not only recalled their previous meeting but recognized him as Sir Erebus.

He was dressed in evening black, with a diamond shining brightly in the folds of his neckcloth. How handsome he was, and how wonderfully exciting. She felt her heartbeat quicken, but strangely she felt no fear, and she stretched a hand out to him as he approached the bed. His warm fingers closed reassuringly over hers as he gazed down at her. "One month from now the nineteen years will have come full circle," he said softly.

"Nineteen years?"

"Your mother sought to keep you from me, but now she has gone, and my path is clear."

"I don't understand."

He put his hand to her cheek. "There is nothing to fear, my sweeting, for you will come to me. I'll be your king, and you'll be my queen."

"As in the lavender song?"

"Yes, as in the song. The lavender is still in bloom, and the wheat stands high. The cycle is turning fast."

"What cycle?"

He didn't answer the question but pressed a pomegranate into her hand. "Eat this when the full moon rises at eight tomorrow morning," he said.

"But—"

"When you see the full moon and its blue shadow, you must eat the pomegranate. The blue image is a portent of the second moon that will come this month, the second moon that signals the ending of the cycle."

"I don't know what all this means, and it frightens me a little," she said in a small voice.

He smiled reassuringly. "You do not need to worry your lovely head, for I will take care of you. For now, though, you will remember nothing of me or this meeting, except the things I have instructed you to do." He bent to put his lips to her forehead.

"But I want to remember you," she breathed.

"And so you shall, but only when it is necessary, as now."

Tears filled her wonderful green eyes. "Will you stay with me now?" she whispered, with no thought of how shockingly improper a question it was. But she was not really herself now, having been overcome by feelings—and a force—she had never known before. She was his to do with as he pleased.

"Stay with you now?" His dark eyes took in the curves of her body beneath the bedclothes. "Believe me, there is nothing I would like more, but you must remain untouched."

He drew back from her, and she reached out desperately to catch his hand. "Are you going?"

"I must."

"Will I see you again soon?"

"Tomorrow night, provided you are still attending the celebrations in St. James's Park."

She nodded quickly. "Oh, yes, the Bishop of Fairwells has secured a private pleasure barge on the lake and is to hold a large dinner party on it when the fireworks display commences."

"Yes, I know, for I will be among the guests, but you will not know we have already met."

Her eyes were warm and filled with longing. "Why must it be like this?"

"Because the cycle cannot be complete unless the mysteries are performed exactly as they always have been." He took a strand of her hair between his fingertips. "You are so perfect that I know I can only succeed in what must be done. Sleep now, and forget me until I next wish you to remember."

Corinna closed her eyes, her fingers tight around the pomegranate, and as she sank into a deep sleep, she was filled with love for Sir Erebus Lethe.

* * *

Lammas Day was traditionally when the gathering of the harvest began, so fine weather was needed; instead it was raining heavily. Out in the countryside the reaping could not begin, but the merrymakers of London were not deterred, and just before eight o'clock in the morning the sound of cheers and cracker fireworks in the square aroused Corinna from her sleep. The day's festivities had already commenced, and other fireworks could be heard across London, even though it was daylight and exceedingly wet.

Corinna lay drowsily in the warm bed, her head devoid of all memory of the night's events. Through the ill-drawn curtains she could see the low gray clouds, and her heart sank as she thought of all the wonderful celebrations that would be ruined by such weather. But then, quite suddenly, there was a break in the endless gray and a glimpse of flawless heavens beyond. Low over the rooftops opposite she saw the pale orb of the full moon. No, she saw *two* moons! One pale and creamy, as always; the other, peeping from behind it, a hazy, spectral blue—lavender blue—that was barely visible against the sun-filled skies above the clouds.

She had never seen such a wonder before, although she knew the old sixteenth-century saying "If they say the moon is blue, We must believe that it is true." Well, it was indeed true, for she was looking at it now. She moved her head slightly in order to see better and felt something hard and round against her cheek. Puzzled, she reached for it. A pomegranate? She was astonished. *Who on earth had put it there?*

When you see the full moon and its blue shadow, you must eat the pomegranate. The instruction entered her head, and without hesitation she sat up and took her reticule from the table by the bed. Inside was a little pair of scissors, which would certainly be needed to pare the fruit's hard rosy-gold skin. She hesitated before cutting into it because she knew the pink juice would run and leave black stains on anything it touched, but she soon dismissed such considerations. She simply had to eat the pomegranate!

Without further ado she cut deep into the skin. The delicious juice ran over her fingers and the bedclothes, but still she kept cutting. At last she had a segment she could eat, and as she sank her teeth into the soft, seed-packed flesh she felt a surge of something she could not have described.

Outside someone began to sing.

> *"Lavender blue, dilly, dilly,*
> *Lavender green.*
> *When I am king, dilly, dilly,*
> *You shall be queen."*

Six

*I*n another bedroom at the back of the house, Anthea had also been awakened by the sound of fireworks. Her window faced east over the garden toward South Bruton Mews and always caught the full glory of the early morning sun, but not on this dismally wet Lammas Day. Directly outside, the rain drummed upon the verandah off her bedroom, to which she had direct access by way of French windows. The sound reminded her of the summer evening in 1812 when she had learned that Jovian reciprocated the secret feelings she had formed for him.

It had happened in the gardens of Carlton House, the Prince Regent's London residence. His Royal Highness had been giving a fête for something or other, the reason escaped her now, and many of the guests had been outside in the gardens because the summer night was oppressively hot and muggy and Carlton House itself stifling. A thunderstorm had been threatening, and everyone wished it would break and bring a little welcome freshness to the air.

Her gown that night was a spangled silver net over white silk, a very light and pretty thing that had been made especially for the occasion, but still she felt uncommonly warm as she crossed the royal gardens. She was going to a secluded bench set in a lanternlit bower of deep pink Apothecary's roses—or *Rosa gallica officinalis*, as Aunt Letty would no doubt say.

Sitting there observing the moths and other night insects fluttering around the colored lanterns, she had thought herself quite alone until suddenly there were voices on the other side of the bower. Unwillingly she found herself eavesdropping on lovers, or rather on a casual encounter the lady wished to turn into something much more. Her name was Mrs. McIntyre, a thirty-five-year-old, chestnut-haired beauty who had a string of liaisons to her name. There was a Mr. McIntyre, but as he also indulged in numerous dalliances, they were evenly matched in the Infidelity Stakes. That night Mrs. McIntyre's sights were set upon none other than Jovian, for whom Anthea had long burned a secret torch of unrequited love.

"Oh, come now, Duke," she heard Mrs. McIntyre tease, "what harm on earth can there be in walking together in the gardens?"

"The harm, Mrs. McIntyre, is that such a walk could be construed as something it is not." There had been no slurring of his voice then, no impatience or slight edge to his temper, just an amiable tone to which no woman could reasonably take offense.

"Perhaps it would be intriguing to let it become the thing it presently fails to be," the lady suggested, in a kittenish tone.

"I have no desire to face McIntyre at dawn."

"McIntyre?" The lady laughed. "Good heavens, Duke, if you imagine my husband is in the least interested in what I do, you are very much mistaken."

There was a pause, and then Jovian apparently decided to be firm and to the point. "I am afraid, madam, that you can apply McIntyre's sentiments to my own."

Silence ensued, then came the sharp sound of a slap, followed by the angry rustle of mauve taffeta as Mrs. McIntyre hurried away in high dudgeon.

Anthea had remained as quiet as a mouse throughout and

truly believed her presence was undetected, but suddenly Jovian addressed her. "I know you are there, Lady Anthea."

Her lips parted in dismay, and she didn't reply as he came around to confront her. He folded his arms and smiled in the lantern light as a sudden stir of breeze gently ruffled his blond hair. It signaled the onset of the thunderstorm, although neither of them realized it. How breathtakingly handsome he was in formal evening black, with white lace spilling from his cuffs and blossoming from the front of his shirt. There was a plain ruby pin in his neckcloth, an understated but exquisite touch that demonstrated his superb taste and style.

She fiddled awkwardly with her ivory fan, glad that the night and the lanterns disguised the hot blush that now marked her cheeks. She had never been alone with him like this before, never been faced with the power of her feelings. "I—I was not a deliberate earwig, your grace."

"Did I say you were?"

"No," she admitted, "but—"

"But nothing, my lady," he interrupted. "And please do not call me 'your grace,' for I abhor it."

"I apologize again."

"I am the one who should apologize for having allowed such a scene in your hearing."

"I rather think events were foisted upon you," Anthea replied.

"Maybe, but in the end I was less than a gentleman."

"She was refusing to take no for an answer."

Lightning flashed in the west, followed by a low rumble of thunder, and the breeze picked up a little more as Jovian indicated the empty bench beside her. "May I join you?"

"Of course." Her heart was pounding so loudly in her ears she wondered he could not hear it, and as he sat next to her, she was so desperate not to give herself away that it was difficult to maintain her equilibrium.

He smiled. "Of course, with no intended offense to Mrs.

McIntyre, if you and I sit here like this, our coziness might be construed as something it is not," he murmured.

"Possibly."

"How very noncommittal," he murmured.

"What would you have me say? Shall I be the vaporish miss and squeal for rescue?"

He laughed. "Do you require rescuing?"

She looked at him. "No."

"I know how you feel about me, Lady Anthea," he said then.

"I . . . beg your pardon?" Her cheeks must have deepened to maroon at the very least.

"I know how you feel about me."

"And how, pray, do I feel about you?" she inquired, trying to be arch.

There was a moment's silence, then he said softly, "You love me, Lady Anthea."

She could not help rather pointlessly seeking to save face by denying what was patently true. "You flatter yourself if you think I love you, Duke."

He gave a low laugh. "One thing that is said of me is true, you know. I *can* read minds. I can certainly read yours and have been doing so for some time now. It is most gratifying to know how your heart turns over with excitement if our glances happen to meet."

Unable to cope with her embarrassment, she leapt to her feet with the intention of returning to Carlton House, but he caught her hand to make her stay. "Don't be offended, Lady Anthea, for I am not poking fun. Far from it." He stood, still keeping firm hold of her hand. "You see, if you could read my mind, you would know that I feel exactly the same way about you."

The clasp of his fingers burned through their evening gloves, but somehow she managed to speak. "Does—does it amuse you to tease me?"

"You think I tease?"

"What else? You and I have never been alone together before; indeed we must be termed acquaintances rather than friends; yet suddenly you speak of harboring deep feelings for me."

"Why should I not? After all, your feelings for me go beyond those of a mere acquaintance. Or do you still deny it?" His thumb moved against her palm as if they were flesh to flesh.

The rising wind died for a second, during which a pin might have been heard to drop upon the grass, then the storm resumed with another flash of lightning. A crash of thunder followed almost immediately, and there were a few spots of rain in the air. Other guests in the gardens began to hurry back to Carlton House, but she and Jovian stayed where they were.

"What shall we do, Anthea?" he murmured. "Remain mere acquaintances, or follow our hearts?"

She couldn't, wouldn't, accept that he was sincere. After all, he was one of the greatest prizes in the Marriage Mart, and certainly the most attractive, so why would he fall in love with her? She was an earl's daughter with a fine inheritance, but there were others like her who were also beautiful. "I—I gave you no leave to use my first name."

"True, so I am presuming anyway, so it is only right that you call me Jovian."

Fear of hurt and ridicule remained stubbornly uppermost in her mind. "You are a practiced lover, Duke, and—"

"Jovian," he corrected.

"And—and half the women in society adore you, so if you expect me to believe—"

"That I love you?" he broke in gently, his voice almost lost in the rushing of the wind. His fingers linked tightly between hers. "I have never before told any woman that I love her, nor will I ever say it to another, because you are the only one for me."

"Please . . ."

"Tell me that you love me too, Anthea, for I need to hear you say it."

Her lips moved, but she could not speak.

"Say it, Anthea."

The rain began to fall in earnest, soaking through her dainty gown almost in a moment. It seemed to wash away her foolish restraint. "I love you," she whispered.

He smiled and pulled her close to kiss her full on the lips. She was hardly aware of the storm that now began to rage overhead. All she knew was that his kiss thrilled through her like a charge, as if her body had absorbed the lightning. His lips moved slowly and luxuriously over hers in the skilled kiss of a man of experience, but at the same time it was innocent too, as if this was the first kiss that had mattered to him. There was no artifice or calculation, no feeling that this was the means to an end or a passing fancy; every heartbeat, every fraction of breath, every caress came from the soul, and there was no room left for doubting his motives. Love was what urged him, what urged them both. . . .

Her emotions soared to meet the storm, as if her feet no longer touched the ground. The sensation of flying was so powerful that she felt they were above the rooftops. It was such a wild, exhilarating, rapturous feeling that she wondered what she would see if she opened her eyes. Would they be above Carlton House, Pall Mall, St. James's Park, Westminster Abbey, then even above the storm clouds, so that the moon and starlit heavens were once again spread overhead . . . ?

She didn't look, for fear of destroying the illusion. It was better by far to believe in the utter enchantment of floating above the world in his embrace, with only his arms preventing her from tumbling to destruction like a modern Icarus, wings burned by the moon instead of the sun. She was breathless and excited, her hair was wet and her gown drenched through and clinging to her body like a cobweb that shone with dew instead of spangles. Exultation coursed through her veins, and she did not want the beguilement to ever end, but at last she was conscious of descending to the earth once more and feeling the wet grass beneath her satin slippers.

His arms still enveloped her. Earthly arms? No, she wanted there to be something of the other world about him, something so amazing and magical that being with him would always be like living a fairy tale. "Tell me we flew," she whispered. "Tell me that you just took me over the rooftops toward the moon."

"We flew, my darling, we flew," he averred softly, and bent his head to kiss her again.

She guessed he was humoring her, but the words were what she wanted to hear. "Will we fly again?" she asked, as the kiss ended.

"Oh, yes, I promise you," he breathed.

The deluge continued around them, the dark skies were slashed with lightning, and rolls of thunder made the very earth tremble, but the storm did not matter at all, nor could she have cared less that her hair was wet and spoiled. When his lips first touched hers she had been a green girl, but now her dormant senses had been fully awakened. Her innocence had begun to steal away, but along the sweetest, most spellbinding of paths.

They both realized at the same moment that they really ought to go inside. How they had laughed as they ran hand in hand back to Carlton House, where their bedraggled appearance caused much comment. But she was suddenly impervious to such things; only Jovian would ever be able to hurt her now.

Her joy had known few bounds as that summer gave way to autumn. Society anticipated the seemingly inevitable marriage announcement, which she knew would take place at Christmas, but as the festive season began a change had stolen over him. The Jovian she adored became someone else entirely, a man more likely to be drunk than not, a man whose tongue could be cruel, and whose entire character appeared to have undergone a complete transformation. The face was the same, but all else was different. Her heart began to break, then it shattered, and her happiness seeped wretchedly away into oblivion.

Now, on this wet and miserable Lammas Day, Anthea's heartbreak was as keen and fresh as if time had not passed at all. There would never be another man like the Jovian Cathness she had fallen in love with. No one could ever take his place; certainly not the drunkard he was now.

Seven

*T*ears filled Anthea's eyes as she lay there dwelling upon how it all went wrong, but then her maid knocked softly at the bedroom door, and she blinked the tears away and sat up. "Yes, come in, Dolly."

"Good morning, my lady," the maid said, as she brought her mistress's cup of tea to the bedside, then bobbed a curtsy. She was brown-haired and freckled, with the sort of wide smile that always cheered the spirits. Neat in a pale green linen dress and starched apron, she went to the window to draw back the curtains, beginning her usual aimless chatter. Her best friend Maisie, who attended Lady Farnborough in Curzon Street, had come down with the mumps. She had caught them from her young man, a footman at Lansdowne House, who had in turn caught it from his brother at . . . As Dolly listed the infection's progress from house to house, Anthea began to wonder if the whole of Mayfair was coming down with it. She almost said as much, but decided it might hurt Dolly's feelings.

The medical report was brought to an end when Corinna peeped around the door. "May I come in, Anthea?"

"Yes, of course."

Dolly left again as Corinna came to sit on the bed. She still wore her nightgown under an unfastened peach silk robe, her golden hair was pinned up very loosely on top of her head, and she looked very fresh and lovely . . . except for some dark stains on her fingers and nightgown. "What has happened to you?" Anthea asked.

"Mm?"

"Those stains."

"Oh, just pomegnanate," Corinna replied.

"Pomegranate?"

"Yes, someone left one on my pillow, and I ate it."

"But who on earth would leave a *pomegranate*?" Anthea inquired.

"I have no idea."

"How very odd." Anthea was puzzled, because as far as she knew, there were no pomegranates in the house, it not being a fruit she and her aunt particularly liked.

Corinna shrugged. "Very odd, but it looked so delicious that I absolutely *had* to have a taste." She rubbed ineffectually at her stained fingers, but pomegranate juice was not so easily removed. "I found it just after I saw the two full moons," she added.

"The what?"

"The two moons. There was a brief break in the rainclouds, and I saw them. The second one was blue."

Corinna spoke as if it were the most natural thing in the world, but Anthea was taken completely aback. "Corinna, there is only one moon, and I have never seen it turn blue. I know we talk of blue moons, meaning something rare, but—"

Corinna interrupted. "This second moon was definitely there and definitely blue. You're right, though, so I suppose it was a trick of the weather and the light. I mean, there is usually only one rainbow, but sometimes there are two."

"Yes, that must be it." Anthea was happy to seize upon a logical explanation, but at the same time she thought Corinna was a little odd this morning. Not quite herself, somehow. It was certainly totally unlike her to emerge from her room with black-stained hands and wearing a spoiled nightgown.

Corinna got up and went to open the French windows and

look out at the rain-sluiced verandah and dripping garden. "Oh, I do hope this weather clears up, or the day will be ruined." She inhaled deeply. "Oh, I can smell the roses and the lavender."

"The lavender is over now, so you must be smelling something else. The rosemary, perhaps?"

"No, it's definitely lavender. And anyway, it must still be in bloom because I heard a flower girl singing this morning. Oh—I suppose it could have been dried lavender."

"Probably."

"I do adore lavender," Corinna said, with a sigh.

"Oh? I didn't know that."

"You must do, Anthea, because I'm always saying it."

Anthea declined to respond, for the simple truth was that she had never heard Corinna say anything about liking lavender.

Corinna turned to look at her. "You are lucky to have eyes that color. I wish I did."

"You have the most beautiful green eyes imaginable, Corinna, and I envy you."

"I can't think why." Corinna closed the French windows and came back to the bedside. "All the Prantons are blonde and green-eyed. Mama used to say we had been blessed with the green of spring and the gold of high summer."

"And she was right," Anthea replied.

The rain stopped between half past ten and eleven, and then the sun shone down upon a capital that seemed cleansed after such a heavy downpour. Everything sparkled, and people's hearts lifted accordingly.

Lady Letitia and her two charges spent the early afternoon driving through the streets, observing all the decorations and enjoying the festive atmosphere. Green Park was to equal St. James's Park that night, with a one-hundred-foot Gothic fortress, the Castle of Discord, which would under cover of fireworks wonderfully transform into a glittering Temple of

Concord. Much earlier in the day, Mr. Sadler's brightly colored balloon rose above the makeshift fortress while he scattered countless jubilee programs to the crowds below.

After admiring Green Park, the Daneway House ladies drove on to Hyde Park to see the immense fair that had been set up beneath the trees. There was a regatta on the Serpentine, which would be followed by a naumachia between two miniature naval fleets reenacting Nelson's great victory over the French at the Battle of the Nile. Hyde Park was a crush to end all crushes, although on the whole the crowds remained good-natured. Nevertheless, because people from every level of society were present, Lady Letitia considered it an unsuitable place for ladies of quality, so before long she ordered a return to Berkeley Square.

Anthea and Corinna did not object, for the thrill of the evening was close now. They were to dress in all their finery for dinner on the pleasure barge, which Aunt Letty assured them was large enough for a long dining table to be set beneath an awning. There were to be a number of guests, so for Corinna it would almost amount to a first tentative appearance in society. She was a little nervous about it but eagerly anticipated the novelty and diversion of dining on the lake while watching what was promised to be the most splendid fireworks display London would ever see.

The sun was setting and St. James's Park was crowded when they arrived. Lanterns twinkled on Birdcage Walk and along the Mall, and it was known that the royal family and three hundred guests were watching everything from the windows of nearby Buckingham House. Marquees and stands had been erected in St. James's Park, and a magnificent single-span Chinese bridge had been specially built across the long, straight lake known as the Canal. From the middle of the bridge rose a handsome seven-story pagoda, yellow and black with a blue roof, and at ten o'clock both it and the bridge would glitter with fireworks.

Lady Letitia, particularly splendid in bottle green taffeta and emeralds, ushered her charges into the park as the evening shadows lengthened almost to darkness and the pagoda was being illuminated with newfangled gas lighting. There was applause and admiring cheers from the immense press of people who had come to watch. The three ladies from Daneway House were in good time for the display and strolled through the crowds toward the pleasure boats and barges that awaited the more privileged onlookers.

Anthea wore a sapphire blue silk gown with a low square neckline and gold embroidery at the hem. A gold lace shawl rested loosely over her arms, and her jewelry was a handsome topaz pendant necklace and matching earrings. Her dark hair was in a stylish knot on top of her head. She knew she looked good but was eclipsed by her stepsister.

Corinna had borrowed one of Anthea's gowns, a lemon plowman's gauze sprinkled with golden spots. Her bright blond hair was in a knot like Anthea's but with ringlets falling to the nape of her neck. She allowed her plum-colored shawl to trail prettily along the grass, as was the rage, and admiring male eyes followed her, though few knew who she was.

It was while they had paused to exchange civilities with some of Lady Letitia's acquaintances that a growl of thunder rattled overhead. There were dismayed gasps, and everyone looked up, but the clear skies showed there to be no chance at all of a storm to spoil their fun. No one thought any more of it, including Anthea, until she suddenly saw the hare again and remembered hearing thunder when last she'd seen it on that arctic cold Christmas Eve in Berkeley Square.

This time the creature was only a few yards away on the bank of the Canal, where there was no shelter and the lantern light was so brilliant that it seemed almost purposely illuminated. It was sitting up on its haunches, cleaning one of its long ears with its front paws, like a woman braiding her hair, and Anthea decided there was certainly something almost human about its quick glance.

The hare was so intent upon Anthea's group that it didn't see the swans gliding up behind it. They spread their wings and arched their necks threateningly, but the hare knew nothing until an angry beak jabbed its scut. At this the animal gave a startled squeak and whirled about to face them, crouching defensively on all fours. As the swans began to hiss and surge forward, the hare wisely fled along the water's edge. The last Anthea saw was its fluffy white scut disappearing into the crowds. It might have been invisible for all the notice other people took of it. No one pointed, no one even turned, leaving Anthea with the uncanny feeling that only she and the swans had been aware of its presence.

She was just thinking what a very strange hare it was when a belated echo of Jovian's voice came to her from Christmas Eve. *"Beware, Anthea, for things might soon happen that are far, far beyond your experience."* Maybe those things had started after all, for there had been the oddness of Corinna and the mistletoe and the business of the pomegranate—and now, the hare again.

Lady Letitia escorted her niece and her stepniece on toward the pleasure barge, but Corinna fell slightly behind, watching the swans preening. Anthea turned to tell her to hurry, but at that moment a tall, richly dressed woman of about Lady Letitia's age approached Corinna. The woman was clad in a light brown brocade pelisse over a cream muslin gown and wore a wide-brimmed brown hat that concealed her face, but Anthea thought there was something familiar about her. Then it came to her. Surely this was the woman who had been behind her in the fog as she returned from the encounter with Jovian by the king's statue!

The woman spoke to Corinna, who turned quickly, her lips parting as if completely shocked, but then she nodded. The woman turned and melted away into the crowds, and Corinna hastened to rejoin the others.

"Who was that?" Anthea asked.

"I—beg your pardon?" Corinna avoided her eyes.

"The woman who just spoke to you."

"Oh, she mistook me for someone else, that's all."

Anthea knew it wasn't true. If the woman had really made a mistake, Corinna would have shaken her head, not nodded. On top of all the other odd little incidents, the realization that Corinna was hiding something made Anthea feel distinctly uncomfortable. Something untoward was going on, and she wished she knew what it was.

Eight

At last Lady Letitia, Anthea, and Corinna boarded the Bishop of Fairwells's lantern-lit pleasure barge, which was one of the largest on the lake. Beneath a delightful red-and-white-striped awning at the stern, a long, beautifully decorated dining table had been laid with silver cutlery, fine plates, and crystal glasses. Lighted candelabra and lavish epergnes of flowers and fruit provided the finishing touch to a splendid setting.

The bishop's guests had been promised an excellent view of the fireworks display, as the boat would sail close to the pagoda bridge. There would be twenty people in all, including, of course, Lord Henley, so lively debate was not only guaranteed but had already commenced as the three ladies boarded the vessel. The other guests were chattering as well, so there was quite a lively atmosphere.

Corinna's courage faltered on being confronted by so many strangers to whom she would soon be introduced. Seeing her sudden nervous pallor, Lady Letitia told Anthea to take her aside for a while, so Corinna was ushered to the bow, where a young lady and gentleman were in intimate conversation, their heads bowed close as they stood in the shadows. Anthea hardly noticed them as she made Corinna sit quietly on a cushioned bench.

Corinna gave her a rueful look. "I'm sorry, Anthea, but when I saw all those people . . ."

"I understand, Corinna, so please don't apologize. It is one thing to have been brought up on an aristocratic but socially isolated Irish estate, and not too bad to join one of Aunt Letty's intimate little dinner parties, or to visit a London art gallery where one or two people are introduced. But it is something else entirely to be suddenly faced with a gaggle of people of the capital's highest society, all of whom will scrutinize every inch of you, then discuss you afterward." Anthea smiled at her. "You do not need to worry, you know, for you are very lovely, you look as delightful as a fashion plate, your manners are all that anyone could wish, and you cannot help but shine."

"You flatter me, I fear." Corinna fidgeted with her plum shawl. "You are very kind to allow me to use your wardrobe, but I cannot *wait* to have my own."

"The dressmakers of London are working as hard as they can on your behalf."

Corinna fidgeted with the shawl again, then cast a sideways glance at the couple in the shadows. "It doesn't help that Viscount Heversham is here with his new love."

Startled, Anthea looked as well, and sure enough it was the viscount, who was so absorbed in his redheaded companion that he had not noticed Corinna. Or if he had, he was unconcerned.

Corinna drew a long breath. "Well, I cannot blame him, I suppose. I didn't exactly give him cause to hope."

"And now you wish you had?"

Corinna hesitated. "I don't know," she replied frankly, "but I *do* know that I don't like seeing him with someone else. Maybe I am simply a dog in the manger." She looked ashore, raking the crowds intently, almost as if expecting to see someone.

"Whom are you looking for?" Anthea asked.

"Mm? Oh, no one. At least . . ." Corinna's brows drew together in puzzlement. "Well, I don't *think* I'm looking for anyone in particular, yet somewhere at the back of my mind I feel I am. Oh, dear, you will think me quite mad if I continue like this. I am in such a lather of nerves right now that I hardly know what day it is."

Anthea smiled. "It's Lammas Day, my girl, and we are about to enjoy a sumptuous dinner and watch the most fantastic fireworks display the world has ever seen. Surely that is cause for pleasure, not apprehension!"

At that moment Lady Letitia hurried up to them. "Anthea, my dear, I fear I have unwelcome news. The bishop informs me that the only guests still to arrive are Jovian and Sir Erebus Lethe."

"Oh." Anthea's heart sank, for she did not think she could endure to see Jovian in his cups again.

Corinna's interest quickened, however, and after a barely perceptible toss of her head at Viscount Hevensham and his ladylove, she rose to her feet. "I am feeling much better now, Lady Letitia."

"I'm so glad, my dear. Society can be very intimidating, I fear, but I know you will carry it off. The next time will not be so bad, and soon you will enjoy it to the full." Lady Letitia looked at Anthea, who had not said anything since learning of Jovian's inclusion in the party. "Are you all right, my dear?"

"Not really. I would much rather not see Jovian."

Her aunt touched her arm. "We will stay well away from him."

Anthea didn't reply. Her spirits had plummeted, and she wished to go home.

Lady Letitia guessed her thoughts. "It would be unconscionably ill-mannered to depart simply because Jovian *may* misbehave in some way. We are obliged to wait until he *does* misbehave." But then she saw Jovian and Sir Erebus approaching the barge, pausing on the way to speak to some other gentlemen. "Well, we shall soon see what transpires, for they are here now," she murmured, "and, oh dear, I'm afraid Jovian appears less than sober."

Anthea gazed unhappily at the man who maintained such an unfair hold upon her heart. He was matchlessly handsome and elegant in evening clothes, yet so obviously in drink that Sir Erebus had to support his elbow to keep him from swaying. But even in this state there wasn't a man in London who could hold a candle to the twelfth Duke of Chavanage. Deeply flawed he might be, but outwardly he would always be closer to perfection than any of his peers.

For a moment his glance met hers, and something reached out to her, as if the old Jovian were still there, hidden deep within the shell he had become. But almost immediately she again saw only the drunkard who had trampled upon her soul. She turned away, trying in vain to shut him out, but he remained in her head, a sad echo of a future that had once offered only joy.

Then she thought she heard him say her name, as if he stood at her side, yet he was still ashore and now gazing toward Westminster Abbey, which was just visible in silhouette against the dark eastern sky. His face was withdrawn, not quite to the point of lack of interest in the proceedings, but certainly as if his mind were elsewhere. Possibly he was wondering when his next drink would be forthcoming, she thought uncharitably. Oh, how *angry* she was with him; how bitter, disappointed, and let down. He had failed her, and she wished she could despise him as he deserved.

Suddenly she pulled her shawl around her shoulders. "I must speak to him," she said.

"Is that wise, my dear?" Lady Letitia's expression spoke volumes as to how *unwise* it was.

"I will not be long," Anthea declared, and before anything more could be said, she hurried along the lantern-lit deck and then ashore. Within seconds she was approaching Jovian, who turned immediately, as if sensing her.

"Goodevenin', *hic,* Anth-thea." His voice was muzzy, yet his gray eyes were surprisingly alert.

"Please tell me you do not mean to come on board in such an inebriated state!" she declared, emotion making her almost strident.

He glanced at Sir Erebus, who was deep in conversation with one of the other gentlemen, then said in a quiet but imperative tone. "It would be better if *you* stayed ashore, Anthea." Suddenly his diction was firm and clear, without a hint of liquor.

She stared at him, as much taken aback by the improvement in his voice as by what he said, but then Sir Erebus turned. "Is anything wrong, Lady Anthea?" he inquired.

Jovian hiccuped, then laughed too loudly. "Methinks sh—*hic*—she's been at th'brandy, Lethe, for I v-vow she's asked me if—*hic*—she should go on the barge or not. As if *I* would know!" He swayed alarmingly and clutched Sir Erebus's shoulder for support.

Anthea was stung. "Oh, there is no point in speaking to you at all, sirrah, for you are beastly drunk as usual. I pray you do not come near me again tonight."

"I didn' c-come near you now. You c-came to me, remember?" He raised an imaginary glass to her.

Sir Erebus disentangled himself from Jovian and came to draw her hand gently over his arm. "I'll see that he leaves you alone, Lady Anthea. Now, please allow me to escort you," he said kindly, and ushered her toward the boat again.

His genuine concern brought sudden tears to her eyes. She blinked them back. "Forgive me, Sir Erebus, I am afraid I still find it difficult to believe the duke is so changed."

His fingers rested briefly over hers. "I quite understand, Lady Anthea. Believe me, he does not mean to be as he is; I fear he just cannot help himself."

She halted. "You are his friend, Sir Erebus, do *you* know what happened to him? Why did he suddenly turn to drink like this?"

He exhaled slowly. "I don't know what lies behind it, Lady Anthea. I have known him since I became his neighbor about twelve months ago, but he has not confided much that went on before our acquaintance. He may have always been a drinker, albeit secretly at first."

"No, I'm sure not." She would have known. Wouldn't she?

"It is none of my business, I know, Lady Anthea, but my advice is that you forget him."

"He is already in the past as far as I am concerned," she fibbed, determined that the statement would very soon be true. She had to *make* herself accept that the Jovian Cathness she had loved had gone forever.

"There are other fish in the sea, Lady Anthea," Sir Erebus said softly, as they reached the railed plank to the pleasure boat. The inflection in his voice could not help but command her attention, and she knew he was telling her he was one such fish. He raised her hand to his lips. "I trust we shall meet again, soon," he murmured, smiling again.

"I trust so too, Sir Erebus," she replied, politely but rather unwisely. She did not mean to encourage him but was swept along by the moment and grateful for being rescued from her self-inflicted confrontation with Jovian.

She went back on board and found Corinna and Lady Letitia waiting anxiously. "What was all *that* about?" Lady Letitia demanded crossly.

"I . . . I just asked Jovian not to come near us."

"And he agreed, I trust?"

Anthea glanced ashore. "Not exactly, but Sir Erebus promised to see that he keeps away," she murmured.

"Ah, the gallant Sir Erebus," Lady Letitia murmured. "*Such* a gentleman, and no mistake."

Corinna sighed. "And so annoyingly interested in Anthea. I wish he liked me even half as much."

"So much for your equivocation over Viscount Heversham," Anthea replied, with what she hoped was a light laugh. "Besides, Sir Erebus only spoke to me because I was silly enough to try reasoning with Jovian. I am quite sure that when he meets you, I will very soon be forgotten."

Lady Letitia's eagle eyes missed nothing of her niece's inner distress, so she diverted Corinna's attention by taking her to meet someone. Anthea returned to the bow, which was now completely deserted, and sat on the bench to compose herself. But her unsettled mind dredged up the past, in particular the terrible night that Jovian's cruel tongue had finally forced her to end matters between them.

It happened at Lord and Lady Farnborough's 1812 Christmas ball. . . .

Nine

The ballroom at the Farnborough residence in Curzon Street was a separate building that stood in the snowy, lantern-decked garden behind the house, and the Christmas ball was always a special occasion. The ball of 1812 was no different. Music sounded sweetly, there was a great deal of conversation, and all in all the occasion was an outstanding success for Lady Farnborough—except for the atrocious wine, of course. It was a mystery to Anthea why such an experienced and talented hostess should lavish money on everything except the wine.

The ball was in full swing when Anthea noticed Jovian's absence. Her already low spirits plummeted a little more as she looked around in vain for his blond head among the sea of guests beneath the shimmering chandeliers and exquisite Christmas decorations. Things had been awkward between them for days now because he had been constantly drunk or suffering the aftereffects. She did not know what was wrong, and he would not confide in her; indeed, at times his retorts had been sharp to the point of unpleasantness. As a result, instead of happily contemplating the imminent announcement of their forthcoming marriage, she was beginning to have serious misgivings about proceeding at all.

It did not seem possible that he could change so much in such a short time, almost overnight, in fact. The nonpareil with whom she had fallen so desperately in love, and whose kiss had made her feel as if they floated above the London rooftops, appeared to have been replaced by a changeling. The sunny paradise of the past months had suddenly begun to grow cold and wintry.

She noticed Aunt Letty talking to Lord Henley and hurried to ask them if they had seen Jovian. It was impossible not to observe that Aunt Letty's glance slid uncomfortably away, or that Lord Henley cleared his throat before answering. "He . . . er, he went back to the house about half an hour ago." Such truthfulness earned him a warning dig from Aunt Letty's elbow, but it was too late, and already Anthea was hurrying out of the ballroom into the chilly gardens, where the colored lanterns cast rainbow pools of light on the snow.

The gemstones on her gauzy violet gown glittered as she hastened along the sand-scattered path, and the sound of carol-singing carried from the street, so that ever afterward she would associate Christmas and carols with those moments leading up to the shattering of her heart and happiness.

She reached the house and entered by way of the French windows of the billiard room. A number of gentlemen were at play and nodded to her as she passed. Had she seen the glances they exchanged afterward, she would have known what to expect.

Jovian was in Lord Farnborough's firelit library, lounging idly on a brown leather sofa with a full glass of whisky in his hand and a half-empty decanter within easy reach on the floor. He had loosened his neckcloth and discarded his coat. Seeing her in a mirror as she entered the room, he raised the glass. "Ah, so you have f-found me," he muttered thickly.

"So it would seem," she replied in the clipped tone that had been so prevalent over the past few days.

"I th-thought to escape your nagging tongue and sour v-visage," he said, sitting up slowly and drinking half the glass of whisky as if hoping the action would displease her.

She gazed at him. "Oh, Jovian, what has happened to you?" she whispered.

His glazed eyes were hard in the firelight. "I have just grown t-tired of you, my l-lady. I don't like your face, your v-voice, your damned name, or any—*hic*—thing about you." He raised the glass again and drank what was left in it.

Salt tears pricked her eyes. "Do you really mean that?" she asked, just preventing her voice from breaking.

"Oh, go away, my lady, for I have h-had enough of your whining complaints. I'm s-sick of you, your conversation, your person, and—*hic*—your prissy standards. I vow you will be as comfortless as a prayer b-book between the sheets! A man can drink as he pl-pleases and should not be expected to do otherwise, simply because a damned w-woman doesn't like it!" He reached for the decanter and poured another full glass, although much was spilled because his hand was unsteady. "A wife such as you, my d-dear Anth-thea, would stifle the very life out of m-me. Look at you, you're too skinny and flat, your hair is dull, and th-there is no kindness in you for a fellow's afflictions."

Each cruel word stabbed her like a dagger, and there were tears on her cheeks as she stood her ground. "Afflictions? Is that what you call your disgusting drunkenness? We are alone in here, Jovian, and I see no one coercing you to raise that glass to your lips. That is not an affliction; it is a deliberate and more than willing choice."

"What a n-nag you are, to be sure. *Hic*." He looked at her as if he truly did despise her.

"And what a shabby, pathetic excuse for a man you are," she breathed. "You have no dignity or manners, and if you continue like this, you will soon have no friends at all."

"Nag, nag, nag."

"Well, I'll spare you my presence now and for ever more. I may have loved you only days ago, sirrah, but I despise you now. Consider our association to be at an end."

"Gladly."

Stifling a sob, she left the room, closing the door upon him and upon her lost happiness. She heard the crash of the glass as he hurled it after her.

Anthea's unhappy meditation about that awful Christmas was ended when Corinna, at Lady Letitia's behest, came to tell her the guests were now assembling at the table. Doing her best to look bright and cheerful again, she accompanied her stepsister to the table under the awning, and within moments everyone was seated, including Jovian and Sir Erebus. Men with rowing boats hauled the larger pleasure craft out onto the water, then returned to the shore until needed to bring them to shore again. Soon the bishop's dinner party had commenced, and it proved to be very recherché indeed, an émigré French chef having been secured at considerable cost.

Corinna spent the meal casting surreptitious glances at Sir Erebus, to whose dark good looks she was drawn so much that she almost ached. She had yet to be introduced to him but felt as if she had known him forever. It was the strangest feeling, mostly agreeable, but sometimes — just sometimes — very unsettling indeed. Once or twice she shivered, although the night was warm. The shivers were on account of Sir Erebus, but she could not imagine why.

Jovian was seated well away from Anthea and did not grace her with so much as a single look. She, on the other hand, was guilty of keeping him under close observation, and what she observed was the number of times he refilled his glass. She hardly dared imagine how slurred and incomprehensible he was by now. Certainly she heard his voice droning loudly now and then and saw Sir Erebus endeavoring to reason discreetly with him.

A number of people looked on disapprovingly, for Jovian was embarrassing, not amusing. Why couldn't he realize that? Why, oh why, had he been invited tonight? And why was it her lot to *still* feel such pain on his account? For every time she looked, she saw his former self standing forlornly in the long shadow cast by his disagreeable new self. The real Jovian was still there . . . if only he would come out of hiding and overthrow the vile usurper.

Everyone had reached dessert when ten o'clock arrived and the first fireworks were signaled. The display went from glory to glory, with Roman candles, girandoles, jerbs, tourbillions, squibs, pots de brin, and amazing sky rockets soaring from the shining pagoda. There were fountains of glowing sparks that were almost too beautiful to be believed, and the air was filled with hissing and crackling. Drifts of smoke floated across the park, and cascades of light spilled from the bridge parapet to dance on the water. In the distance were fireworks elsewhere in the London skies, especially from nearby Green Park, where the Castle of Discord was undergoing its transformation into the Temple of Concord.

The bishop's guests had soon left the table for the deck rail in order to have the best view possible. Sir Erebus was among them, leaving Jovian the only person still seated. But then, as Anthea observed with silent helplessness, that was where the decanters were located. Corinna's yearning gaze followed Sir Erebus's every move, but if he glanced toward her at all, it was only in search of Anthea, who began to feel a little uncomfortable as she realized that she was the unwilling recipient of the admiration so longed for by her stepsister.

Anthea observed that longing looks were not only passing from Corinna to Sir Erebus, but to Corinna herself from Viscount Heversham. The mystery of the redheaded lady had been solved, Lady Letitia having discovered that she was the viscount's married sister, Lady Ellison. It seemed Lord Ellison was a wayward husband whose latest affaire de coeur had caused his wife many tears, and she had fled to her adoring brother for sympathy. A placatory message from Lord Ellison had been handed to his wife just before the pleasure barge left the shore, and now she was all smiles and dimples again, leaving her lovelorn brother to belatedly realize how he had neglected his own affairs of the heart. He gazed at Corinna, only too aware that her favor had now been bestowed else-where. Anthea felt very sorry for him but could not help thinking he had handled everything badly. He should have told Corinna who the lady was and certainly should not have devoted his attention so completely to family matters that he abandoned Corinna altogether.

The watching crowds clapped and gasped as scintillating explosions lit the indigo heavens above London, and the lake reflected the show, rippling like liquid jewels in the light breeze that sprang up to gently cool the smoke-filled air. The breeze caused the flotilla of hitherto motionless pleasure craft to drift inch by slow inch toward the bridge, although no one noticed.

Anthea was intent upon the fireworks when suddenly she heard Jovian's voice. *"Be ready, Anthea. Be on your guard."* It was so clear that she whirled about, expecting to find him at her shoulder, but he was still seated at the table with his back toward her.

Then he spoke again. *"Listen to me, Anthea. Go to the stern, and take Lady Letitia and your stepsister with you."*

There was no drunken slur; he was perfectly articulate. She hesitated, confused by the constant changes in him and shaken too by his ability to somehow speak inside her head. What was happening? Why go to the stern? What was he talking about?

Anger touched his voice. *"Do it, Anthea! I may not have power enough to prevent what is otherwise bound to be, and I want you to be as far away as possible."*

The urgency of the command made her breath snatch, and without further ado she hurried to Aunt Letty and Corinna, the latter now all blushing delight because Sir Erebus had joined them. Anthea blurted the first thing that came into her head. "Aunt Letty, I . . . don't feel well. Will you come and sit with me at the stern, where it's quiet?"

Lady Letitia was immediately filled with concern. "Why, of course I will, my dear. We both will, won't we, Corinna?"

It was a subtle way of telling Corinna that a young lady of just nineteen should not remain alone with a gentleman she hardly knew, but even so Corinna pouted and resisted. "Oh, but Lady Letitia—"

"That is the end of it, my dear," was the prompt reply.

Sir Erebus came to the rescue. "Allow me to come with you, ladies; then if anything is required, I can be your page-of-all-trades."

Corinna was delighted. "Oh, how gallant you are, Sir Erebus," she breathed.

Lady Letitia did not argue with his suggestion but put an arm around Anthea's shoulder and ushered her past the deserted dining table to the stern, where there were comfortable sofas and chairs. Anthea allowed her aunt to fuss around her and accepted the glass of iced water that Sir Erebus brought from the table. She stole a glance at Jovian, and for the briefest of seconds he smiled at her. A wellspring of loving emotions rose through her veins, for he was the old Jovian, the one who had plucked her heartstrings and played wonderful melodies with her senses; the old Jovian, whom she had adored so very, very much. And whom she adored still, no matter how hard she tried not to.

Suddenly there were cries of renewed wonder from the onlookers. Smoke had begun to belch from the pagoda, and everyone expected another extravaganza, but then the pagoda shifted slightly, and flames began to leap from it. Soon the blazing edifice lurched over the water in the direction of the drifting flotilla and at last there was an uncertain stir as people realized that not only was something gravely wrong with the display, but the breeze was carrying the vessels toward danger! The crowds ashore however, still believed it was part of the show, and they cheered and clapped.

Some alert gentlemen on the vessels began to shout ashore for the rowing boats to put out and haul them to safety again, but the crews shouted back that they had been hired to row *after* the display was at an end, not halfway through it.

Sir Erebus became uneasy. "Can you swim, ladies?" he murmured.

Lady Letitia looked at him as if he were mad. "No, sir, I cannot, and even if I could, do you imagine I would jump in the water in *these* costly togs?"

"High fashion may be obliged to give way to necessity," he replied.

Corinna's face puckered, and her little chin wobbled. "Are we going to drown?" she whispered.

Lady Letitia would have gathered her close, but Corinna rushed to Sir Erebus and flung her arms around his neck. "Oh, you must save us, Sir Erebus! You simply must!"

"You will be safe, Miss Pranton," he answered soothingly, hesitating before venturing to put his arms lightly around her. He was clearly uncomfortably aware of Lady Letitia's watchful glare.

With a creaking and groaning that was really quite awful to hear, the blazing pagoda finally toppled into the lake. Sparks flew, flames flared, and there was hissing and steam as burning timbers were extinguished, but the wild conflagration had already spread to the bridge, which was soon alight from end to end. And *still* the pleasure boats drifted inexorably toward it, faster now because the breeze chose this of all times to increase.

The smoke was quite choking, and Anthea could feel the heat on her face. The acrid taste was in her mouth, her eyes stung, and she was very frightened. She found herself looking to Jovian for protection, but as she turned toward him she saw him reach almost casually for a decanter of brandy. He refilled his glass but did not drink it; instead he sat back in his chair, his hands flat upon the table before him, his eyes closed, as if with intense concentration. Then he raised both his arms toward the sky. His lips moved, but if he spoke aloud, she could not hear him.

Billowing curtains of smoke drifted across the deck, sometimes concealing him, sometimes exposing him as clearly as in a painting. His arms were still held high, and his hands trembled; then suddenly she thought she felt the boat shudder. Had they struck something submerged in the water? But, no. Inch by amazing inch, all the drifting vessels began to move in the opposite direction, against the breeze and away from danger. There were cries of astonishment all around, because what was happening was clearly impossible.

Lady Letitia cried out with relief. "See, we're drifting away again! I don't know how it can be, but we are safe once more!"

Anthea continued to watch Jovian. He lowered his arms, and even in the leaping light of the flames she saw how tired and drained his face had become. Had he just made the boat change direction? Was it possible? All the amazing stories about him came rushing back . . . that he could fly and make bottles move. Was this another instance? Could he make a flotilla of pleasure craft drift against the prevailing breeze?

She got up to go to him but then halted as he took the glass of brandy and swallowed the contents. After that he slumped forward, his head on his arms. Her heart hardened; and bitterly, she turned away from him again.

Sir Erebus at last managed to give Corinna into Lady Letitia's comforting embrace and turned to Anthea with a smile. "Are you all right, Lady Anthea?"

"Yes."

He came closer and lowered his voice so that only she could hear. "Lady Letitia has intimated that she wishes to invite me to dinner. Would an acceptance on my part be welcome to you?" It was as near a statement of intent as any gentleman could reasonably give without stepping over the invisible lines of etiquette and propriety.

Thinking of Jovian and that glass of brandy, Anthea was again guilty of seeming to encourage Sir Erebus. "Yes, sir, it would be welcome to me."

Events in St. James's Park were the inevitable talking point as the ladies returned to Daneway House, but while Lady

Letitia and Corinna were concerned with the terrible fire,
Anthea could only think of Jovian's secret but momentous
part in their deliverance. To Sir Erebus Lethe she gave no
thought at all.

Ten

There was no unwelcome rain the next morning, the sun shone brightly, and the weather was perfect, and at breakfast Corinna announced she would go for a walk. She had begun to go out now and then on her own, so no one thought anything of it.

Anthea barely noticed what her stepsister was doing, because in the cold light of day she realized how incautious she had been with Sir Erebus. How could she have been so foolish? She knew he admired her, and now he probably thought she admired him too. Oh, it was all Jovian's fault! If he hadn't drained that last glass of brandy and then collapsed in a drunken stupor, she would have been much more prudent! She gazed guiltily at the toast rack beside the little bowl of nasturtiums on the table, for it was no good blaming Jovian. She had been stupid and would now have to deal with the problem as best she could.

After breakfast, when Corinna had been gone some ten minutes, Anthea decided she would feel better if she took an airing of her own. Donning her best blue velvet spencer and a white-sprigged muslin morning dress, she tied a blue-ribboned straw bonnet beneath her chin and then left the house. Her route took her down Berkeley Street, then west along Piccadilly, before crossing toward the entrance to Green Park to see the Temple of Concord.

A fully-laden traveling carriage waited at the curb, facing west. It was a gloomy vehicle, in unrelieved black, drawn by four equally black horses, and it put Anthea so in mind of a funeral equipage that she paused to look. There was no one inside, and she supposed the occupants were stretching their legs in the park before setting off on a journey. The coachman was clad in black too, and he sat so still that he might have been a statue.

Repressing a shudder, Anthea hurried into the park, a place of trees and small herds of cattle and deer. Unlike the disaster in St. James's Park, the celebrations here had been faultless, and the Temple of Concord stood majestically in the middle of an expanse of open grass. As Anthea approached to take a closer look, she suddenly noticed Corinna talking to a woman beneath some trees about a hundred yards away. There was no mistaking her buttercup-and-gray clothes and golden ringlets; nor was there any mistaking that the woman was the same person who had approached her the previous evening, albeit now wearing beige instead of brown.

The more Anthea studied the stranger, the more certain she became that it was also the inhospitable woman in Berkeley Square on Christmas Eve. Whoever she was, she talked urgently while Corinna listened. Then the latter suddenly stepped back as if utterly shocked.

Realizing her stepsister was distressed, Anthea began to hurry over, but she had gone only a few yards when Sir Erebus Lethe suddenly appeared from nowhere in front of her. He wore a sage green coat and cream cord breeches and smiled as he doffed his gleaming top hat to bow. "Lady Anthea, I am afraid you were so engrossed that you didn't hear my greetings."

"Your . . . greetings?" Anthea tore her eyes away from the scene beneath the trees to look at him instead.

"I spoke three times before it became necessary to place myself directly in your path."

"Forgive me, I—I am a little distracted."

"So I notice. May I inquire why?"

"My stepsister is over there with a lady I do not know, and she seems very upset."

"Really?" He turned, his ebony walking stick swinging idly in his kid-gloved hand.

"I don't know who the woman is," Anthea went on, "but she spoke to Corinna last night in St. James's Park. Corinna said it was a case of mistaken identity, but . . ."

"Perhaps it still is. Would you like me to go over and see if—? Ah, the woman is departing anyway."

"So she is." Anthea breathed out with relief as the woman pressed something into Corinna's hand, then hastened out of the park to the black traveling carriage, which promptly drove away toward Hyde Park Corner. Followed by Sir Erebus, Anthea ran across the grass. "Corinna? Corinna, are you all right?"

Corinna turned with a guilty start. "Anthea? And . . . and Sir Erebus? Wh-what are you doing here?"

"I simply came for a walk and decided to look at the Temple of Concord. Sir Erebus stopped to talk to me." Anthea looked curiously at Corinna's right hand, which was tightly clenched around something.

Sir Erebus bowed courteously. "Good morning, Miss Pranton. Lady Anthea is concerned that you are in some distress."

"Distress? Oh, no, I'm perfectly all right."

"That's a fib," Anthea observed frankly. "Are you going to tell me she has again mistaken you for someone else?"

Corinna's eyes slid away. "Er, yes, actually. She became a little persistent, but at last I managed to convince her of her error."

"Error? Yet she gave you something, didn't she?" Anthea pointed at her stepsister's hand.

Corinna's fingers uncurled reluctantly, revealing a beautiful gold locket, oval and daintily engraved with an ear of wheat. Anthea stared at it, for it was not a bauble but looked very old and expensive indeed. "Corinna, that woman simply *gave* it to you?"

"Yes."

Anthea held her gaze. "The truth, if you please, for perfect strangers do not hand out such things willy-nilly."

Corinna went very red and glanced at Sir Erebus, who immediately withdrew to a discreet distance.

"Well, Corinna?" Anthea prompted.

"The locket was my grandmother's."

"Your—? How do you know that?"

"Because the woman you saw me with just now is my aunt, Abigail Wheatley."

Anthea stared.

Corinna was close to tears. "I'm sorry I fibbed, Anthea, but I am so shocked I really don't know what to think. I thought my mother's twin was called Flora, but it seems her name is Abigail and she is very much alive. It also seems that my mother was never married to my father, and that she was still a Wheatley when she fled from home. Pranton really is my father's name, but I have no right to it because I . . . I was born out of wedlock, Anthea. My mother lied to me. Oh, the shame of it . . ."

As Corinna burst into tears, Anthea wished her own suspicions about Chloe Pranton's first marriage had not been so sadly confirmed. She held her sobbing stepsister and murmured sympathetically. "Oh, what shall I do, Anthea?" Corinna wept. "I dare not hold my head up in Society now, and Lady Letitia is bound to send me packing!"

"What nonsense is this?" Anthea cried, shaking her a little. "Neither Aunt Letty nor I will think any the less of you, so stop fearing the worst. Besides, no matter what went on before, you are now the Earl of Daneway's stepdaughter, and don't you forget it."

"I . . . I suppose you're right." Corinna summoned a weak smile and fished a handkerchief from her reticule.

"Of course I'm right, and if you imagine an admiring

gentleman will be deterred by such a thing, I think you are very much mistaken. It is your beauty that will draw them and your charm and vivaciousness that will win their hearts. And if they need anything else, your close connection to my family will do the trick." Anthea paused. "Corinna, you only know all this about your background because Miss Wheatley, or whoever she is, has chosen to tell you. What if she is wrong? What if she is even being malicious?"

"But why would she do that?"

"I don't know, but then I don't know her, either. She may have escaped from Bedlam."

"Don't be horrid, Anthea. She told me she resides in the house the Wheatley family has lived in for two hundred years."

"And what house is that?"

Corinna cleared her throat. "I, er, don't actually know the name of it."

"You don't *know*? Then how . . . ?"

"There is no mystery," Corinna broke in quickly. "She simply forgot to mention it. She said that it was so out of the way in back lanes that the best way to get there was to ask for directions at the local inn, the Cross Foxes. She said the landlord would supply a guide."

The details passed Anthea by. "How did she find you?"

"She overheard two other ladies mention me by name in St. James's Park last night. They said Lord Daneway had married my mother in County Fermanagh and spoke of me being blond with green eyes, so she felt sure I must be her niece. She says I am the very image of my mother at the same age."

"And you believe her?"

"Yes, I do," Corinna replied.

"What else did she tell you?"

Corinna drew a deep breath. "That there were many papers and diaries in her possession that will tell me all about my family, and if I wish to know more, I am invited to visit. She says she fully understands that you and Lady Letitia may wish to accompany me, and that she has more than ample room to accommodate you as well. She is very aware of propriety and what is expected."

Anthea was startled. "Where are we invited?"

"Her home in Gloucestershire. That's where she is going now."

The fact that Gloucestershire was Jovian's home county passed briefly through Anthea's mind but was forgotten again almost immediately. "Corinna, you knew who she claimed to be last night, didn't you? She asked you to meet her here today."

Corinna lowered her eyes quickly. "Yes," she confessed.

"Why didn't you tell me? I would have come with you, and—"

"I thought it was something I ought to do on my own," Corinna interrupted defensively.

Anthea felt guilty and pulled back a little. "Forgive me, I didn't mean to sound overbearing. Well, what do you want to do?"

"Do?"

"About this invitation to Gloucestershire."

Corinna looked urgently at her. "I dearly want to examine those papers and diaries. Do you think Lady Letitia will allow it?"

"I will be honest, Corinna. I have no idea, but Aunt Letty sets great store by propriety, and no matter what, this Miss Wheatley has so far displayed precious little. Why on earth didn't she simply write to you or to Aunt Letty? That would have been the correct approach." Then Anthea smiled. "But, if Aunt Letty is agreeable, I am, too."

Corinna beamed and hugged her. "It is all arranged. She expects us to leave London on Saturday the twenty-seventh and to arrive at her house late on the Sunday."

Anthea gaped at such precipitousness. "You've already accepted? Oh, Corinna!"

"I couldn't help myself, Anthea. I was alarmed when she

approached me again, but her talk of family documents quite carried me away, and when she pressed my grandmother's locket upon me, I just had to accept the invitation."

"Not only on your own behalf, but on mine and Aunt Letty's as well," Anthea pointed out.

"Anthea, you know your family background through and through and are secure in such knowledge. Can you imagine what it is like to have a great void where one's past is concerned? Suddenly I may not even be named Pranton, for if my mother did not marry my father, then I am Corinna Wheatley. To be able to discover the truth means everything to me, and I think I will die unless I can go."

"That is surely a little dramatic," Anthea replied, "but I suppose I can understand what you feel. Please do not think the matter is settled, however, for even if Aunt Letty agrees, she will first write to Miss Wheatley, as is the done thing. And the twenty-seventh may not suit, and another date have to be arranged instead."

"My aunt was rather insistent upon the twenty-seventh," Corinna replied doubtfully.

"I am sure it is not carved on tablets of stone." Anthea linked arms with her. "By the way, where in Gloucestershire does your aunt live? The Cotswolds?"

"No, a place just north of Bristol in the vale of the River Severn. Near a town called Cathness," Corinna replied; then her brow creased. "Isn't that the Duke of Chavanage's family name?" she asked.

Anthea had halted in dismay. "Yes, it is. Cathness Castle, his country seat, is there." Of all the places in England Abigail Wheatley might have lived, why did it have to be there?

Corinna was concerned. "Oh, Anthea, will this make it impossible for you to come too?"

"I don't know."

"But as the duke is here in London, why should you not go to Gloucestershire?" A new thought occurred to her, and Corinna's glance slid briefly toward Sir Erebus, who still waited a polite few yards away. She lowered her voice, although it was not necessary. "Anthea, if Sir Erebus is the duke's neighbor in the country, *he* must live near Cathness too."

"That is true, which means that he may well know your aunt, although he gave no intimation of recognizing her. Still, it will not do any harm to ask." Anthea took Corinna's arm, and they went to join Sir Erebus, who straightened expectantly.

"Your sisterly confab is at an end?" he inquired.

As it happened, Sir Erebus did not know Miss Wheatley, but as he explained, he had only lived near Cathness for a little over a year. However, he did know the landlord of the Cross Foxes. "Ah, yes, his name is Obed Dennis, and he is an excellent fellow." Then he added, "Regarding Miss Wheatley, it occurs to me that the Duke of Chavanage is certain to know of her. I can ask him, if you wish."

Corinna's face brightened. "Oh, *would* you?"

He smiled. "But of course, Miss Pranton, and I am sure that what he has to say will assure Lady Letitia that the invitation may be safely accepted."

"Oh, I *do* hope so. I long to go to Cathness."

Sir Erebus smiled again. "And Cathness will make you very welcome, Miss Pranton," he murmured.

Anthea was sure some other meaning was hidden in those words, although she could not imagine what it could be.

His smile continued. "Well, ladies, what is your immediate plan?"

"To return to Berkeley Square," Anthea answered.

His dark eyes brushed hers. "May I escort you?"

Corinna answered for her. "That is most kind of you, Sir Erebus."

"I offer my services gladly, Miss Pranton, and then I will go directly to the duke. A running footman will be sent to Daneway House the moment I learn anything." His gaze returned to Anthea, lingering a moment longer than necessary, which made her feel awkward. Oh, *how* she regretted those unguarded words last night.

Lady Letitia was as startled as Anthea to hear of Miss Wheatley and her news, and was at first inclined to be disapproving of the lady's methods. The gift of the locket made her frown, she was exceedingly doubtful about the wisdom of going to stay with a stranger, and the connection with Jovian and Sir Erebus made matters worse, as did the absence of a proper address. But what shook her most of all appeared to be that Corinna's perplexing new relative lived in the vicinity of Cathness.

At first Anthea was inclined to think it was because of Jovian, whom Aunt Letty may have liked well enough in the past but who was now entirely unsuitable because of his overindulgence in tipples of one sort or another. Gradually, however, Anthea realized that there was something else behind her aunt's attitude. Inevitably Anthea wondered about the past love affair she was sure had existed. Had Aunt Letty perhaps been in love with Jovian's father?

Knowing nothing of Anthea's secret pondering, Lady Letitia wagged a finger at Corinna. "You, miss, were in error to accept an invitation without consulting me first. The proper rules must be followed."

Anthea felt the need to support her errant stepsister. "Aunt Letty, I know that it is a little, well, unconventional, but we will soon learn all that is necessary. Sir Erebus is going to speak to Jovian and then send word here."

"Nevertheless . . ."

"And Sir Erebus may not know Miss Wheatley herself, but he spoke very highly of the landlord of the local inn."

"Did he indeed?"

"Yes, Aunt Letty."

Lady Letitia fidgeted. "I will give it consideration, but no decision will be made until I am in possession of all the facts.

A letter will be sent to Miss Wheatley, care of the Angry Foxes, and—"

"The Cross Foxes," Corinna corrected, with youthful zeal.

Lady Letitia bristled. "Whatever the vulpine temper, miss, I will not permit anything without being considerably more reassured than I am right now. Is that clear? I will *not* have you accepting invitations here, there, and everywhere without consulting me first. Your conduct today has been lamentable, Corinna, and I will not tolerate it. Have I made myself clear?"

Corinna was contrite. "Yes, Lady Letitia," she said meekly.

"That had better be so, for I mean what I say."

"Yes, Lady Letitia."

"And you will not, I repeat, not, go out alone again for the time being, until I am satisfied that this has been an isolated episode." Lady Letitia's eagle eye fixed Corinna. "And while I think of it, in your eagerness to quit London, have you overlooked the matter of Viscount Heversham, who was not after all playing you false with another?"

Corinna's lips parted, for indeed she *had* forgotten that unfortunate gentleman; indeed, he had ceased to matter now that she was so preoccupied with the much more exciting Sir Erebus.

Lady Letitia searched her face. "There is no need to reply, for I can read you like a freshly printed page. Exit the viscount, stage left. Enter Sir Erebus Lethe."

Corinna lowered her eyes. When put like that, it made her sound a flighty piece, and no mistake.

"So instead of inviting the viscount to the modest dinner party I am shortly to hold," Lady Letitia continued, "I will ask Sir Erebus instead."

Corinna's suddenly bright eyes were raised once more. "Will you really? Oh, thank you, Lady Letitia!"

"Hmm."

It seemed an age before the running footman brought the promised note, which was wisely addressed to Lady Letitia. She broke the seal and read it out to Anthea and Corinna.

*Dear Lady Letitia, I have spoken to the Duke of
Chavanage about Miss Wheatley, and he tells me
she is a highly respected lady of means. He agrees
that her home is rather difficult to find because it is
in the many lanes between Cathness and the River
Severn, and he supports me in assuring you that the
landlord of the Cross Foxes is a very upstanding,
helpful man who will be more than willing to assist.
Miss Wheatley's home is only about three miles as
the crow flies from both Cathness Castle and my
country seat, Wycke Hall, so should anything be
required, you are not to hesitate to approach the
duke's servants or mine. I have already dispatched
a note, advising my household to be helpful should
they be asked. I have the honor to be, etc. Erebus
Lethe.*

Lady Letitia refolded the note. "What a very charming and
gracious man Sir Erebus is, to be sure," she murmured, then
went to the window, looked out, and drew a deep breath. "No
matter what else may be said of Jovian, his word is still to be
trusted on matters like this. Very well, provided I am content
with Miss Wheatley's response to my communication, we
will go to Cathness."

Corinna could have danced with joy, and Anthea shared
her delight, but a glance at Aunt Letty's contemplative expression as she gazed out at the square told again of secret
thoughts. Memories? Ghosts from the past?

Eleven

*L*ady Letitia wrote to Miss Wheatley, in care of the Cross Foxes in Cathness, and soon received a polite reply. An address was still wanting, but the writer's hand was educated and the paper very expensive, and Lady Letitia was most impressed by the sentiments expressed. She also approved of Miss Wheatley's assurances about her home and servants and the fact that she had several maids who had in the past attended ladies of considerable consequence. Any secret reservations that Lady Letitia might have had about going to Cathness were now well and truly buried from view, as she arranged their departure for the day Miss Wheatley had wished, Saturday, August 27th.

Lady Letitia's select little dinner party took place on the Friday, a day that had not gone well from the outset. The veritable epidemic of mumps that had been spreading through Mayfair at last reached Daneway House. In the morning a footman complained of feeling unwell, and by the evening a number of other servants were affected, including the three ladies' maids. Their swollen faces were a sure indication of what was wrong.

Fortunately Lady Letitia, Anthea, and Corinna had all had the disease during childhood and were therefore unlikely to contract it again, so the visit to Gloucestershire was not in jeopardy. They would, of course, have to travel without the services of their maids, but they were confident from Miss Wheatley's letter that she could provide them with suitable replacements. "Aunt Abigail's abigails," as Corinna said laughingly.

Housemaids helped the ladies dress for the dinner party, which went ahead because the cook was quite well and there were sufficient remaining servants to assist her and wait at the table. The other dinner guests, Sir Erebus, along with the Bishop of Fairwells and Lord Henley, three gentlemen to three ladies, replied to Lady Letitia's hasty warning notes that they too had contracted the illness when young and were therefore still quite happy to attend.

The dining room was on the ground floor at the rear of Daneway House, with French windows that stood open to the garden so that the scent of flowers drifted on the evening air.

A lavish epergne, heavy with fruit, stood on the table between candelabra that cast warm light on crystal glasses and polished silver cutlery. The best Sèvres dinner service had been brought out, as had the finest wines, and the cook had done Lady Letitia proud with both white and brown soup and then a choice of loin of veal, gammon of bacon, or venison, all served with potatoes and peas. For dessert there were apricot tarts, jellies and creams. It was, as the bishop remarked afterward, a meal fit for the Prince Regent himself.

Lady Letitia would have been well pleased with everything, had it not soon become clear to her that Sir Erebus was not interested in Corinna but in Anthea, who tried to discourage him with politeness. Corinna was hurt and disappointed, for she still burned with attraction for him. It felt to her almost as if she had loved him forever, yet in fact she hardly knew him at all. Anthea felt dreadful for her stepsister and wished Sir Erebus in perdition for paying such marked attention to the wrong young lady.

When the meal was at an end, the gentlemen elected to follow the custom of remaining at the table while the ladies adjourned to the drawing room on the floor above. Before accompanying her stepsister and aunt upstairs, Anthea first slipped out into the gardens for a little fresh air. The bishop and Lord Henley were embroiled in another of their interminable political debates, and after a minute or so Sir Erebus joined her outside.

Until he appeared at her side, Anthea had been enjoying the night air and the sounds of London beyond the garden walls. The fountain splashed prettily, the roses and the honeysuckle were sweet, and a good moon had risen over the nearby rooftops. It was the second moon of the month and only a few days short of full. The light it cast was cool, clear, and—dared she think it?—vaguely blue, no more than a slight tint that prevented it from being its usual ghostly self, but discernible for all that.

She was dismayed when Sir Erebus came up to her, for the last thing she wanted was for him to make an overture that she would be obliged to rebuff. Surely he must realize by now that she simply was not interested in him!

"I cannot leave you all alone out here, Lady Anthea," he said.

"It is kind of you to be concerned, Sir Erebus, but I quite like being alone." Would he take the hint?

"Are you looking forward to Gloucestershire, Lady Anthea?" he inquired.

"Yes." Maybe a monosyllabic response would work.

"Ah, but I suppose you will have been there before?"

She looked at him. "Why should you think that?"

He cleared his throat. "I . . . er, presumed you might have been there with the duke. With Lady Letitia as well, of course," he added hastily.

"I have indeed been to Gloucestershire before, Sir Erebus, but only to pass through on the way to stay with relatives in Monmouthshire"—she studied him—"not that it would have been any business of yours if I had." *Surely* he knew his attentions were not welcomed?

"Lady Anthea, do you know that the duke still loves you?"

She became irritated. "What may or may not be between the duke and me is absolutely private and certainly not your concern, Sir Erebus."

It was a snub that froze his face for a second, but then his smile returned. "You are right to chide me, Lady Anthea, for I have been most presumptuous. I fear you may be even more displeased when I tell you I have made plans to return to Gloucestershire myself."

"Oh?" Her heart sank. Just how far must she go to cool his ardor?

"Yes, because from tomorrow London will hold no charm for me."

What else was she supposed to understand from such a remark than that he was following her? "Sir Erebus, you are perfectly at liberty to go where you choose."

"I trust that you, Lady Letitia, and Miss Pranton will call upon me at Wycke Hall?"

"You are kind to invite us," she replied, omitting to accept.

The mysterious hint of blue in the moonlight revealed something in his dark eyes, a nuance that she could not quite interpret, but when he spoke again it was to compliment her. "What a perfect picture you are among Lady Letitia's matchless flowers. Why, I do believe this aster is the same color as your eyes." He bent to pluck a flower, then held it out to her.

She couldn't bring herself to refuse, but what she accepted wasn't an aster at all but a sprig of mistletoe! In her mind's eye she saw a similar sprig that Corinna had insisted was a narcissus. Had Sir Erebus been responsible for that, too? Yes, of course he had! His gaze was upon her, attentive and anticipatory, his whole demeanor one of keen expectation. What was he hoping? That a spell just cast would bring her into his arms? She met his eyes squarely . . . but inside she was greatly disquieted that this might be another of the strange occurrences of which Jovian had warned.

Disbelief replaced his eager anticipation, and he turned away slightly to hide the ugly emotions on his face. "May I ask if anyone has given you lavender within the last year?" he asked, in a tight voice.

"As it happens, someone did. In January."

He turned back to her, his nostrils flared and his lips pinched white around the edges. "The duke?"

"Does it matter?"

"It matters, believe me," he replied shortly.

"Very well, yes, it was the duke. Now, if you don't mind, I have endured sufficient interrogation." She made to walk past him, but he caught her arm and prevented her.

"Was it fresh lavender?"

"Let me go, Sir Erebus," she demanded.

"Just answer the question!" he snapped.

"How dare you!"

"Tell me!"

He frightened her, so she told him what he wanted to know in the hope that he would let her go. "Yes, it was fresh. From a field at Cathness, or so he said."

He had changed completely, and his rage communicated itself through his grip. With Jovian she had often sensed another world, somewhere magical and bright but never threatening; Sir Erebus had become the opposite, portending the clammy darkness beneath the earth.

She tried to pull free of him, but he seemed not to hear, only releasing her when the bishop's curious voice came from the open doors of the dining room. "Is everything all right, Lady Anthea?"

"Yes, Bishop, it is." She looked disdainfully at Sir Erebus. "I wish you to leave immediately, sir."

"Lady Anthea, if I have behaved badly I—"

"You have indeed behaved badly," she breathed, "and I am not requesting you to leave, I am *telling* you to!"

He hesitated but then politely inclined his head. "As you wish."

"And any further approaches from you will be firmly rejected; is that clear?"

"I will mend the breach between us," he said softly.

"No, sirrah, you will not," she responded, then whisked her skirts aside to walk away from him. Lord Henley had now joined the bishop, and he looked quizzically at her. "Are you quite sure all is well, m'dear?"

"Yes, Lord Henley, but Sir Erebus is leaving."

"Ah." Political differences momentarily forgotten, the two elderly gentlemen drew themselves up and gave Sir Erebus looks that ought to have withered him on the spot.

"Your presence is no longer welcome, sir," the bishop said coldly, and without another word Sir Erebus walked through to the entrance hall, where a vigilant footman was ready to hand him his top hat, gloves, and tortoiseshell-handled cane.

Anthea was relieved when the outer door closed. What a horrible man he really was! Aunt Letty would have to be told about his disagreeable conduct, and Corinna would have to be persuaded to no longer view him through the rosy haze she did at present. Shaking a little, she smoothed her gown with her palms, trying to reassemble her shattered poise.

What was all this about? Sir Erebus had clearly expected her to accept the illusion that the mistletoe was an aster, and, as a result of her accepting what he gave, something to his benefit would result. When that did not happen, he became enraged. It seemed to be connected with the bunch of lavender from Jovian.

Alarm ran through her, for if that was what he had expected tonight, what had happened with Corinna? Was that how he made certain of her adoration? Had he seduced her? Please don't let that be so! But then she grew calmer, for in her heart of hearts she knew that Corinna was simply infatuated with him. Oddly so, perhaps, but she was still the same sweet, innocent Corinna as before.

Anthea was disturbed about everything, for what was happening was unlike anything she had known before. Then Jovian seemed to whisper to her. *"Beware, Anthea, for things might soon happen that are far, far beyond your experience . . ."*

Outside on the pavement Sir Erebus's face had twisted savagely. "You aren't protected from me that easily, my pretty," he breathed, and struck his cane so ferociously against the wrought iron railings that the sound rang across the square.

Twelve

*L*ady Letitia was horrified to hear what had happened and vowed to tell all her friends and acquaintances what a lecherous monster Sir Erebus really was. However, Anthea persuaded her from such a course, pointing out that Sir Erebus could ruin her reputation by claiming his advances had been invited. Better by far to confine the story to those present, a suggestion with which all eventually agreed, even Corinna.

At first that young lady had been desperately upset to discover her idol's feet of clay. Her evening had simply gone from bad to worse because of Sir Erebus, and she dissolved into tears but was soon restored to smiles by Lord Henley, who told her that she was too much of an ornament to society to remain alone for long. He also swore he had heard Viscount Heversham declare his unrequited love for her, which certainly gave her food for thought. It was to be hoped her reflective expression signified renewed interest in the lovelorn viscount, Lady Letitia thought.

Anthea tossed and turned in her bed that night as she tried unsuccessfully to banish Sir Erebus and his mysteries from her mind. The window had been left slightly raised, and the lightest of soothing drafts took away the stuffiness from the room. When the curtains moved gently, it seemed the moonlight was still perceptibly blue. The hall clock chimed, and as the last note died away she heard low voices in the passage.

Puzzled, she sat up. A door closed, and she thought it was Corinna's. Was something wrong? She got out of bed to see. A night candle cast a lonely light over the passage, and all seemed quiet now, except— She strained to listen. Yes, there were voices in Corinna's room, and one belonged to a man!

Shocked, she hurried along to her stepsister's door and knocked urgently. "Corinna?"

Silence.

"Corinna?"

A drowsy voice stirred. "Mm? Yes? What is it?"

"Are you all right? I heard voices."

"Voices?" Corinna came to the door and looked sleepily at her. "I must have been talking in my sleep."

"True, but I hardly think you would sound like a man."

Corinna's jaw dropped. "What are you saying, Anthea? That I have a sweetheart in my room?" Her green eyes flashed defensively. "Well, if that's what you think, please feel free to search for him!"

Anthea was embarrassed. "If you must know, I was afraid there was an intruder, and that you were trying to reason with him."

"I—I didn't think. I'm so sorry." Shamefaced, Corinna tried to make excuses. "Maybe you heard a maid with one of the footmen, or maybe someone else has mumps and needs attention. Oh, I don't know anything, except that it wasn't me." She smiled and gave Anthea a peck on the cheek. "Go back to bed, now. We have a long journey tomorrow and need to be fresh for it."

Lady Letitia's door opened, and she peered out. Her gray hair hung in plaits from beneath her night bonnet, and she was ghostly in her voluminous robe. She held up a lighted candle and peered shortsightedly at them. "Why is everyone up and chattering at this hour? Is everything all right?"

Her voice was slightly nasal, and her eyes were red, and

Anthea was concerned to realize she had been crying. "All is well, Aunt Letty. I heard a noise, but think I was asleep and dreamed it."

"Very well, my dears. Good night to you both."

As Lady Letitia began to draw back into her room, Anthea hastened to her. "All may be well with us, Aunt Letty, but clearly the same cannot be said of you," she said quietly, so her voice would not carry to Corinna.

Lady Letitia hesitated. "It is nothing, my dear, just an old maid's foolishness."

Anthea put a gentle hand on her aunt's sleeve. "It's Cathness, isn't it? Something happened there."

Lady Letitia looked at her in surprise. "You are sometimes too perceptive for your own good, miss. Well, I will never divulge the sorry tale, so please do not press me. It is something that must be left to lie."

"Aunt Letty—"

"Good night, Anthea," Lady Letitia said firmly, and went into her room.

As the door closed behind her, Anthea went back to Corinna, who looked curiously at her. "What was all that about?"

"Oh, nothing important."

Corinna smiled. "I'm not entirely empty-headed, Anthea. I've already guessed that Lady Letitia was once very much in love, and that Cathness has something to do with it. Do you think it was the previous duke?"

Anthea pursed her lips. "To be honest, that's what I wondered too, but as she does not intend to speak of it, I doubt if we will ever know."

They said goodnight, and Anthea returned to her room, but before getting into bed, she looked out at the curious blue moon. There was an unaccountable atmosphere tonight, as if something momentous but not very benevolent were imminent. She flung the curtains back and raised the sash fully. Cool air swept over her, bringing with it the fresh, bewitching scent of lavender—although where it came from she couldn't imagine, for the plants in the garden were no longer in bloom. She breathed the fragrance.

"Anthea?" Jovian spoke quietly in her head. *"I'm over here on the stables."*

She was shocked to see him on the ridge of a roof by the mews lane. He was dressed in evening clothes, his blond hair was silvery in the faintly blue moonlight, and he lounged against the wall of a tall adjacent building as if it were quite natural to be where he was.

"To me it is," he said then.

He could not only speak to her but knew what she was thinking too!

"Yes, Anthea, I can do both."

She fixed him with a glare, thinking that if he spoke the truth then he would know how many questions she wished to put to him.

"And I will answer what is necessary, but if you expect a complete explanation about everything, I fear you will be disappointed."

You always disappoint me, she thought.

"I know, my darling, but I love you and I always will." He straightened and walked casually down the sloping roof to the boundary wall between Daneway House and the neighboring property, then along the wall until he was as close as he could get to her window. He smiled up at her. "How lovely you are in the moonlight," he said, speaking naturally.

"This is not real moonlight, but something very different," she replied, glancing up at the sky. "Why is the moon that color?"

"Because the time has almost come."

"What time?" she asked quickly.

How it happened she didn't know, but suddenly he was sitting casually on the outer ledge of her window, one leg drawn up, the other swinging idly, as if he were on the ground floor, not the third. It was too far from the garden wall to the window ledge for him to have jumped or climbed, and besides, she'd barely had time to blink. She drew back uncertainly. "How . . . did you do that?"

He smiled. "Come now, Anthea, surely you aren't surprised? Not after Carlton House and St. James's Park."

"I know I should be used to it, but I don't think I ever will be." She looked at him. "You still haven't explained what time you were referring to."

"The time that Lethe and his cohorts have been anticipating for nineteen years, when the lavender blooms out of season, the harvest is ready, and there are two full moons in August," he said softly.

Her skin turned to gooseflesh. "I don't want riddles, Jovian; I want answers I can understand."

"Believe me, Anthea, if you knew those answers you would wish you did not."

"Why?"

"Trust me where this is concerned."

"Trust *you*? That is too much to ask, for you cannot exist without strong drink and become cruel and heartless when you have it inside you. I would as soon trust a rat."

"I suppose I deserved that, but if you imagine I have willingly drunk myself into oblivion these past months, you could not be more wrong. Every glass I have downed has been a torture to me. I want none of it but have no choice."

"No choice? Did someone hold the poisoned goblet to your lips and force you to sip? I think not. You drank because you *wanted* to, and I despise you for pretending otherwise."

He breathed out slowly. "You are entitled to your opinion, wrong as it may be. But speaking as a relatively harmless rat, I sincerely hope you realize that Lethe is of the plague-carrying variety and thus very dangerous indeed."

She searched his face. "From which remark I suppose you witnessed what happened in the garden after dinner?"

"I did not need to, for I know him. He showed his true vile colors tonight—well, some of them." He swung his leg over the ledge and stood in the room with her. "Never place faith in him, Anthea."

"How unflatteringly you speak of him; yet I thought he was your good friend."

"He is no friend of mine. Believe me, it is for good reason that he is called Erebus Lethe."

"The son of Chaos and the River of Forgetfulness?" Unwillingly she recalled how earlier that evening she had associated Sir Erebus with the clammy darkness beneath the earth.

Jovian put the back of his fingers to her cheek and drew them gently upward in a caress that aroused joyous memories. "Anthea, I wish none of all this had happened, and that we were as before, but it *has* happened . . . or at least has begun to happen. . . . The truth is more fantastic and sinister than anything you can conceive, and I am desperate to prevent it from proceeding. To that end I have come to you tonight to tell you not on any account to go to Gloucestershire in the morning. Stay away from the town of Cathness, and be sure that your stepsister does as well. Remain safely in London until this moon is over."

She stared at him. "What on earth are you talking about, Jovian?"

"*On* earth? Oh, how droll, to be sure," he murmured.

Suddenly she was angry. "You and Sir Erebus are both quite mad. Tonight he was ridiculously angry when he learned you had given me fresh lavender."

"Had he tried to give you a flower?"

She was confused. "Yes, an aster, except that it was really mistletoe."

He seemed unutterably relieved. "So at least I can be sure you are protected," he murmured.

"Protected? From him?"

"Yes."

A rumble of thunder spread across the sky, again from clear heavens. Would she now see the hare? That was what had happened before. Jovian glanced at the window, a look of bitter frustration on his incomparable face. "Is it real thunder, Jovian, or more akin to blue moonlight?"

The faintest of smiles played upon his lips. "It is not real thunder, but merely the way she—" He didn't finish.

"She? Who do you mean? Is it something to do with the hare?"

Their eyes met again. "It doesn't matter," he replied. "But what does matter is I love you above all others, Anthea, and will protect you in whatever way I can. You *must* trust me, my darling, for I am all that stands between you and wickedness itself."

He crushed her to him in a kiss that seemed wrenched from his very soul. His parted lips moved richly over hers, and he stroked her through her nightgown. Her senses reeled into that ecstasy from which she could never escape, the ecstasy she shared only with him, no matter how he sinned against her. Her lips softened beneath his, and her body melted into a luxurious warmth that would have denied her the will to resist had he laid her on the bed and made love to her. But instead he released her.

"Anthea, I do not intend to explain any of this unless there is no choice, but one thing I must know now. Did Lady Letitia and Corinna touch the lavender I gave you?"

She blinked. "Did they what? I . . . well, no. When I returned to the house, I gave it to a maid to put in a vase; then it was taken up to my bedroom."

The ghost of a smile raised the corner of his lips. "I'm honored," he said softly, "but we are wandering from the path, I fear. Lethe now knows that you are protected, which will not have pleased him at all, but he can be equally sure that Lady Letitia and Corinna are still at his mercy. Well, it is not important where your aunt is concerned, but your stepsister is in the utmost jeopardy. *There will be danger if you go to Cathness, so I beg you not to leave London.*"

The last sentence sounded in her head, for she was suddenly alone in the room, with just the night air moving the curtains. And outside it seemed she heard the hare's mocking cry.

Thirteen

The day of the journey was perfect for traveling, although such fine weather meant the roads would inevitably be dusty. Still, better dusty than wet, for at least a good pace could be maintained.

But the comfort of the journey was not Anthea's prime consideration as she went down to breakfast with Lady Letitia and Corinna, for she was too disquieted by Jovian's plea of the night before. He had been so earnest, so intense, so . . . believable, that she could not ignore him. Somehow she had to prevent the journey from taking place, but without causing undue alarm—or outright disbelief, which might be the case. It would not be easy, especially at the eleventh hour, and if Corinna ever spoke to her again, it would be a miracle.

It had been decided the previous evening that they would not dress until after breakfast, so they all appeared at the table in their robes and wraps. Lady Letitia did not look her best, and Anthea felt sure she had cried again during the night. Corinna thought so too, as was evident from her frequent glances at her ladyship's rather red eyes.

Given Aunt Letty's mood and the gravity of Jovian's warnings, it was some time before Anthea was able to muster the courage to say her piece. "You will both be angry with me, I know, but . . . I really do not wish to proceed with this journey."

Two pairs of eyes stared at her. Lady Letitia recovered first. "Is it not a little late to mention this?" she said, with considerable disapproval.

Anthea swallowed, "I—I know, and I was going to say something before, but Corinna was so anxious to go that I held my tongue. Now, however, I just can't go on."

Corinna was hugely dismayed. "Oh, Anthea, *please* don't do this! I am eager beyond belief to spend some time with my aunt, and—"

"But what do we really know about this woman? She might be an adventuress, intent only upon getting her hands on any of Papa's fortune that you may have," Anthea interrupted, and regretted the latter words the moment they tripped from her tongue, for Corinna was devastated.

"Is that what you think of me, too, Anthea? That Mama and I dug our grasping fingers into his title and fortune? And maybe that I am only here now in an endeavor to do the same?" she cried, tears leaping to her lovely green eyes.

Lady Letitia gave Anthea a furious look and then got up to put a comforting arm around Corinna. "No, dearest girl, of course we do not think such a dreadful thing," she said gently.

"But—but if Anthea thinks that of my aunt, she *must* think it of me too! All her smiles and outward fr-friendship have been false!"

Anthea felt awful. "1 don't think that, Corinna, please believe me. I just have an awful feeling of apprehension and want to stay here. Maybe I am being silly, but I just can't help it."

Lady Letitia tutted. "I suspect it is your time of the month or the full moon, Anthea," she said sharply.

Anthea lowered her eyes at the mention of the moon. She was ashamed of herself for speaking without thinking how her words might be interpreted.

Lady Letitia continued to chastise her. "Anthea, when I expressed uncertainty about Miss Wheatley, you and Corinna promptly talked me out of it, so it is hardly reasonable of you to present such concerns again at this stage in the proceedings."

Corinna was still distressed. "I think you are very mean, Anthea, and I will never forgive you for this."

"I'm sorry, Corinna, truly I am, but my doubts have been multiplying, and now I cannot bear it any more. I have become very uneasy about this whole thing and honestly believe we should make more thorough inquiries about Miss Wheatley before we visit her."

Lady Letitia was not at all amused. "This is intolerable, Anthea, and I am deeply disappointed in you. Such misgivings should have been expressed at the outset. I, too, have reasons for not wishing to go to Cathness again, but for Corinna's sake I have managed to overcome them. It is therefore my opinion that you should be capable of the same consideration toward your stepsister. Besides, I cannot agree with your doubts about Miss Wheatley. Her letter to me was couched in most proper and gracious terms, and she impresses me as a lady of excellent character and quality."

Corinna glared reproachfully at Anthea and nodded her agreement with Lady Letitia's sentiments.

Anthea knew she was losing the battle. "Aunt Letty, I—"

"Enough, Anthea! You may stay here if you choose, but Corinna and I will proceed to Cathness as planned."

Stay behind and leave them to travel into danger? Anthea knew she couldn't possibly do that. "I . . . I will come too," she said in a small voice.

"Very well, but you will hold your tongue in future, unless you have something sensible to say."

Having mishandled the whole thing, Anthea nodded. "Yes, Aunt Letty."

It was a quarter of an hour short of midday when the three ladies emerged from the house to enter the waiting traveling carriage, a handsome navy blue vehicle drawn by four well-matched chestnut horses.

Corinna took Lady Letitia's arm to step across the pavement, thus obliging Anthea to follow behind on her own. This slight was done deliberately, for although Lady Letitia had mellowed toward her niece since breakfast, Corinna remained very upset and had, as the saying goes, sent Anthea to Coventry, for not a word would she say, even though Anthea had striven to put matters right. Anthea was very troubled as she tried to make herself comfortable for the bumpy miles ahead. She was in a terrible quandary, and did not know how to cope with it.

The coachman, named Longton, stirred the horses into action, and the carriage jolted away from the curb. As it drove smartly north around the square toward Oxford Road it passed a flower girl, who Anthea noticed was selling asters. That was all, just asters. Yet her street call was about a different plant entirely. "Who will buy my lavender? Six bunches a penny! Lavender, sweet lavender blue!"

Startled, Anthea sat forward to lower the window glass and look out. The call changed immediately. "Asters, beautiful asters! Pink, white, red, and blue!"

Anthea glanced at Lady Letitia and Corinna. "Did you hear that?" she asked.

"Hear what, my dear?" inquired her aunt.

"The flower girl on the corner called out 'lavender,' yet is selling asters."

"I only heard her mention asters."

Corinna nodded agreement. "I did too. I know I thought I heard 'lavender' being called before, but not this time. Anyway, it's even later in the month now, and even more unlikely."

Lady Letitia looked perplexedly at Anthea. "Oh, you are being odd today, child. Why on earth would she sing about *lavendula vera* at the end of August?"

"I . . . don't know." Anthea gazed out the window as the

carriage turned west along Oxford Road and Longton brought the team up to a spanking pace as they left London.

The first change of horses was made at the Red Cow in Hammersmith, a famous sixteenth-century hostelry that stood directly on the road. It had a high pitched roof with red tiles and vast stables to accommodate the considerable amount of traffic that halted there, which included the mails and numerous stagecoaches. When Lady Letitia's equipage drew up in the busy yard, Anthea alighted to walk a little. It was a firm habit of hers to do this on long journeys, and only a torrential downpour would have kept her seated inside.

Hardly had she stepped down to the cobbled yard when she saw Jovian ride slowly past the inn in the same direction they were going. He was mounted on his fine dappled gray thoroughbred and wore his pine green riding coat. His close-fitting cream breeches clung to his hips and thighs, and the admirable shine on his top boots caught the sunlight as he reined in and turned in the saddle to look directly at her. When he removed his top hat to incline his head, she was distressed to see him rock in the saddle. Then he called out drunkenly.

"Go h-home, Anthea. Be s-safe." Then he glanced behind him in the same haunted manner she'd noticed before. He must have seen something, for he kicked his heels and urged his horse on toward the west. Was he leaving London for Cathness Castle?

Anthea ran out to the road, but all she saw were traps, wagons, coaches, carriages, drovers, even a donkey cart. Jovian had disappeared into the dust and vehicles. Soon afterward the carriage left the Red Cow with fresh horses. It did not pass Jovian along the road, nor did she mention having seen him.

The countryside was mellow beneath the late summer sun, and the harvest was well advanced, although not by any means complete. Rows of reapers with scythes or sickles made their slow, methodical way across golden wheat fields or mowed through fine ripe barley. They were followed by binders, who in turn were followed by women and children gathering the gleanings or propping the sheaves into little stacks known as stooks.

Anthea sometimes heard the men chanting to help keep their rhythm, "Mow high, mow low, mow levelly O." At other times she heard pipes and tabors playing, and occasionally she even saw morris dancers, bells jingling and handkerchiefs fluttering as they, too, helped keep the all-important rhythm. It was hot work for all concerned, and much cider was imbibed from horn cups filled from each man's two-quart wooden bottle, called a costrel. Close to midday Anthea saw women bringing out bread, cheese, and more cider, and everyone sat down for a well-earned rest.

Variations on these scenes were observed all along the way, together with prosperous dairy farms, flocks of sheep, excellent turnpikes, leafy lanes, grand houses, and gracious parks. It was all a constant reminder of just how rich and fertile a land England was.

In the evening they reached the little town of Hungerford on the border between Berkshire and Wiltshire. Lady Letitia's diligent preparations meant that comfortable accommodation awaited them at the Bear Inn, which had stood on its site since the thirteenth century. Renowned for the cleanliness of its accommodation and the quality of its table, it was considered one of the best hostelries in the two counties.

After enjoying a fine dinner of salmon, peas, and potatoes, followed by gooseberry tart, the three tired ladies went gladly to their rooms. Corinna had now relented a little toward Anthea, so they shared one room, while Lady Letitia had the other to herself. They all three missed the services of their maids. Putting clothes away, unpinning hair, and all the fiddling services they took for granted now had to be undertaken by themselves, which led Lady Letitia to mutter that the Almighty had obviously created mumps as a punishment for idle gentlewomen.

At last, however, all three travelers were asleep between the Bear's freshly laundered sheets.

Fourteen

The peace of the night was marred by a storm. Lightning split the darkness, and thunder shuddered through the inn. Rain poured in rivulets along the street, dripped from eaves, and gurgled in pipes and drains. The smell of wet earth filled the air, and the leaves of a tree glinted wetly in the light from a lantern on the corner outside Anthea and Corinna's room.

Anthea slept through it all, but just as the thunder at last began to fade into the distance, her slumber was once again disturbed by voices in the room. Corinna and a woman were talking. Anthea stirred sleepily. "Mm? Who's there . . . ?" she mumbled, still not really awake.

The woman fell silent, but Corinna was too anxious about something to be wary. "Don't go, please . . ." The woman didn't respond, so she pleaded again. "Please stay, I beg you." Still there was nothing, and Corinna whispered, "I will remember what to do. Every single word is engraved on my heart." Then came smothered sobs as she hid her face in her pillow.

Thunder rolled far away, and the eastern horizon was lit now and then by flashes of lightning. Anthea awoke properly and lay there for a second or so, trying to assemble her thoughts. She was too drowsy to be sure what she had heard. Puzzled, she sat up, then looked at Corinna, who was still crying quietly into her pillow. She put a gentle hand on her step-sister's shoulder. "Corinna? Whatever is wrong?"

Corinna gave a start, then sat up too, the lantern outside casting sufficient light for Anthea to see her face. She seemed bewildered, as if she did not know where she was, but then gave Anthea a puzzled little smile. "Why did you awaken me? Is something wrong?"

"Well, actually I thought there was something wrong with you."

"Me?" Corinna's expression was utterly astonished. "Why? I was fast asleep, so why should you think there was something wrong?"

"You were crying."

"Was I?" Corinna instinctively put her hands to her eyes. "Good heavens, so I was."

"I thought I heard voices again, you know, like that night back at Berkeley Square; only this time you were talking to a woman."

Corinna was taken aback. "A *woman*? Look, Anthea, it really must be that I talk in my sleep." She gave a little giggle. "Maybe the next time I will be a yapping terrier or a yowling cat."

Anthea smiled, too, but she had to force herself. The strange occurrences had followed them from London, and she was more aware than ever of the seriousness of Jovian's warnings; yet at the same time her faith in him had been shaken by seeing him drunk at the Red Cow. The remote rattle of thunder sounded again, and a stir of breeze crept around the slightly open window to move the curtains as they settled to try to sleep again.

Minutes later there was an almighty crash from the corner of the room, followed by the splash of water on the wooden floor. Anthea and Corinna sat up again with startled cries. "What was that?" Corinna gasped.

"I don't know." Anthea pulled the bedclothes right up to her chin and peered nervously around the shadowy room. Her gaze fixed upon the washstand in the corner, for the bowl and water jug no longer stood on it as they should have done. Slowly she sat forward to look at the floor. Sure enough, broken china lay there in a pool of water. "It was the bowl and water jug," she said hesitantly, "but they were really heavy, so how on earth could they just fall?"

"I don't know," Corinna whispered fearfully, beginning to draw the bedclothes up to her chin as well.

Another draft found its way around the window, and this time sucked strongly through the bedroom so that the door creaked. It was open! Anthea's heart almost stopped, for she knew she had closed it very firmly when they retired. Someone had been in the room!

Corinna heard the door too. "Oh, Anthea, we've had an intruder! Do you think he stole anything?"

"He?"

"Well, burglars and thieves are usually male, aren't they? Look, I really wasn't talking to anyone, male or female, so please don't start all that again."

"I had better take a good look," Anthea said, and tossed the bedclothes aside to stand up. She tiptoed around the shards of china and the pool of water, then looked warily out into the passage. There seemed to be no one around, and the night light at the far end was burning calm and steady, as if the draft had not reached that far into the inn.

She was about to draw back into the bedroom when she saw wet paw prints on the passage floor. They led two by two away from the room toward the staircase. She had seen them before in the frost of the Berkeley Square garden and knew they belonged to the hare. Such a creature, abnormally clever or not, was unlikely to have opened the door by itself, so maybe she had not closed it properly after all.

Corinna's querulous voice sounded from the bed. "Anthea? I'm frightened in the dark on my own."

"I'm coming." Anthea closed the door firmly and returned to the mess on the floor. There was nothing she could do about the water, which she hoped was not dripping into the dining room directly below, but she collected the fragments of china and put them carefully in the hearth of the little fireplace.

"Perhaps we ought to look through our things and see if a thief has been at work," Corinna suggested, but Anthea could see in the faint light from the outside lantern that nothing had been disturbed. She looked all the same, but of course everything was where it should have been.

"Maybe it was one of the inn cats," Corinna ventured.

"Yes, that must be it," Anthea replied, getting back into the bed.

Lady Letitia was the first to leave her room the next morning, Sunday. The bells of Hungerford church had rung very early, awakening her after a very bad night, so she did not feel her best as she crossed the staircase landing toward the passage to Anthea and Corinna's room. Memories jostled in her head, and she chided herself for an excess of sentiment; after all, it had all happened so long ago that she really ought to have put it away by now.

But then an exchange of greetings between two gentlemen at the bottom of the stairs brought her to a shocked halt.

"Hugh? Damn it all, old fellow, I cannot believe I've bumped into you after all this time!"

The man called Hugh answered in an unmistakably Welsh voice. "Joseph? *Duw,* man, I thought you'd gone to perdition years ago!"

Lady Letitia put a hand to the passage wall to steady herself. To suddenly hear again that name and the sweetest of Celtic accents twisted a knife in her heart, and fresh tears stung salt in her eyes.

Anthea and Corinna emerged from their room at that moment and halted in dismay on seeing her in such distress; then Anthea ran to her. "Aunt Letty? Are you unwell?" she cried anxiously.

"Don't fuss, my dear, for there is nothing wrong." Lady Letitia tried to look carefree and bright, but her lips quivered again, and the tears began to pour down her plump pink cheeks.

Corinna came hurrying up as well, and in great concern both young women ushered Lady Letitia to their room and made her sit on the edge of their bed. Anthea took a little vial of sal volatile from her reticule and passed it briefly under her aunt's nose, and after a moment or so, Lady Letitia was able to collect herself a little. She dabbed her eyes with a handkerchief and then struggled to give them a rueful little smile. "Such nonsense first thing of a morning," she muttered.

"Clearly it isn't nonsense to you," Anthea said kindly, sitting beside her and taking her hand.

"What is it, Lady Letitia? Are you sad?" asked Corinna.

Lady Letitia pressed her lips together to stem a new flood of tears; then she managed to nod. "Yes, Corinna, my dear, I am. Memories have been plaguing me ever since this business of going to Cathness arose, and then just now, when I heard that name again . . ."

"What name, Aunt Letty?" Anthea asked.

"Hugh."

Anthea was puzzled. "But . . . wasn't Jovian's father also called Jovian?"

Lady Letitia smiled. "Oh, it wasn't the duke, my dear, but one of his gardeners at Cathness Castle."

Corinna's eyes widened, for a gardener was surely even lowlier than a governess.

"He spelled his name the Welsh way, *H-u-w*," Lady Letitia went on, her eyes dreamy as she thought of her great love. "Huw Gadarn was the most handsome, charming, delightful man I have ever known. He set my life alight, and I wish with all my heart that I had not allowed myself to be torn away from him by disapproving parents. But I was young, and very much under their thumb."

"Tell us about it, Aunt Letty," Anthea urged gently, feeling sure that it was something her aunt needed to talk about, after keeping it secret for all this time.

Lady Letitia thought for a moment and then nodded. "Very well, for perhaps it is something you should know, if only to understand why I am so anxious for both of you to be happy. We are not all granted the experience of true love, but you, Anthea, discovered it with Jovian." She smiled at Corinna. "And I think you will find it with Viscount Heversham, my dear, for he is desperately in love with you, and I think you do not yet realize that you return his feelings. Oh, yes, do not roll your eyes like that, for I know more of these things than either of you give me credit."

"How did you meet Huw Gadarn, Aunt Letty?" Anthea asked.

"Many people do not know now that in 1795 I was marked to be Jovian's father's second wife."

Anthea was startled, for it was the first she had heard of it, and she was sure that Jovian did not know of it either.

"Jovian's mother had died in childbed," Lady Letitia continued, "and negotiations had been trundling along for several years between the duke and my parents——your grandparents, Anthea. The duke had at first seemed very keen on the match but had latterly begun to drag his feet. This resulted in my father's annoyed demand that a betrothal take place forthwith. The duke agreed, so my parents took me to Cathness Castle, where we were to stay for a week or so before the announcement."

Lady Letitia paused for several seconds, and Corinna was desperate to hear more. "What happened, Lady Letitia? Oh, do tell!"

"Well, the duke was older than me, fine of feature, and amiable of character, but although he and I liked each other, we knew we were not suited for marriage. We knew because we were each deeply involved with someone else. From the moment I arrived at Cathness I plunged into love with Huw. It was a wonderful, exhilarating affair that made it impossible for me to contemplate marrying another. Our different backgrounds made no difference to the way we felt. We met whenever and wherever we could and were so unbelievably happy together that nothing else mattered. It is because of him that I am so interested in plants and gardening. He had a way of explaining everything that made it all so clear and compelling that I could not help but be swept along by his enthusiasm."

Corinna sighed wistfully. "Oh, how romantic," she breathed.

"Romantic, but doomed," Lady Letitia said.

Anthea was curious. "You said the duke was involved with someone else too?"

"Yes. I never saw her or knew her name, but she was a local woman of good breeding."

"How did you find out about her?" Corinna asked.

"The duke told me. Oh, don't look so shocked, for he had no choice. You see, I was returning to the castle after one of my nighttime trysts with Huw, when I saw a small traveling carriage drawn up by the lodge. I might not have taken any notice had it not been that the duke was standing by its door obviously saying farewell to a lady. It was a quiet night, and I could hear the lady sobbing. The duke kissed her hand with such passion that I thought he would devour it, but then the carriage drove off up the road toward Cathness town. She leaned out to wave to him until the carriage reached a bend in the road; then he turned to come back to the castle. I was standing too much in the open to conceal myself and so had no option but to wait there until he reached me. It was then that we talked properly for the first time and acknowledged that it would be wrong to marry. He revealed that he knew about Huw, but he didn't sneer or speak of it as an appalling misalliance; indeed, he said that it ill became him to criticize as he had just assisted his own secret love to flee the area."

"Flee? Was she married to someone else?" Corinna inquired.

"I'm not sure, but there was certainly some obstacle to

marriage. The duke loved her dearly, and I am sure she was with child by him, but no vows were taken. Anyway, the next morning the duke and I confronted my parents with our decision. It was a difficult scene, as you may imagine."

Anthea searched her aunt's face. "And that was the end of it all?"

"Not quite. That same morning, as preparations were being made for our immediate return to London, my father found out about Huw and me. Papa was not the easiest or most tolerant of men, and he had a terrible argument with the duke, whom he accused of aiding and abetting my ruin. Huw was threatened with lynching—by Papa, that is—and I was hauled away from Cathness with embarrassing haste, lest I lose my character completely. I was desperately heartbroken and wrote many a letter to Huw, but someone at the castle must have been in my parents' pay, for all were intercepted and returned unopened. Huw would have answered had he received them, I'm sure."

Corinna's green eyes filled with sympathetic tears. "And you haven't seen or heard from him since then?"

"No." Lady Letitia drew a deep breath. "I thought I was over it long ago, but this visit to Cathness has resurrected it all, and when I heard that name and a Welsh voice . . ." She didn't finish.

Anthea looked earnestly at her. "Is he still at the castle, Aunt Letty?"

"Huw? Oh, I doubt it. He was such a fine gardener that he was almost bound to have moved on. By now he will have a wife and family, and I will have been forgotten."

Anthea smiled a little. "And maybe neither of those things has happened. Let me put it this way, Aunt Letty. Would you like to see him again? Because while we are in Cathness, it would be quite in order for us to visit the castle."

Lady Letitia hesitated and then shook her head. "Perhaps it would be better to leave the past alone, my dear. People change. I know I have, and Huw probably has too."

Corinna glanced at Anthea and then spoke to Lady Letitia. "Are you quite sure you are up to continuing this journey, Lady Letitia? I . . . I mean, if you find it difficult and Anthea doesn't want to go anyway, I can hardly expect—"

Lady Letitia hastened to reassure her. "Not at all, my dear. I have piped my eye now and feel a great deal better for it."

Anthea's hope of a return to London had risen with Corinna's offer but was now dashed once more.

"Are you quite sure, Lady Letitia?" Corinna pressed.

"Quite sure, my dear."

Anthea said nothing, for to renew her own objections at such a juncture would look and sound very heartless indeed.

Lady Letitia got up from the bed. "There, I am myself again now, so maybe we should go down to breakfast without further ado. After all, we do not want to make too late a start."

The carriage drove on from Hungerford in fine weather, and all sign of the overnight storm soon evaporated beneath the warm sun. Longton kept the team moving along at a good pace, so they made excellent time toward Marlborough.

Before that town, however, they passed through the rolling northernmost acres of Savernake Forest, once the hunting grounds of medieval kings and princes. In those days the great tract of oak and beech woodland had stretched all the way from Marlborough to the shores of the Solent on the south coast. Savernake was smaller now, but still vast, and its leafy glades fringed the road as Longton drove toward the next inn. He was concerned about one of the horses, which he was convinced was going lame. At last he had to investigate and drew the carriage up at the side of the road.

The three ladies alighted to take a little stroll while he made certain of the horse. The tree-cooled air was fresh and pleasing, with the overtone of earth, leaves, and wildflowers that always pervaded woodland. Birdsong rang through the glades as Lady Letitia and Corinna debated fashion, in particular the new rage for wearing colored skirts held up with straps over a white bodice. Lady Letitia did not like it at all, but Corinna thought it a delightful mode that she hoped to be allowed to wear.

Anthea took off her bonnet and swung it idly by the ribbons as her attention wandered to the scenery around her. There were nuthatches darting up and down tree trunks in search of beech nuts and early autumn crocuses raising their pale mauve heads in the shade. Among the first fallen leaves, she noticed lovely but deadly fly agaric toadstools, with their red caps and scattering of white specks like pieces of crushed sugar loaf. Sylvan shadows dappled the ground, and from time to time she was sure she glimpsed fallow deer moving deeper into the trees.

A green woodpecker gave its laughing call somewhere overheard, and it was all so timeless and everlasting that had a Norman king ridden toward her with his hunting retinue, she might not have been entirely surprised. She fell behind the others, just savoring nature's beauty, then paused to watch a scarlet, black-spotted ladybird beetle on a sun-warmed ivy leaf. As if fearing her attention, it suddenly flew off with a faintly whirring sound that made her smile. She watched it skim away between the low-hanging branches of an oak tree and then gasped as she saw Jovian walking toward her.

Fifteen

T he speckled sunlight shone on Jovian's fair hair because he wasn't wearing a hat, and he had flung his coat over his left shoulder so that his white shirt was bright amid the luxuriant green foliage. He paused and gave her one of those lazy smiles that filled her with feelings she knew a proper young lady should conquer. "We meet again, Anthea," he said softly.

"What . . . what are you doing here?"

"Taking a stroll through the woods, which is presumably what you are doing."

He came over to her and stood so close that she could have put loving fingers to his face. The almost irresistible desire to touch him made her self-conscious. "Er . . . Longton thinks one of the horses may be lame," she said, "and we are just taking a little walk while he makes sure the animal is well enough to proceed."

"The horse is not lame, Anthea. I just needed to halt your progress."

"Yet another of your many talents?"

He smiled a little. "One of the many talents I still endeavor to cling to."

Anthea wasn't sure if he was sober or not, for although his voice was clear enough, there was something about his eyes that almost made him seem to be looking right through her.

He read her mind. "No, my darling, I am not drunk, nor do I intend to be again."

"Would that I could believe that."

"Why have you ignored my warnings, Anthea? Why are you *still* en route for Gloucestershire?"

"You know why. Corinna's aunt lives there, and—"

"Corinna has no aunt."

Anthea's lips parted. "Yes, she does! I've seen her several times, Corinna has spoken to her, and Aunt Letty has received a letter from her. Her name is Miss Abigail Wheatley."

He gave a short laugh. "Well, I suppose the name is particularly suitable."

"Meaning?" Anthea prompted.

"Work it out for yourself, my lady. An abigail is a servant, and a wheat lea is a wheat meadow. She is a servant of the wheat meadow, and her duties will be performed when the blue moon is full and the harvest rites are carried out."

"What?" Anthea stared at him, then gave an incredulous laugh. "Oh, come now, isn't that a little far-fetched even for you?"

"It is the truth. Damn it all, Anthea, I cannot believe that after all my warnings you are being idiotic enough to proceed with this cursed visit."

She looked away. "I *tried* to dissuade Aunt Letty and Corinna, but I bungled the whole thing and only succeeded in making them angry with me. They made it clear they would continue without me, which I could hardly allow to happen. So here we all are."

"En route for what? This nonexistent Miss Wheatley?"

She was angered. "How can you possibly say that when you yourself recommended her?"

"I did no such thing." He was taken aback.

"Oh, yes, you did. I may not like Sir Erebus Lethe or trust him one inch, but I have no reason to think he lied about speaking to you on our behalf. You told him Miss Wheatley was respectable, and that the landlord of the Cross Foxes is an excellent and reliable person who will see us safely to her home."

Jovian took her by the shoulders. "Lethe did lie, Anthea. He had to in order to ensure that you—and especially Corinna—would go to Cathness. Miss Wheatley may not be fact, but I know Obed Dennis of the Cross Foxes certainly is. I know him for a scheming villain of the first water, and Lethe's supporter to boot. However, I would no more recommend the Cross Foxes than I would fly to the—" He broke off.

"To the moon?" she finished for him. "Well, that brings us to another aspect entirely, doesn't it?"

"No, Anthea, for it is all the same circle." He closed his eyes for a moment and exhaled slowly. "Look, I don't want to quarrel with you, nor do I want to frighten you, but I *am* desperate to protect you."

"But you will not tell me what I am to be protected from. Sir Erebus? Well, it seems you have already done that with the lavender."

"Nothing is absolute, Anthea, and while the lavender will safeguard you from much, there remain things against which it is powerless."

"Things?"

"Don't ask me more, I beg of you, for it really is better you do not know." He brushed a curl from her forehead. "Forgive me these riddles, but I swear I will give you the answers if it becomes imperative."

"And when will that be? When we reach Cathness?"

"I fear so," he replied quietly. "Lethe will be there, but so will I."

"And I will see you?" A glad light sprang to her eyes, for with him she could be strong.

"Of course you will," he breathed. "You are precious to me, my darling, for you are my beloved, the queen to my king, my soul's other half, and I will be your shield until I breathe my last."

The sweet words of love brought a lump to her throat and tears to her eyes. "Oh, Jovian . . ." she whispered.

Emotion darkened his eyes, and he opened his arms to her. "Come to me," he bade softly.

She obeyed gladly, and he enclosed her with a fierce embrace, holding her so close that her body molded to his. Her arms slid around his waist, and she savored his lean warmth and the hint of costmary that always clung to his clothes. As she lifted her parted lips to meet his, she had no thought of being seen by Aunt Letty or Corinna.

At last he drew back and looked into her eyes. "You are my redemption, Anthea. Were it not for you, I might not have had the will to fight Lethe's ancient evil."

"Is it the real Jovian I have redeemed? The Jovian of this moment, not the one who sees and feels everything through a cruel blur of strong drink."

"I have always been the Jovian of this moment, but—believe me, please—intoxication was forced upon me to prevent rebellion against the cycle." Seeing the questions in her eyes, he pressed a finger to her lips. "I have already said more than enough. Would to God you had been able to call off this journey, for then the whole primitive business could not have taken place."

A stir of thunder sounded in the distance, again without any trace of cloud on the horizon. He glanced behind him. "It is known I am here. I do not have much time now, so hear me well. Do not shrink from trying again to make the others return to London. They may not be pleased with you, but believe me when I say it is worth that risk. The best thing all around will be for you all to go home to Berkeley Square, but if that cannot be, then you must not let Corinna out of your sight. Do you understand? Stay with her at all times."

Another roll of thunder sounded, much closer this time, and Anthea glanced instinctively at the sky, but of course it was blue and clear. She lowered her gaze to Jovian again, but he was no longer there, and as she looked all around she was just in time to glimpse the hare bounding away between the trees.

Then Corinna's voice sounded from the road. "Anthea? Where on earth are you? We must drive on if we are to reach Cathness by tonight!"

"I'm coming. I must have wandered further than I realized!"

"Do hurry!"

Anthea returned to the carriage, preparing herself to do as Jovian advised, but she knew that this time it would be more difficult than ever to broach the subject of going back to the capital. She believed Jovian when he said Corinna in particular was in danger. It did not matter that he had refused to explain anything, or that what he did say seemed more conundrum than common sense, because in recent days her faith in him had been reestablished. The Jovian with whom she had fallen in love was with her again, and to him she would gladly entrust her life.

The carriage set off again, more briskly now because, to Longton's mystification, the apparently lame horse seemed miraculously restored. Anthea did not know how to say the necessary words, for when she looked at Corinna's excited face and remembered how Aunt Letty had overcome her own difficulties to proceed with this visit, her own foolish objections seemed immaterial. Nevertheless, if Jovian said she had to try, then try she would.

Lady Letitia noticed her preoccupation. "Is something bothering you, my dear?"

"Not exactly . . ."

"Which means there *is* something wrong," Lady Letitia declared. "Well, out with it."

Corinna looked at her too. "Yes, Anthea, please tell us."

"I . . ."

"Yes?" Lady Letitia waited attentively.

There was nothing for it but to plunge in. "I am still bothered about going to this Miss Wheatley."

Corinna stared in disbelief, and Lady Letitia tutted very crossly indeed. "This really is too bad of you, Anthea!"

"I can't help it, Aunt Letty. I just have a terrible feeling of foreboding. Please abandon the journey and let us return to London."

Corinna burst into tears. "Oh, I think you are more than horrid, Anthea!" she sobbed.

Lady Letitia thought the same. "This is monstrous, Anthea, and I will not tolerate another word. You had the opportunity to stay behind, yet chose to accompany us, so if you imagine I am about to give credence to your vague talk of foreboding, you may think again!"

"But, Aunt Letty—"

"Enough!"

Anthea flinched and did not say any more. A heavy silence fell, and she resigned herself to being sent to Coventry again as the carriage drove out of Savernake into the town of Marlborough. She felt like screaming at her aunt that Corinna would be in peril if they went to Cathness, but how could she say that without also admitting that she did not know what the danger really was? It had something to do with Sir Erebus Lethe, something to do with harvest rites, and something to do with a cycle, but she could not sensibly explain anything.

No one said anything as the carriage left Marlborough and Wiltshire to enter Gloucestershire, and the atmosphere was oppressive by the time they reached the quaintly named town of Chipping Sodbury. It was usually a busy place, but today being Sunday, it was virtually deserted as Lady Letitia's equipage moved slowly up the wide, sloping main street. Suddenly there came from behind the sound of a swift but light vehicle; then a furious Longton had to haul his team swiftly to one side as a smart yellow phaeton overtook them at breakneck speed. Drawn by dark high-stepping horses, it was tooled with reckless verve by a gentleman in a blue coat. His top hat was fixed firmly over his forehead for fear of losing it in his rush, and he skimmed the phaeton dangerously close to the carriage, a frowned-upon maneuver known as feather-edging.

Longton was so livid he stood up to brandish a fist and bel-low shocking abuse after the gentleman, who glanced briefly back. Corinna had lowered the window glass to see what was happening. "Oh, no, it's Sir Erebus!" she cried.

Anthea was conscious of a horrible feeling in the pit of her stomach. Jovian had warned her that Sir Erebus would be in Cathness, but even so this sudden confirmation of the fact was a disagreeable shock.

Lady Letitia was dismayed. "Oh, dear, I would much pre-fer him to be in London. However, if he drives in that repre-hensible fashion, he'll be at Wycke Hall before we reach Cathness, and with luck our paths will not cross again."

"With even better luck his driving will overturn him into a deep, particularly disgusting duck pond," Anthea observed, forgetting she was in Coventry.

"That is not charitable, my dear," Lady Letitia chided, then gave a mischievous smile. "A duck pond would be just the thing, though."

Corinna's was not a vindictive nature, and she too smiled at Anthea's remark. The ice was suddenly broken, and Anthea found herself back in the body of the kirk, as a Scottish friend of Aunt Letty's had been wont to say.

Sir Erebus may have driven on, but he had clearly recog-nized the carriage, and he was waiting beneath an oak tree at a fork in the road. He hailed Longton, whose inclination was to drive on past the hated yellow phaeton and its owner, but the coachman now recognized Sir Erebus as having been a guest at Daneway House, so he knew he must seek Lady Leti-tia's wishes. He halted the carriage well short of the oak and climbed down to approach the lowered window.

"Begging your pardon, my lady, but Sir Erebus Lethe awaits just ahead. Do you wish to acknowledge him, or should I drive by?"

Lady Letitia was about to say they should drive by, when

it occurred to her that here was a chance to tell Sir Erebus exactly what she thought of him. "I will speak to him, Longton."

"As you wish, my lady."

The coachman returned to his seat, and as the carriage moved on once more, Anthea and Corinna exchanged appalled glances. Lady Letitia saw. "Don't misunderstand, my dears, for I intend to singe the scoundrel's ears!"

The carriage halted again at the fork, and Sir Erebus stepped forward to open the door. "Good afternoon, ladies. How very pleasant it is to encounter you."

No one answered. Anthea noticed that he had one hand behind his back, and she was a little curious, but then she fixed her gaze to the floor. Corinna looked briefly at him, her expression one of very mixed emotions. She could not remain indifferent to him, in spite of his conduct toward Anthea. Something inside her seemed to yearn for him, and she could not help herself. Yet, at the same time she despised him. It was all very confusing, and she wished things could have been different. If only he were a true gentleman, and if only his admiration had fallen upon her instead of Anthea, then this could have been a happy moment; instead it was disagreeable and embarrassing, and she wished the carriage would drive on.

Seconds of embarrassing silence passed, but as Lady Letitia bristled and prepared to give him a piece of her mind, they all heard chanting in a field on the other side of the road, where a circle of reapers stood on the stubble around the last stand of wheat.

"Make the earth abundant, give us fruits, and ears of wheat, and a goodly harvest, O Demeter. . . . Make the earth abundant, give us fruits, and ears of wheat, and a goodly harvest, O Demeter. . . ."

As it was repeated over and over, Anthea's brows drew together. "Demeter? But she is a Greek goddess."

Lady Letitia nodded. "Yes, with supposed dominion over

harvests. I must say I had no idea the country folk of England regarded her as a deity."

Sir Erebus spoke. "Demeter is worshipped everywhere at this time of year, Lady Letitia, as you will discover when you reach Cathness."

Lady Letitia gave him an icy look. "Do not attempt to worm yourself back into favor, sirrah, for it will not wash. How dare you presume to greet us on the king's highway as if nothing had happened! You are without conscience or honor, and I do not intend to have anything more to do with you."

He seemed totally bewildered. "I don't understand in what way I have offended, Lady Letitia."

"Don't attempt to pull the wool over these eyes, sir. You do know, and it ill becomes you to pretend otherwise. To call you a gentleman would be a great untruth; to call you a scoundrel would be accurate in the extreme."

Sir Erebus let her speak, then smiled ingenuously. "If I am guilty in your eyes, Lady Letitia, please allow me to apologize." He took his hand from behind his back and held out a little posy of honeysuckle picked from a nearby hedge.

Anthea saw that it wasn't honeysuckle at all, but mistletoe, and knew she had to prevent her aunt from accepting it. Leaning forward quickly, she snatched the posy from him and tossed it away. Her reward was a look of fury that momentarily flashed in his dark eyes.

Lady Letitia, who would not have accepted the honeysuckle anyway, looked at her in astonishment. "Whatever is the matter, my dear?"

"Forgive me, Aunt Letty, it's just that . . . that I saw a large wasp, maybe even a hornet, on one of the flowers."

Anthea could almost *feel* Sir Erebus's malevolence fixing upon her, but then he conjured a cool smile. "How very observant to see a wasp that wasn't there, Lady Anthea."

This was too much for Lady Letitia, and she swung her reticule and clouted him soundly on the side of the head. "Stand away from the carriage this very instant!" she commanded, ready to set about him again if he didn't obey. She had a strong arm and accurate aim, so he moved hastily back, and Lady Letitia immediately instructed Longton to drive on, then slammed the door.

The carriage jolted forward once more, and Lady Letitia almost snorted with displeasure. "What an unmitigated monster! What a disgrace to his rank!"

"Indeed so, Aunt Letty," Anthea answered, wishing she knew exactly how much of a monster Sir Erebus really was, but unless or until Jovian divulged the whole truth, no one would know.

"Good heavens, Corinna has fallen asleep!" Lady Letitia exclaimed.

Anthea looked, and sure enough Corinna's eyes were closed. Her head rested against the back of the seat, rocking lightly to the motion of the vehicle, and she was oblivious to all around her. Only minutes ago she had been very much awake; now she was in the very arms of Morpheus. Anthea recalled Corinna being awake when Sir Erebus opened the carriage door but could not recall anything about her from that moment on.

No one could have known that Corinna's was no ordinary sleep, but something much more sinister. They would discover it soon enough, but by then it would be too late, Jovian's frequent warnings would not have been heeded, and Corinna would be in the clutches of Sir Erebus Lethe.

Sixteen

*C*orinna was still asleep in the early evening when the carriage reached the quiet, almost bewitchingly beautiful countryside near Cathness. It was a secret corner of England, a sun-soaked vale of rich soil, ample streams, long summers, and mellow winters, nestling between the Cotswold Hills to the east and the slopes of the Forest of Dean to the west.

Here was a pastoral haven where the late summer hedgerows were sweet with honeysuckle and lush with juicy blackberries. Wild hops and clematis festooned the roadside, and myriad orange-red rose hips shone in the golden light of evening. The cider and perry orchards were fruitful, the sheep were contented in lush pastures, and the red-brown cattle—mostly the rare and almost extinct Old Gloucester breed—were plump and glossy in the meadows. It was all so tranquil and timeless that Anthea likened it to an arcadian masterpiece by one of the world's greatest artists.

Even the harvest scenes impressed as more picturesque and delightful than in other places, and although Anthea did not hear any further alien prayers to Demeter, there was nevertheless an ancient, somehow mystical atmosphere. Was it that the wheat was more golden and the farms more prosperous? That the warm air was more shimmering and the people more merry? Whatever it was, the mood was almost unearthly, and it was made more entrancing by the sound of singing and music that came from virtually every field. Had the distant sweetness of Pan's pipes carried on the balmy breeze, Anthea would hardly have been surprised.

The shadows were growing long as the first outlying cottages of Cathness came into view. The last time Lady Letitia had seen the cottages was in 1795, when her parents had taken her home by force in order to end her love affair with Huw. By cruel chance, it had been a sunny August evening then, too, with harvest time all around. Lady Letitia braced herself for more memories.

Cathness had existed long before its first recorded charter of 1070, and it seemed to be part of the land itself, rather than put there by the hand of man. There were buildings from every period, and some were so rambling, low, and venerable that even Lady Letitia, very much in control of herself, was forced to declare they must number among the oldest in the entire kingdom. Every property seemed to be in good repair, which spoke well of Jovian as a landlord.

Anthea was apprehensive as the carriage drove down the long high street. When would something happen? Would danger be lurking in the shadows of the next alley or lane? Or lying in wait at the Cross Foxes Inn, where the landlord, Obed Dennis, was part of the darkness that was Sir Erebus Lethe? So many secret fears coursed through her that she felt quite sick with nerves as Longton drew up outside the inn.

The Cross Foxes stood about halfway down the street, not far from the town pump, and displayed a colorful sign of two running foxes, red and beautifully painted, set in a diagonal cross on a background of vibrant yellow. Sunday or not, it was a thriving establishment, with much coming and going in the yard at the back and the sound of male conversation and laughter issuing from the open windows. A columned porch flanked with stone foxes jutted into the roadway, and everything was freshly painted and in as good repair as the rest of the town.

Corinna was still deeply asleep and unaware of anything,

but Lady Letitia looked out approvingly. "What a very handsome inn," she declared. "I can well understand why both Jovian and Sir Erebus speak so highly of it and its landlord."

Anthea couldn't answer, for she was too worried that in this case outward appearances might be deceptive. But at least she was forewarned, although whether or not that made her forearmed, too, was another matter.

Tables had been set outside on the cobbles, and sun-browned countrymen were seated at them with tankards of ale and cider, served to them by a plump young maid in a blue linen dress. Her brown hair was twisted up beneath a frilly mobcap, and as the carriage halted, she hastened into the inn. Something made Anthea decide to alight. She did not really know why, except that she preferred to be eye to eye with Obed Dennis when he emerged, which he did a few seconds later, wiping brawny hands on a striped apron.

He was a large, exceedingly muscular man with a genial face, rosy cheeks, and no hair at all. His eyes were small, nondescript, and almost lost amid cheerful wrinkles, and there was a broad smile on his lips. All innkeepers graced their lapels with a nosegay, and his boasted scarlet poppies and blue cornflowers. Anthea disliked him on sight—or was she influenced by Jovian's strong words of caution?

He bowed politely to Anthea. "Welcome to the Cross Foxes, ma'am." His accent was broad Gloucestershire.

"Thank you, sir," she answered, "but I fear I am not seeking your hospitality, more your assistance with directions."

He smiled again. "Directions? Certainly, ma'am. If 'tis 'elp you wants, then Oy'm your man."

"I wish to know how to reach the home of Miss Wheatley."

For a moment his face became quite still, then a little puzzled, and she was aware of eyes upon her from the inn doorway and the nearby tables. The innkeeper's glance flickered to her dark hair, then back to her bluer-than-blue eyes. "But *you* can't be Miss Pranton . . ." he said. There was an accompanying stir among the other men, as if she had been caught in a lie or even imposture.

Anthea felt uncomfortable. "That is perfectly true, sir. I am not Miss Pranton," she replied. "I am Lady Anthea Wintour. Miss Pranton is in the carriage." She indicated Corinna's sleeping figure.

He saw Corinna's golden hair, and his grin returned. "Ah, yes," he declared, his manner becoming what Anthea could only describe as hugely thankful, which emotion was shared by the other men. An important question had apparently been answered. But what had the problem been?

A man at one of the tables muttered beneath his breath, *"Make the earth abundant, give us fruits, and ears of wheat, and a goodly harvest, O Demeter."*

In the carriage Corinna awoke with a start, and in such confusion that Lady Letitia sat forward to reassure her, but Anthea, sharp of hearing, turned swiftly to the man. "Why did you say that?" she demanded.

It was Obed Dennis who replied. "Oh, pay no 'eed to Rufus, moy lady, for you knows what's said of folks round these parts, that we be Gloucestershire born and bred, strong in th'arm and thick in th'ead." He brandished a fist, then tapped his head and laughed uproariously.

Anthea did not think it funny, and he stopped laughing, cleared his throat, then gave her a courteous bow. "Forgive moy levity, moy lady. No 'arm were meant. Allow me to make amends." He plucked a cornflower from his nosegay, and held it out to her in an apparently charming and gallant gesture.

But she did not see a cornflower, just mistletoe, and shook her head. "Thank you, but I would prefer not to accept it, sir. Flowers make me sneeze. In fact, they make us all sneeze." She felt Aunt Letty's startled glance upon her, but she was determined to obstruct any intention he might have of presenting the mistletoe to anyone in the carriage.

The innkeeper's eyes narrowed, and he tossed the mistletoe away. "Moy mistake," he murmured.

"You were not to know," she replied.

"Oy certainly knows now."

"Yes, you certainly do," she retorted, giving him a narrow-eyed look to match his own.

"Oy'll see as you gets directions to Miss Wheatley's, moy lady. Allow me to 'elp you back into your coach, then Oy'll send my boy Billy out to sit with your coachman an' show 'im through the lanes."

"Is it far?"

"Far? Oh, a couple o' moyle past the castle, but 'tis complicated, if you knows what Oy mean," he replied, extending his hand to assist her. When she was seated, he paused to look up into Corinna's wonderful green eyes; then he inclined his head to her. "Welcome to Cathness, Miss Pranton." Lady Letitia was not acknowledged at all.

Corinna drew instinctively back, and Lady Letitia bestowed a thoroughly disapproving look upon him. His inn might be all that was to be recommended, but he himself did not pass muster at all! She misliked being ignored, disapproved of what she saw as his forwardness toward Corinna, and didn't much care for the way he had spoken to Anthea.

His smile did not waver as he slammed the carriage door and went back into the inn, pushing past the crowd of men pressing to stare out at the carriage—or rather, at Corinna. There was no doubt that *she* was the sole object of their interest.

Lady Letitia regarded Anthea. "My dear, since when have flowers given you the sneezes?"

"I just didn't want his horrid cornflower."

"That is understandable," her aunt murmured, her gaze shrewd. "What is going on, my dear? You were most odd about Sir Erebus's honeysuckle, and now the cornflower . . ."

"Oh, it's just my mood," Anthea replied, then looked urgently at her aunt and Corinna. "Don't either of you accept flowers from *anyone* while we are here," she said. "Please promise me."

They stared at her. "Why?" Corinna asked.

"I . . . er, don't really know; it's just a feeling I have. It will make me feel much happier if I know you will refuse such gifts."

Corinna smiled. "Then I shall do as you ask, Anthea, for it will not do for you to be unhappy."

"Of course I will comply too," Lady Letitia said, but gave Anthea another curious look. Moods had nothing to do with it; something was going on! There was clearly far more to the sudden fuss to abandon this journey and return to London. Well, one way or another, the truth would be exposed, for Letitia Wintour was nothing if not dogged when it came to getting to the very heart of something. And in this instance, other people's secrets were fair game.

A moment later Billy Dennis, barefoot, freckled and ginger-haired, ran out to clamber up with Longton. The tired horses were stirred into action again, down the street, past the pump, and then out toward the western edge of the town. The road narrowed to a lane as an imposing church steeple appeared above the trees ahead. The parish church was at a right-angled bend in the lane, facing a little pocket-handkerchief green edged with thatched cottages. The raised churchyard was scattered with timeworn tombs and gravestones set amid ankle-deep grass that waved and rippled in the stir of the evening breeze. Beyond the church could be seen the magnificent Tudor outline of Cathness Castle, the lodge and heraldic gates of which were on the bend beside the church lych-gate.

Lady Letitia looked at the lodge, recalling the night she had seen Jovian's father saying farewell to his secret lady. She could not look at the castle itself because of the more poignant memories of Huw.

Anthea looked at the castle of which she might so easily have become mistress. Maybe she would yet. Who could say?

Corinna smiled at her. "Would you have liked to be Duchess of Chavanage?"

The smile was returned, but Anthea didn't answer.

After the church, the lane wound into a patchwork of rich farmland that in prehistoric times had been under seawater. That was how Cathness had acquired its name, for the land upon which the town stood had originally been a ness or promontory that reached out into the then much wider tidal estuary. The Severn was several miles to the west now, hard against the hills of the Forest of Dean.

Anthea lowered both window glasses to allow the scent of flowers, especially the honeysuckle, to drift in. The air was drenched with its fragrance and with the dry, vaguely dusty smell of wheat harvesting. Singing and music still carried from beyond the hedgerows, and thoughts of danger and dark forces were temporarily banished from moments so perfect that Anthea knew she would remember them forever.

The carriage turned at a crossroad, then at another, before taking the left lane at a fork. Several forks later, as they crossed a stone bridge over a stream, it hadn't occurred to Anthea that it was already far more than a couple of miles since they'd left the Cross Foxes. Deeper and deeper into the vale they went, and Anthea felt the strange enchantment of the countryside coiling around her. The hazy scenery was golden and ripe beneath the slanting rays of the fading evening sun. But suddenly a sickening foreboding engulfed her. It was as sharp as unsweetened lime cup at an overheated ball, but nowhere near as pleasant, and she knew that Jovian's prediction of peril for Corinna was about to come true.

They were about to pay a heavy price for failing to act on his warnings.

Seventeen

The carriage turned at yet another crossroad, and suddenly Lady Letitia noticed a handsome holly bush she had seen before. They had come full circle! Startled, she got up to lean out the window. "Longton? We've been this way once already!" she cried.

The coachman reined in immediately. "My lady?"

"We've been this way before," she repeated. "I recognized the holly bush back there. Just where is this boy taking us?"

The coachman took Obed Dennis's offspring by the scruff and climbed down with him wriggling in his grasp. "Right, you young varmint, what's the game, eh? Taking us to be robbed, are you?"

Corinna recoiled in alarm, and Lady Letitia muttered something trenchant about rascally boys benefiting from a good wallop on the backside. Anthea was in such a ferment of trepidation that her mouth had run dry and she trembled. She felt as if a great invisible circle — Jovian's cycle — were turning, and she could only watch helplessly as it swept over Corinna standing unknowingly in its path.

Billy Dennis, who was only about ten, with scruffy clothes and a face that had not been washed in far too long, looked fit to burst into tears. "Oy ent done *nuthin'* wrong!" he protested in a rustic accent to match his father's. "Oy jus' lost moy way, tha's all! Oy said royt 'stead've left and was afeared to let on!

Please doan 'urt me! There ent no robbers, I *swears* it on the Lavender Lady!"

Longton shook him. "You swear it on the what?"

"The Lavender Lady."

"And who might she be?"

The boy's glance shifted to Anthea, then his lips clamped shut, and he hung his head.

Longton looked at Lady Letitia. "What do you wish me to do, my lady?"

"Well, as we need local assistance to get out of this maze, I see no course but to give the child the benefit of the doubt. And I suppose anyone should be allowed one mistake." Lady Letitia looked sternly at the boy. "Do you know where we are now?"

Billy didn't reply and earned himself a cuff on the ear from Longton. "Answer her ladyship, or I'll beat you black and blue!" he threatened.

The child answered hastily. "Yes, my lady, Oy knows where we be."

"Good, then please let us continue. I would prefer to be at journey's end this side of Christmas."

Billy turned as if about to clamber back up on the carriage, then ducked out of Longton's grasp and ran like the wind down the lane. Anthea was almost resigned as she watched him go. It had begun, and there was no stopping it. . . . Corinna and Lady Letitia cried out in dismay, and the coachman began to give chase, but Billy scrambled over a gate and disappeared across a field of grazing brown cows.

Corinna and Lady Letitia alighted as Longton, knowing he stood no chance of catching the fleet-footed child, gave up the chase. After a moment Anthea climbed down too. What would happen now? she wondered, so conscious of invisible forces surrounding them that it seemed the very air tingled with electricity. She glanced again and again at Corinna, upon whom she had been instructed to keep a very close eye. Oh, how she wished Jovian were here; how she wished she could feel his arms around her again, keeping all danger at bay. . . .

Lady Letitia was exasperated by Billy's flight. "What on *earth* does that child think he's up to? You may be sure that I will pay his father a visit!"

Corinna pulled a doubtful face. "If you ask me, the innkeeper told the boy to leave us stranded," she said.

"Oh?" Lady Letitia thought for a moment. "You may be right," she said then.

"You . . . don't think they really do plan to rob us, do you?"

Lady Letitia hastened to reassure her. "Of course not, my dear, that sort of banditry doesn't happen in England, only in barbaric places like France. It's probably just a silly prank. If so they will rue it, you may count upon that."

"And we still have no idea where my aunt's house is," sighed Corinna.

Longton returned and heard what she said. "Well, I certainly don't know where it is, Miss Pranton. That slippery young mongrel kept saying it was just ahead, but we never seemed to get any closer. If I ever see him again, I swear I'll remove his scrawny guts to have as garters."

Lady Letitia sympathized with his sentiments. "I may even assist you in the surgery," she murmured, then declared, "Oh, I will be glad when this journey is over."

Corinna nodded. "So will I."

Her aunt suddenly noticed Anthea's silence. "Anthea? Have you nothing to say?"

"I . . . well, no, not really," Anthea replied hesitantly. What *could* she say? That terrible events were in motion, and wickedness lurked behind every leaf and blade of grass in this lonely lane?

Corinna gazed around at the scenery. "Well, we may be lost, but you have to admit that the countryside here is particularly lovely — although perhaps a little mysterious," she added.

"You feel that too?" Lady Letitia inquired.

"Oh, yes, most definitely." Corinna drew a deep breath. "I feel as if I am on the brink of something quite wonderful."

Anthea had to bite her lip to prevent herself from bursting into tears. *Jovian, I need you, please come now.* . . . But he didn't come.

Lady Letitia sniffed. "The brink of something wonderful? Corinna, my dear, I sincerely hope it will be a restorative cup of tea at Miss Wheatley's residence, followed by a good hearty meal."

Longton looked at her. "What shall I do, my lady? Drive on in the hope of finding a house or cottage? Or try to find the way back to Cathness?"

"Oh, drive on for a while, I suppose," Lady Letitia replied. "If we don't find anything in the next ten minutes, we'll have no choice but to try to return to the town. It goes against the grain, but I fear we will have to seek accommodation, although *not* at the Cross Foxes!"

"Very well, my lady."

Longton assisted them back into the carriage, then wearily resumed his seat, but they had not proceeded more than a few hundred yards when Anthea again heard chanting. It came from behind a hedgerow that was blushed pink by the disappearing sun, and she glimpsed a scene exactly like the one they had observed when Sir Erebus had halted the carriage. A circle of twenty or so reapers stood in the center of a harvested field that was dotted with stooks. The men's heads were bowed, they clasped their sickles and scythes before them, and their long shadows stretched away over the stubble. Watching from the far end of the field was a gathering of the women, children, and older men who had been gleaning and binding the sheaves.

The chanting carried clearly. *"Come to us, O Harvest Maiden. Protect us from the Lavender Lady. Come to us, O Harvest Maiden. . . . Come to us, O Harvest Maiden. Protect us from the Lavender Lady. Come to us, O Harvest*

Maiden. . . ." Then the circle parted, and the men formed a long line that faced the carriage, allowing a clear view of the last stalks of wheat around which they had been standing.

Corinna saw as well. "Isn't that little bit of uncut wheat called the neck?"

"I have no idea," Lady Letitia replied.

"Yes, I'm sure it is. In some parts of the country there is a ceremony called 'Crying the Neck,' in which they throw their sickles at the last stand of wheat because they believe a baleful female spirit is hiding in it. I thought they called her the White Lady, but here she seems to have changed color to lavender. Anyway, until she is driven away, their harvest isn't safe."

Lady Letitia looked at her in astonishment. "How do you know all that, my dear?"

"Oh, Mama told me. She said there were all sorts of traditions, superstitions, and archaic beliefs associated with harvest."

"Well, if she came from these parts, I can well believe she knew what she was talking about. It almost makes me wish to turn my back on botany and study anthropology instead."

Corinna had to smile. "But Lady Letitia, that would not do, for unlike plants, people are inclined to answer back."

Lady Letitia eyed her severely. "And you, Miss Chit, are a prime example of *that*!"

The lane led around two sides of the field, so the harvest ritual remained in view for quite some time. At first Anthea did not notice that the line of men was somehow always facing her square on, but then she realized they were turning in time with the carriage's pace. It meant they were always looking at it, no matter what, and all the time she could hear their droning chant. Her stomach tightened more and more as the agony of suspense intensified. She almost wished it would all begin in earnest . . . whatever it was.

A new scent replaced the warmth of honeysuckle and harvested wheat that had filled the air for so long. Now there was lavender, fresh, piquant, and to Anthea as strong as though she had dabbed her skin with the oil. She looked through the other carriage window into the glinting crimson-and-gold dazzle of the sunset and was astonished to see a haze of purple-blue lavender. Row after row of the shrub stretched across a field, flowering as abundantly and fragrantly as if it were the beginning of summer, not the end. Was this the lavender that had blown as sweetly at Christmas too?

She thought of Jovian's description of the mysterious nineteen-year cycle. *The time . . . when the lavender blooms out of season, the harvest is ready, and there are two full moons in August. . . .*

Corinna suddenly spoke urgently. "I don't feel at all well, Lady Letitia; in fact, I think I'm about to be very sick!"

Lady Letitia was alarmed and hurriedly leaned out to call Longton. "Stop the carriage, if you please! And quickly, for Miss Pranton is unwell!"

"Yes, my lady!" The carriage jolted to a halt, and Corinna, now very pale and wan, climbed swiftly down and walked a few steps back to a gnarled old oak tree they had just passed. She stepped into the poppies and deep grass that grew beneath the overhanging branches and put a steadying hand against the trunk, then bowed her head, as if awaiting the retching to begin.

The chanting had stopped in the field, but only Anthea noticed as she and her aunt alighted too. Lady Letitia went to Corinna. "Oh, my poor dear, the motion of a carriage can be unsettling at the best of times, but in these winding, rather uneven lanes, I fear it is worse than ever. My legs feel a little wobbly too. Most disagreeable."

Anthea saw the reapers departing, along with their audience, among whom she spotted the miscreant Billy Dennis. Everything was now utterly quiet, except for the occasional sound from the carriage team. Night was imminent, with the shadows reaching so far that they merged together and seemed to mask what remained of the sunset.

Corinna closed her eyes. "This is dreadful," she whispered.

"Can I get you anything, my dear?" Lady Letitia inquired.

"No. Just let me stay here a minute or so."

"Very well." Lady Letitia returned to Anthea and then noticed the field of lavender for the first time. She stared at it. "Impossible," she declared. "*Lavendula vera* should be over and done with by the beginning of August; yet I appear to be looking at a crop as fine as Mitcham in June."

"But Jovian gave me fresh lavender on Christmas Eve," Anthea reminded her.

"Which he claimed to have picked here, but more likely it came from a hothouse at a Chelsea market garden. Anthea, he made a dilly of you. A lavender blue, dilly, dilly, in fact!" Lady Letitia chuckled, for Huw had once told her that dilly was the Gloucestershire dialect word for fool.

Anthea tried to smile too, but then from nowhere a quotation from *Macbeth* came into her head. *By the pricking of my thumbs, / Something wicked this way comes* . . . There was a familiar echo of thunder from the cloudless sky, signaling that the hare was close by. Corinna! She whirled about, but there was no one beneath the oak tree or along the lane in either direction. "Where's Corinna?" she gasped.

Lady Letitia turned too. "She must have gone around the carriage," she said sensibly. "Corinna, my dear? Are you all right?"

There was no answer, and Longton cleared his throat. "Begging your pardon, my lady, but Miss Pranton is not by the carriage at all."

"Then she must have climbed back in," Lady Letitia declared, and went to see. But the carriage was empty. Puzzled, she too looked up and down the lane. "She *must* be here somewhere," she murmured.

Anthea's heart had begun to hammer in her breast, and she felt as cold as ice. Corinna, oh, Corinna . . .

Lady Letitia called much more loudly, but there was only silence. Longton stood up and gazed all around, concentrating on the continually gathering shadows, but there was nothing.

Corinna Pranton seemed to have vanished off the face of the earth.

Eighteen

Corinna's sudden disappearance left Anthea feeling numb. It was all her fault. She had failed to prevent the journey continuing here to Cathness and failed to watch Corinna closely enough. If she had been Sir Erebus Lethe's faithful handmaiden, she could not have aided him more.

Lady Letitia blamed herself as well. She was Corinna's guardian and chaperon and would rightly be judged careless. Oh, how *could* she have been so negligent as to allow Corinna to be—to be what? There was no knowing what had happened, because no one had heard or seen anything. Had she been abducted? Was kidnap, not robbery, the plan they should have suspected when Billy Dennis ran off and left them? Would a ransom be demanded for Corinna's return?

Anthea saw her aunt's distress and hurried to comfort her. "Please don't upset yourself, Aunt Letty, for it isn't your fault."

"Isn't it? Oh, I should never have let her out of my sight. Why, just this morning I was foolish enough to let you wander off in Savernake Forest. Anything might have happened to you. . . ."

"But nothing did happen to me, Aunt Letty. Besides, where Corinna is concerned, we were both here with her, and Longton was too. None of us saw anything." Anthea felt worse by far as she tried to encourage her aunt; after all she had *known* something would happen and yet said nothing. The only way to have prevented this would have been to return to London as Jovian had begged.

Lady Letitia strove to concentrate. "Might she have strolled a little for the fresh air, stumbled over something, and tumbled into that ditch on the other side of the lane?" She pointed a quivering finger.

"But surely we would have heard?" Anthea replied. "And wouldn't she have cried out if she fell?"

"Maybe, but we cannot be certain. She may have been knocked unconscious!" Lady Letitia clutched Anthea's arm. "Oh, I dare not look, my dear. You must do it for me!"

Hopeful that her own fears might be unfounded after all, Anthea hastened across the lane to inspect the ditch, which was overhung by the luxuriant hedgerow. A blackbird flew off in noisy alarm as she approached, and the loud cries were piercing after the silence. Darkness was coming on by the second now, every branch and leaf was in silhouette, and the western sky was a smudge of deep crimson. The grass at the edge of the ditch was undisturbed, and the lower hedgerow had not suffered any broken twigs or damaged leaves. It needed only a glance to tell that Corinna had not fallen here or even stepped on to the verge.

"She isn't here, Aunt Letty—" she began, then broke off as she saw a gap in the hedgerow. It was very narrow, a mere foot of space between a hawthorn and a crab apple tree, and she could see that it was very unlikely indeed that Corinna could have gone through it without tearing some leaves, but nevertheless . . . "There's a way into the wheat field," she said. "I'll just go through to see if there is any sign of her."

"Oh, do be careful, my dear."

The hedgerow rustled and shook as Anthea pushed her way into the harvested field, which now stretched eerily into the darkness. She shivered a little as she stood there, for an echo of the chanting seemed to drift on the air, but it was only imagination. But suddenly she wasn't frightened, and she knew it was because Jovian was close by. She turned instinctively, and he was there. "Oh, Jovian!" she whispered, and ran into his waiting arms.

He crushed her body to his, and their hearts beat close as they shared a long kiss that ached with love and desire. She needed him so much that tears were wet on her cheeks and lips, and her fingers shook as she pushed them longingly through his fair hair. The wretchedness once suffered at his hands might never have been, because once again there was only the immeasurable love that had been kindled when first they met.

But then chill reality returned to her, and she pulled out of his arms. "I'm sorry, I—I'm so sorry! I couldn't make them abandon the journey, and now . . . and now Corinna has gone," she said brokenly, trying not to let her voice carry through the hedgerow into the lane.

"I know, my sweeting, I know," he whispered back, taking her face in his warm hands and kissing her lips again. They might have been one in that lingering moment.

As their lips parted again, she looked into his eyes. "You know where she is, don't you? You were expecting this and know what has happened to her?"

"I did not know exactly how it would be done, but, yes, it is more or less what I expected."

"Tell me, please," Anthea pleaded.

"Lethe has her, probably at Wycke Hall but possibly at the Cross Foxes."

"But why? What reason does he have?"

He glanced around, then looked intently at her in the virtual darkness. "All I will say for the moment is that she is Persephone to Lethe's Hades."

Anthea started with shock, for she knew the myth of Persephone, Demeter, and Hades. "How—how can I possibly believe that?"

"Because it is true. I will tell you everything when you are at the castle," he replied.

"The castle? But we don't know where—"

He put a finger to her lips. "It is just the other side of the lavender field, barely a quarter of a mile as the crow flies."

"If it is so close, why haven't we seen it already?"

"Because the sunset dazzled in that direction. You will see it well enough now. If Longton drives on a short way he will find an entrance to the lavender field. Leave the carriage there and walk the rest of the way. Don't dawdle, for it is not wise to be out at night anywhere, let alone here."

"But Corinna—"

"—is safe enough until the peak of the full moon the day after tomorrow."

She gazed at him in the darkness. "What happens then?" she asked fearfully.

He didn't answer the question. "Just do as I have instructed, and when you reach the castle, tell Sebbriz that—"

"Who?"

"Sebbriz, my—er, steward."

The way he spoke told her that the steward ranked along with Sir Erebus, Obed Dennis, and Abigail Wheatley. "He is one of their number, isn't he?" she inquired.

"Yes. He is Cerberus."

Anthea's heart seemed to stop, for Cerberus was the mythical hound of Hades, a monstrous, many-headed creature that guarded the entrance to the nether world.

Jovian put his lips to hers again, a gesture that was meant to—and did—reassure her. "He will not harm you, my darling, nor will anyone. You are to tell him the gist of what has actually happened, that you were deserted by your guide, that Corinna has gone, and that you are seeking my assistance. This will be accepted, and you will be given shelter. Later, when you and I can be alone, I will explain absolutely everything."

Lady Letitia was becoming anxious. "Anthea? Is something wrong?" Her voice shook, and it was clear she feared a second calamity.

Anthea called back. "I'm all right, Aunt Letty. Please don't worry. I'm just having a really good look, just in case. But I haven't found anything."

"Please come back, my dear."

"All right." Anthea looked up into Jovian's eyes again. "I love you," she said softly.

"A love that is more than reciprocated," he replied.

They kissed again, clinging together as if the parting might be their last; then she slipped reluctantly from his arms and went back to the hedgerow. She paused to glance back at him, but he had already gone, so she continued through the foliage into the lane, where she found her aunt pacing distractedly up and down.

"Oh, *there* you are!" Lady Letitia cried, running forward to catch her by both hands. "Don't you venture out of my sight again, for I could not endure it if you disappeared too!"

Anthea looked across the lavender field. Sure enough, beyond a small wood of Scotch pines, she saw the beautiful outline of Cathness Castle against the western horizon. There were some lights at the upper windows and in a single-story wing that projected to one side, presumably the kitchens and other such offices. "Oh, look! It's the castle!" she cried, hoping to sound surprised.

Lady Letitia and Longton turned. The coachman stared, then scratched his head, unable to believe he had driven mile upon mile, only to end up a little over four hundred yards from the bend in the road by the lych-gate and lodge. Lady Letitia was overwhelmed with relief. "Oh, some good fortune at last, for we are bound to receive assistance there," she breathed. "But how can we get out of these wretched lanes?"

"The best thing is to leave the carriage and walk straight there," Anthea said, this time determined to impose Jovian's instructions.

"Walk?" Lady Letitia was horrified.

"Yes, Aunt Letty. It cannot be far. Maybe there is a way to get there through the lavender field a little farther on down the lane, where we can get the carriage off the road. Then we can take the horses, our night cases, and our valuables with us, so there will only be the carriage itself and some less important luggage if any thieves should come."

Longton thought she spoke good sense and climbed down before Lady Letitia could argue. "Let me assist you back into the carriage, your ladyships. I carry a lantern for emergencies, so we can easily light our way to the castle," he said, trying not to sound too hasty, for this place gave him cold shivers, and he imagined a murderous robber behind every tree and wheat stook.

As if on cue at just this fearful train of thought, there was another gloomy drum roll of thunder. The coachman glanced up nervously, and Lady Letitia flinched. Only Anthea knew what it was, and she glanced around for the hare. Sure enough, it was there, eyes shining, ears pricked as it crouched among the poppies through which Corinna had walked to the oak tree. It bared its teeth, as it had before in the garden of Berkeley Square, before scrambling beneath the overhanging hedgerow into the lavender field.

No one else saw it, for Longton was already ushering Lady Letitia into the carriage. Then he helped Anthea, too, and resumed his seat to drive on down the lane in search of a way into the lavender field. At last he found what Jovian had spoken of, a wide break in the hedgerow that gave sufficient access for two fully laden farm carts to pass through side by side. He maneuvered the cumbersome carriage out of the lane and onto the wide border of long grass that ran around the field, then climbed down to assist the two women again.

The lavender was a pale gray-mauve haze, and the air unbelievably warm and scented. Everything was as quiet as — as the grave, Anthea thought. For a moment they all stood there listening intently, and if a twig had snapped or another blackbird flown off in alarm, Lady Letitia was sure she would have expired of fright.

As Longton unharnessed the horses, tied the overnight

bags and jewelry cases together to fling over their backs, and then took out a lantern from the box beneath the carriage to light with his tinderbox, Lady Letitia went back into the lane for a last look. She was hoping against hope to see Corinna hurrying toward her through the darkness. But nothing moved at all.

Longton managed to light the lantern, and Anthea called softly to her aunt. "Come on, Aunt Letty. We mustn't linger here."

Reluctantly Lady Letitia returned. "We—we can't just go and leave Corinna."

"But she isn't here anymore, Aunt Letty, and we don't know where to look. We must seek shelter at the castle. Someone there will know what to do. Maybe even Jovian himself."

"You think he is here, my dear?"

"I—I think he may be, for there are lights at some of the castle's upper windows."

"Maybe Huw Gadarn is still there too, my dear, and I do not think I could bear to see him again. He may have lived in happiness since we parted, whereas I . . . well, I have wasted my life in heartbreak, have I not?"

"You haven't wasted your life, Aunt Letty, and if Huw shared your love, then maybe he is still alone too."

"That is very doubtful, my dear, and we both know it." Lady Letitia took a shaky breath. "Oh, dear, the very last thing I wished to do was return to the castle, for whatever reason, but it seems I must. So many memories, so very many memories . . ."

Longton was restless. "We should be going, because every second we dally—"

"Yes, I know," Anthea replied, and gently ushered Lady Letitia out of the lane.

A few moments later, with the women leading a horse each and Longton taking charge of the remaining two, the little procession began to make its way by lantern light along the edge of the lavender field toward the castle.

The moon had begun to rise, and its cool blueness was the very opposite of the fiery sunset that had gone before.

Nineteen

*T*he light moved with the swaying lantern, the horses snorted occasionally, and the heady fragrance of the lavender was like an opiate as the benighted travelers proceeded toward the castle. There was such a dreamlike quality about everything that Anthea wondered if she was really asleep and might awaken at any moment.

Then, strange new feelings began to steal through her, as if the finest lavender oil flowed through her veins, and her clothes were fashioned from lavender flowers and leaves. She had become an ethereal being, with hair of spun silver, and bare feet that brushed the cool grass without actually touching the ground. Glancing at the center of the field, she was startled to see a vision of herself, ghostly blue in the first beams of moonlight, walking back toward the lane; and for a moment, distant and muted, the chanting drifted to her ears.

The fanciful sensations only subsided when she followed the others through an open gate into the little wood of Scotch pines at the edge of the park. Longton paused before entering the trees. "Now then, we must be careful to stick to the path, your ladyships, for I do not know how His Grace feels about poachers. We don't want to step into snares or traps set by his keepers."

Lady Letitia nodded. "Well, if the present duke is anything like his father, the keepers will be very active," she said, turning to look back the way they had come, hoping in vain to see Corinna running after them. But there were only night shadows in the light of the rising moon.

They made their way between the tall, leggy pines, where the thin canopy was high and whispered very faintly. Holly and brambles grew in abundance, making Anthea think of the Sleeping Beauty, around whose enchanted castle rose a briar thicket so high and dense that no one but her prince could reach her.

They had only just reached the middle of the wood when Jovian's urgent whisper alerted Anthea to danger. *"Have a care, my darling, for Lethe is riding toward you! Get out of sight, for we need him to be well on his way!"* Almost immediately the sound of a slowly cantering horse approached from the direction of the castle. She acted without hesitation. "We must hide! Over there, behind those holly bushes!"

Lady Letitia dithered. "But it may be someone who can help us. . . ."

"And it may not! We might be taken for poachers, or at the very least trespassers, and keepers have been known to fire guns first and only ask questions afterward. Now come *on*!"

Swiftly Anthea led her horse through the thorny undergrowth toward the shelter afforded by the prickly holly foliage, praying as she went that no traps or snares lay in her way. Startled into unquestioning compliance, Lady Letitia and Longton followed, and they had all just led their horses out of sight when a lone horseman appeared along the path.

Sir Erebus rode at a leisurely pace, but he suddenly reined in to glance around, as if sensing eyes upon him from the shadows. Everyone froze and kept soothing hands on their horses' muzzles, and all was quiet as he continued to look around. Anthea held her breath as she watched him through the spiky leaves; then to her relief, he rode on and the sound of his horse's hooves died away into the darkness.

Lady Letitia breathed out shakily. "That man gives me the

shivers," she said, then looked curiously at Anthea. "You guessed who it was, didn't you?"

"I—suspected it might be him," Anthea replied lamely.

"Hmm. Well, his presence would seem to indicate that Jovian is at home, for Sir Erebus is his friend—although heaven alone knows why!—and I suppose it is only to be expected they would call upon each other here in the country."

"Sir Erebus is not Jovian's friend," Anthea replied unguardedly.

"Oh? But I thought—"

"So did I, but Jovian loathes Sir Erebus and does not trust him an inch."

Lady Letitia was astonished. "Well, that is indeed a turn-up for the books, for I was under the impression that the two were bosom companions," she murmured, "especially as it was through Sir Erebus that we learned of Jovian's recommendations concerning Miss Wheatley." When Anthea didn't comment, Lady Letitia went on, "When did you learn of Jovian's thoughts upon Sir Erebus?"

"I . . ."

"An answer, if you please."

Anthea struggled for words. "It was at the Red Cow."

"In Hammersmith? But we hardly stopped there at all."

"I know. He was riding past and we spoke for a moment or so. He told me then." It was part truth, part fib, but was all Anthea could think of.

Lady Letitia was astonished. "And you did not see fit to mention it?"

"Well, it was a little difficult. You were being cool with me, and Corinna wasn't speaking at all. So I thought it better not to say anything." Anthea crossed her fingers behind her back. "Anyway, it's not important. Come on, we *must* get on to the castle."

Lady Letitia sighed and nodded. "Very well, but oh, these brambles have played the very devil with my skirts."

"Pulled threads are the least of our problems," Anthea

replied, as she led her horse behind Longton so that this time it was her aunt who brought up the rear.

At last they emerged from the wood beside an expanse of grassy park, at the other end of which the castle stood amid the gardens once tended by Huw Gadarn—perhaps tended by him still. Lights still shone in the low wing and at the upper windows, but there seemed no one around. Longton turned to Anthea and her aunt. "Begging your pardon, your ladyships, but do you know if His Grace keeps guard dogs?"

"I have no idea at all," Anthea answered.

Lady Letitia wasn't sure. "Once again I have to say that his father did, but I have no idea about the present duke. However, Sir Erebus would seem to have passed safely enough."

The coachman pursed his lips. "That's true. Well, just to be sure, I'll hold the lantern up high, to show we aren't up to no good."

Brandishing the lantern aloft as obviously as he could, he followed the path across the open park, and after a moment Anthea and her aunt continued too. As they neared the castle they found a deep grassy ditch barring their way. Called a ha-ha, it was there to protect the extensive gardens from deer or cattle in the park and did not spoil the view from the castle as would a wall or fence.

The path led along the top of the ditch toward the lodge and main drive, and incredibly the lantern still seemed to go unnoticed, even though it swayed brightly. No one seemed aware there were intruders in His Grace of Chavanage's grounds, which was all very lax, Lady Letitia thought, recalling how difficult she had once found it to slip away to meet Huw without anyone knowing.

The ha-ha ended at the main drive, which led past the impressive south frontage to a Tudor gatehouse straddling the way into the courtyard beyond. The gatehouse was covered with ivy and climbing roses and resembled a little half-timbered house. Tears welled in Lady Letitia's eyes as she saw it again. Nineteen lonely years had passed since last she had seen those small diamond-leaded windows. Nineteen years . . . the length of Corinna's entire life. "Oh, Huw, *cariad*." The Welsh word for sweetheart came to her as easily and lovingly now as it had then. "What a fool you were, Letitia Wintour. You found true love and let yourself be torn away from it."

Anthea heard her aunt's voice. "Did you say something, Aunt Letty?"

"No, my dear. At least, nothing worth repeating." *Just the words of a penitent old maid who would have behaved very differently if she had her time over again. . . .*

Everything remained quiet as they left the path to follow the drive instead. Longton led the way past the castle frontage, where more ivy and roses flourished against south-facing walls that enjoyed so much sunshine summer and winter alike that an orangery had been built against them, its line of gothic arched windows exactly in keeping with the rest of the castle. There was a faint light inside, and they stopped hopefully, thinking someone must be there, but although a candle had been placed on the tiled floor, the place seemed deserted.

The wavering flame cast a very poor light with confusing shadows, but it was sufficient to reveal that the orangery had fallen into sad disrepair. It no longer appeared to serve its proper purpose, all the plants except one small tree having withered or died. Anthea became aware of a movement by the living tree and after a moment realized a woman was picking fruit from it.

She was thin and a little angular, and Anthea estimated from her figure and manner that she was about forty. A lace shawl over her hair hid her profile, her brown long-sleeved gown appeared to be of fine quality, and Anthea saw the glitter of diamond earrings as she turned slightly to place fruit in a basket over her arm. Who was she? It seemed unlikely she was Jovian's latest love; she was too well dressed to be his housekeeper; and, as far as Anthea knew, he had no other female relatives.

Lady Letitia took it upon herself to rap loudly on the glass. The woman gave a frightened start and looked around, but the upward cast of the candlelight distorted her features. Seeing faces outside, she gathered up her skirts and hastened away with her basket, causing a draft that made the candle smoke and then go out.

Lady Letitia was indignant. "Well, *really*! What a very foolish creature she must be to scuttle away like a frightened rabbit."

Or hare, Anthea found herself thinking, although she did not quite know why, but then the woman was forgotten as a rough male voice—foreign but in perfect English—shouted loudly from the direction of the gateway. "Who are you? What do you want?"

Men with torches had emerged beneath the gatehouse, and it was their leader who had addressed the newcomers. By the flickering light of the torches Anthea saw that he was swarthy and of almost shaggy appearance, with wavy bronze-colored hair that was long enough to just brush his broad shoulders. He had dark eyes, a large pointed nose, and a receding chin, and when he spoke again, she was put in mind of a dog's hollow bark. "Answer me! Who are you? What is your business here?"

Lady Letitia recovered from her startlement. "No, sirrah, who are *you*?" she demanded, finding him presumptuous in the extreme.

"I am the Duke of Chavanage's steward, Sebbriz."

The mythical guard dog, Cerberus, Anthea thought. He seemed human enough, and yet—there *was* something oddly canine about him.

Lady Letitia's thoughts were surprisingly similar. "Sebbriz? Cerberus, more like," she whispered to Anthea, "although to be sure the fellow appears to have just two legs and one head, and I cannot imagine Cathness Castle is the entrance to Hades."

"Is Huw Gadarn among the men?" Anthea whispered back.

"No, definitely not. Even after all this time I would know him anywhere."

Sebbriz did not like the whispering and came closer, followed by the others. "If you do not tell me who you are, I will have you thrown into a dungeon," he threatened, in an accent that Anthea, who had once been introduced to a gentleman from Athens, now recognized as Greek.

Lady Letitia eyed the steward. "The dungeon? How very medieval, to be sure. Very well, Mr. Sebbriz, I will identify myself. I am Lady Letitia Wintour, sister of the Earl of Daneway, and this is my niece, Lady Anthea. Our male companion is my coachman, Longton. We were on our way to stay with a Miss Wheatley when we became lost. Now my stepniece, Miss Pranton, has disappeared, and we have come in desperation to seek His Grace's hospitality and assistance."

Unexpectedly, the steward's grim face broke into a smile, and Anthea felt he had known who they were all along. "Ah, welcome to Cathness Castle, my lady," he said smoothly. "I crave forgiveness for my curtness, but I had no idea I was addressing so fine a person. His Grace is in residence, and I am sure he will gladly extend his help and hospitality to you."

"Well, that's a little better," Lady Letitia replied, mollified, "although I fear that you and the other servants here are guilty of gross dereliction of duty. We might have been robbers or murderers; yet, we have all but reached the castle doors without being detected. I will be having strong words with the duke."

"My lady." The steward's smile did not waver, and he bowed deeply. "Please come this way." The other men parted as he turned to lead the weary travelers beneath the gatehouse into the confines of Jovian's castle, so beautiful in daylight, so mysterious and daunting after dark when the moon was blue.

Twenty

*F*ootsteps and hooves echoed beneath the gatehouse as Anthea, Lady Letitia, and Longton followed Sebbriz into a graveled courtyard where wall torches and clipped bay trees in large terracotta pots created an entirely Tudor atmosphere. To Anthea, it was like stepping back in time. A farthingale, a ruff, and a red-curled wig looped with strings of pearls would have been more in keeping with these surroundings than their modern fashions.

Cathness Castle possessed some of the most magnificent mullioned oriel windows she had ever seen, certainly as fine as those at Hampton Court. Formed of five curved-bay levels set with leaded glass, they were not only very handsome but admitted a great deal of sunshine. At present the ground floor was in darkness, but hooped chandeliers on the upper floor revealed paneled walls, exquisitely ornamented plaster ceilings, and sumptuous Elizabethan furniture of a grandeur to suit Gloriana herself.

In the far corner of the courtyard, the principal entrance was approached up a flight of worn stone steps, at the foot of which everyone halted while the luggage was quickly unloaded from the horses by Sebbriz's men. As two of the men then assisted Longton in leading the animals away to the stables, Sebbriz started up the steps, expecting the two women to follow, but Lady Letitia remained obstinately where she was.

"What of the carriage that we have been obliged to abandon?" she asked.

Sebbriz was glib. "No harm will come to the carriage or its contents, my lady."

But Lady Letitia, accustomed to the business of London thieves and pickpockets, was not so easily fobbed off. "Sir, I am sure there are villains even in Cathness."

"Certainly not, my lady. We do not even require a constable."

Confounded, she stared at him. "No constable?" she repeated.

"No, my lady, nor are there magistrates. Cathness does not need them. Disputes are heard by the manorial court of record, presided over by His Grace or occasionally by me. That is the way."

"Indeed? Well in the eleventh duke's time there were constables, magistrates, justices of the peace, and all other officers of the law. There were also proper courts of every description, not a manorial hodgepodge that has been cobbled together in order to usurp absolute power. The full panoply of the law is required in a town where the children are disobedient ne'er do wells, for such offspring reflect very badly indeed upon the adults and are proof positive that a mere court leet alone cannot successfully administer the required penalties." Lady Letitia was at her most scathing and unreasonable.

"Billy Dennis is but one boy, my lady, and he will be severely reprimanded if found at fault."

"*If?*" Lady Letitia glared with gimlet eyes. "My good man, are you presuming to question my word?"

Anthea quickly interrupted. "How did you know about Billy?" she asked the steward.

His eyes slid briefly to hers. "I was at the Cross Foxes not long after you called there," he said smoothly. "Obed Dennis happened to mention that his boy, who I assure you is of excellent character, had gone with a fine carriage to direct it through the lanes. I merely put two and two together now."

Anthea did not believe a word. Sebbriz knew about Billy Dennis because he was part of whatever it was that involved Sir Erebus Lethe, and therefore — she was sure — party to Corinna's disappearance. But mindful of Jovian's instructions to go along with whatever transpired, she did not press the matter further.

Lady Letitia, however, was unaware of such considerations. "May I remind you, sir, that boys of excellent character do not leave travelers stranded in the middle of nowhere with darkness coming on."

The steward ignored her and continued toward the entrance. "Please come this way, and I will conduct you to His Grace."

"Well, *really!*" Lady Letitia was incensed and considered making a battle of it, but, on seeing Anthea's pleading look, she gave in. "Oh, very well, but the duke will hear of this fellow's gross ill manners!"

Sebbriz must have heard, but her ire was water off a duck's back — or in his case a dog's back — for he did not even deign to glance back as he reached the doorway and went inside.

Anthea agreed with her aunt but was too eager to see Jovian to be much concerned about how his servants deported themselves. Jovian made her feel safe, and right now she needed to escape the uncertain darkness and its fearful secrets.

They entered the great hall, where light was beginning to glimmer as several maids hastened to light some of the floor-standing candelabra that stood around. The hall rose right through the castle to the beamed roof. It had gray and white tiles on the floor and richly carved oak paneling on the walls. The floor was empty, but around the edges there was a sparse display of sixteenth-century chairs and tables, on one of which stood a tray with a two chalices and a jug, all beautifully chased silver.

Sebbriz went straight to the tray. "Please allow me to pour

you a refreshing cup of kykeon to welcome you across His Grace's threshold," he said.

"A cup of what?" Anthea inquired.

"Kykeon, my lady. It is a barley and honey wine flavored with mint, and here at Cathness it is traditionally given to visitors."

Lady Letitia would have no truck with stewards presuming to play host. "It may well be a local custom, sir, but this is the first I've heard of it, and before I drink anything at all, I demand to see the duke. Immediately."

"His Grace will come directly and in the meantime would expect me to greet you in a fitting manner," Sebbriz replied, pouring the wine and bringing the chalices to them.

"Fitting manner?" Lady Letitia snorted. "In my judgment there has been nothing at all *fitting* about your manner, sirrah!"

"If I have offended, my lady, I crave your leniency, for I am a foreigner with much to learn of English ways."

"That is clear enough!" Lady Letitia replied tartly.

Anthea accepted one of the glasses, for the man had apologized, and to persist with argument would achieve nothing except her aunt's indisposition due to stress and ill humor. "Be mindful of your headaches, Aunt Letty," she whispered discreetly.

To her relief Lady Letitia accepted the other glass, although with another only too audible comment. "I would like to tell him what he can do with his wretched kykeon, jug and all," she muttered wrathfully.

"I'm sure a maiden lady should not say such shocking things," Anthea replied, with a little smile.

But Lady Letitia was still not quite done with the infuriating steward. "Do not dally around, fellow. My stepniece is missing, probably abducted, and I expect an immediate and intense effort to find her."

"A message has already been sent to the town, so that not

only will Miss Pranton be sought there, but men will come to the castle to join the search from here."

"Already sent?" Lady Letitia was caught off guard, for Sebbriz had not been seen to send anyone anywhere.

"Yes, my lady."

Lady Letitia eyed him, then sipped the kykeon. "Why, this is truly delicious," she declared, and to Anthea's astonishment, drained the entire chalice and then indicated that she wished for some more. The smiling steward, smooth as ever, hastened to comply.

The second drink went the way of the first, and then Lady Letitia yawned loudly. "Oh, goodness, I'm suddenly very tired," she announced.

"Aunt Letty?" Anthea was quite nonplussed by her aunt's extraordinary behavior, but Lady Letitia yawned again.

"I know it's early, my dear, but I am absolutely exhausted and in dire need of a good long sleep."

"But Corinna—"

"The steward has done all that can be done tonight."

Anthea stared at her.

"I cannot stand around awaiting Jovian's pleasure," Lady Letitia went on. "Sebbriz, I wish to be conducted to my room."

It was too much for Anthea. "Aunt Letty, we *must* wait to speak to Jovian first. We cannot simply demand to—"

"Oh, stuff and nonsense, my dear. You *know* Jovian will be only too delighted to extend us his hospitality—when he stirs himself to greet us, that is."

Sebbriz was already at Lady Letitia's side. "Apartments are at your disposal, my lady," he said ingratiatingly.

"That sounds most agreeable."

Anthea was dismayed. "But, Aunt Letty—" To her shock, Sebbriz interrupted her by speaking to her aunt again.

"Do you have maids, my lady?"

"Our maids are in London, sir, suffering a most inconvenient dose of mumps."

The fact that he had so rudely broken in while Anthea was speaking seemed not to worry Lady Letitia at all. In fact, *nothing* seemed to worry that lady now, unlike a few minutes ago when nothing at all pleased her.

Sebbriz was attentive. "Would you like one of the maids here to attend you?" he asked.

"That would be most helpful, sir. I begin to see why His Grace leaves the welcome to you."

Anthea could not believe that her aunt had undergone such a complete change of heart about the slippery steward, for he was odious and impertinent and had richly earned a flea in his ear. But these were not ordinary circumstances. Anthea glanced down at the chalice of kykeon she had still to sample. Maybe this was no ordinary wine. Aunt Letty had begun to behave oddly from the moment she drank this dubious liquid. . . .

Sebbriz snapped his fingers at one of the maids. "Phoebe, you are to attend Lady Letitia."

The maid bobbed a curtsy. She was small, slender, and pale, with blond hair that was almost ash in color, and her eyes were cool and gray. Her gray linen dress was beautifully laundered, and the starched mobcap on her head was pinned in place just so.

Sebbriz bowed to Lady Letitia. "You are to have the Buckingham rooms, my lady. I trust they will be to your complete satisfaction. They were prepared in 1509 for Edward Stafford, third Duke of Buckingham, and—"

"I am aware of the facts, sir, for I have stayed here before," Lady Letitia interrupted.

"My lady." He bowed again, but in a manner that was anything but subservient.

Lady Letitia, as unlike her true self as ever, turned impatiently to the waiting maid. "Lead the way, if you please, for I cannot stay awake. Be quick now."

"My lady." Phoebe hastened to light a candle from one of the candelabra, then conducted Lady Letitia toward an open doorway in the corner of the hall, through which could be seen a grand staircase.

Anthea looked at her untouched chalice of kykeon and decided on no account to drink it. She was about to set it aside, when Jovian spoke again. *"You are protected, so it is safe for you. Its purpose is to make you desire sleep, as things are to take place here tonight that neither you nor Lady Letitia should see. So drink it and behave out of character as she did."*

Aware of Sebbriz watching and waiting, she raised the chalice to her lips and took a taste. It was indeed delicious, and she had no trouble at all in emptying the glass. She felt no effect beyond enjoying a refreshing and delicately flavored wine. The steward replenished the glass, which she immediately drank. Then she pretended to stifle a yawn. "Good heavens," she murmured, "is it the air here? I vow I suddenly feel as tired as my aunt."

"An apartment awaits, Lady Anthea."

"I think that would be most agreeable. It has been a very difficult day."

"Of course, and you may be assured that in the meantime every endeavor will be made to find Miss Pranton. If you should hear horses in the courtyard, it will be the search party preparing to set off to look for Miss Pranton." The steward snapped his fingers at another maid. "Cynthia? Lady Anthea is to have the King Hal suite."

"Yes, Mr. Sebbriz." The maid who came forward was so very like Aunt Letty's that Anthea suspected they must be sisters. Maybe that was why their names had been chosen, for both were titles for the moon. Or maybe being named for the moon had other connotations here in Cathness. Anthea's glance crept to a high window, through which the pale blue beams of moonlight now shone.

Jovian spoke once more. *"I am coming down now, Anthea, and I want you to go along with whatever I say. I will appear to be tipsy, but you are not to cavil about it because kykeon causes amenability. If you point out my failing, Sebbriz will know you are protected, and that will not suit my plans at all."*

Almost immediately there was the flicker of candlelight from the grand staircase, and the sound of unsteady steps. Jovian came into view and entered the great hall. His hair was untidy, he wore no coat, his shirt was undone almost to the waist, and the candle in his hand was at such an angle that the leaping flame smoked and hot wax splashed to the floor. He gave a cheerfully inebriated smile. "Wha's all this, Sebbriz?"

"We have guests, your grace," the steward replied. "Lady Letitia Wintour and her niece, Lady Anthea Wintour. Lady Letitia is tired and has retired to the Buckingham rooms. Lady Anthea was just about to retire to the King Hal suite."

"Ah, sw-sweet Anthea," Jovian murmured, allowing his gaze to wander appreciatively over her. "Where is the d-delightful Corinna?"

Anthea pretended to blink back tears. "Corinna has disappeared in the lanes near here, Jovian. She was snatched from us, and now Aunt Letty and I do not know where she is."

Jovian looked as if he had difficulty grasping what she'd said. "Corinna has disap- —*hic*—peared? Good God."

"Everything is in hand for a search to begin, your grace," Sebbriz said.

"Good. No doubt she'll be f-found quick as a w-wink. *Hic.*" Jovian came closer and made a shambles of taking Anthea's hand and raising it to his lips. "Did you know, Seb —*hic*— briz, Lady Anthea almost b-became my betrothed? We got on f-famously until she t-took offense at my liking for a little s-sip or two. *Hic.*"

Anthea gave him an amiable smile, then put her hand to her mouth as if stifling another yawn.

Jovian waved Cynthia away, spattering hot wax in all directions. "You w-will not b-be required now, for I w-will escort Lady Anthea t-to her —*hic*— room."

Sebbriz nodded at the maid, who gave a quick curtsy and

hurried away, but as Jovian offered Anthea a rather unsteady arm, the steward spoke quickly. "You must not be long now, your grace."

Jovian frowned and waggled the dripping candle at the steward. "Am I, or am I not the k-key to everything?"

Anthea wondered what he meant.

Sebbriz gave an obsequious bow. "You are, your grace."

"Then if I w-want to be—*hic*—a few minutes late, I d-damned well will be."

"As you wish, Your Grace, but the moon is up and you must be there."

"Just h-have my h-horse ready, and all will p-proceed as it should. *Hic.*"

With that Jovian ushered Anthea toward the grand staircase.

Twenty-one

As soon as Anthea thought she and Jovian were out of earshot on the staircase, she halted. "Jovian, I—"

"Not yet, Anthea," he said under his breath. The candle flame leapt, and monstrous shadows rose against the paneled walls as he gripped her arm and forced her to keep ascending.

"But—"

"There are ears everywhere. Wait until we are in your suite." Then in a much louder, completely drunken tone, he declared, "Apart fr-from mislayin' your stepsister, d-did you and Ol' Letty have an agree—*hic*—able journey?"

"We didn't mislay Corinna, Jovian; she simply vanished."

When they reached the top of the staircase, where the candlelight revealed a gallery hung with tapestries, Anthea was sure she saw someone draw swiftly out of sight into a curtain-draped doorway that was flanked by two suits of armor. Jovian saw it too and feigned losing his balance. "Deuce t-take it, my pins are—*hic*—treacherous tonight!"

"Oh, do get on, Jovian, for I am desperate to rest my head a while," she pleaded.

"Would that y-you had always b-been as eager to get me to a b-bed," he muttered, as he conducted her across the gallery toward a particularly impressive double door. "Behold Bluff K-King Hal's suite!" he announced, as he flung them open with a grand gesture.

Much more candlelight suddenly brightened everything, and it was a moment or so before Anthea's eyes adjusted to the change, but then she saw the rooms she was later to learn had been used by Henry VIII during his 1535 royal progress with Anne Boleyn. They were the rooms she had seen from the courtyard and were every bit as splendid as they had seemed. There were highly polished wooden floors and oak paneling, rich furniture and tapestries, and paintings and portraits of all description.

Stained glass in the oriel windows showed off the arms of families with whom alliances had been forged over the centuries. Green velvet curtains, undrawn and looped back, stretched from floor to ceiling, and matching velvet cushions graced the ornate Tudor chairs. Hooped chandeliers provided much of the light, but there were wall-candles too.

Anthea untied and removed her bonnet. "These rooms have been prepared at leisure, not hastily opened in the last few minutes. Besides, I saw the lights from the lane."

"They knew you would come here." Jovian closed the door behind them, then put a finger to his lips as he pressed his ear to the door. He heard a soft step outside, then silence as whoever was there listened as well. Most probably they were ear to ear through the iron-studded wood, he thought, as he gestured to Anthea to give some vocal indication that they were still behaving as before.

She obliged. "Oh, Jovian, what *marvellous* rooms. I vow I almost wish I had married you after all."

"W-we'd have been dreadful together, my sw—*hic*—sweet," he replied with a grin.

The eavesdropper must have been persuaded, for the steps retreated once more. Jovian put his finger to his lips again as he went to draw all the curtains. Only then did he sweep her into his arms. The bonnet fell from her fingers and her fears began to melt away into the sheer joy of cherishing and being cherished by a man who was able to take her to the very borders of another world.

He did not want the kiss to end, but he knew it must and pulled back to take her hands. His thumbs were strong and warm as he caressed her palms. "I will have to leave you in a few minutes, or they will come for me, and I don't want to risk arousing their suspicions about anything at all, no matter how trivial."

For a few heartbeats she was still enveloped in the rich emotions that kept reality at bay, but then the chill facts returned. She searched his face. "But *you* are the duke, not Sebbriz or Sir Erebus Lethe. Why must you bow to their bidding?"

"I will explain when I return later." He pointed toward a section of wall paneling. "There is a secret passage behind there, connecting this apartment with mine. No one will know I am with you, so we will be able to talk to our hearts' content, and I promise you will learn all there is to know."

She took a deep breath. "Is — is Corinna safe? And what of Aunt Letty? She changed so much that I was quite alarmed."

"Corinna will not be in danger until the day after tomorrow, when the moon is full, and Lady Letitia will not come to harm at all. Kykeon will make her sleep and forget things they do not wish her to remember. She will awaken in the morning and not remember anything about your stepsister's disappearance. The kykeon not only induces sleep but removes chosen memories and inserts false facts in their place. She will believe Corinna stayed behind in London and that you are here so that I, on the wishes of your father, can negotiate a match between you and Lethe. If the kykeon had worked upon you, that is what you would also believe. And you would accept it all."

Anthea stared at him. "Kykeon can do so much?"

"Oh, yes, but I made you resistant by giving you lavender from the field here in Cathness."

"How does it make me so?"

"I can resist kykeon and was able to transfer that ability to you through the giving of the lavender. The act of giving and accepting is always significant." He exhaled slowly, before adding, "I then made even more certain of your immunity by adding a small sprig of rosemary to the bouquet."

"What difference does rosemary make?" she asked.

"Rosemary is for remembrance, and thus counteracts Lethe, the River of Forgetfulness. You are therefore safe, except from pomegranate in any form. There is no protective charm or potion for that."

Anthea gazed at him. "When you say such things, I begin to fear I am losing my wits after all. It is so fantastic, so—"

He put a gentle finger to her lips. "You are not mad, and neither am I. You did not imagine that we flew above the rooftops of London, that I somehow reached your window ledge without having to climb, or that you saw the hare that does not behave like a hare at all. I really can speak to you in your head, and a sprig of mistletoe really can appear to be a narcissus, honeysuckle, a cornflower, or anything else. And I really can change the direction of a pleasure boat with just the power of my will. As for Lethe and his evil, well, that too is real. None of it is the product of lunacy."

"You said earlier that it concerns the myth of Demeter, Persephone, and Hades, but that is certainly impossible, for a myth is a myth, and therefore not fact."

"Nothing is impossible, my darling." He turned to point a finger at a chair. His eyes darkened with concentration, and after a moment it shook slightly, rose about three feet, then floated motionless. "What do you see, Anthea?"

She stared. "I see a chair that defies gravity."

"It does more than that. Now what do you see?" He made a circular sign with his fingertip, and the chair turned over and over as if upon an invisible spit. As he allowed it to sink gently back to the floor, Jovian looked at her, his eyes dark and unfathomable. "That was not your madness or my trickery, just a simple piece of reality. Nor am I conjuring more fantasy from thin air when I tell you that harvest time here in Cathness, and in many other places throughout Britain and

Europe, is inextricably entwined with the Greek myth of
Demeter and Persephone. You must believe me, Anthea, for it
is an unavoidable truth."

"I believe you," she answered. To look at him now was not
to know him at all, for he was part of something far outside
the range of ordinary experience, something so different and
rare that—

"—that you feel compelled to accept whatever I say?" he
broke in.

"Well, I . . ." It was very disconcerting to have him knowing what she was thinking almost before she thought it.

He smiled tenderly. "Never be in awe of me, my darling,
for that would change you, and I love you as you are." He
dragged her back into his embrace. "I swear to you that I will
overcome all this wickedness and that none of you will come
to any harm. Tonight I must go along with their rites; indeed
I must seem to be so doing right up until the last seconds, but
I believe I know how to defeat Lethe and erase this savage
business from Cathness."

"You do?"

Footsteps approached the door, and someone knocked
loudly. "You are needed, your grace," Sebbriz's voice said.

"I-I'm almost ready. *Hic.* I'm trying to c-clear my head a
little."

"We must leave in five minutes, your grace."

"Very well," Jovian replied, and as the footsteps walked
away again, he drew Anthea close a last time. "We can send
Lethe and his creatures packing, my darling, and that is exactly what I intend to do. But for now, please try to rest if you
can."

"That is easier said than done." Rest? She was too over-
wrought for that.

"Try anyway, but just remember that the kykeon would
have made you sleep, if things had gone as they intended, so
be alert for the door. The moment you hear someone coming
you are to lie on the bed and give every impression of being

in a deep slumber. It's important, Anthea, because since the night Lethe came to Lady Letitia's dinner party, he has known that I gave you lavender. He *must* be reassured that the lavender was not as potent a deterrent as he feared, and that you are after all susceptible to his will." The sound of horses and voices drifted from outside. "I had better go, but I will return later; on that you have my word."

He went to the door and looked out at the deserted gallery; then he remembered something and came back to her. "Whatever you do, don't drink any red wine that may be brought, or indeed any drink that is any shade of pink, purple, or red," he said, in little more than a whisper, "for they are always mixed with pomegranate juice, against which no one is safe. That is how they were able to gain control of me, and it is how I would have remained had I not chanced upon their method. Now I merely pretend to be drunk when I am expected to be, and I secretly dispose of their brews."

Anthea's fear seeped back. "Why do they want to keep you under control? Oh, Jovian, I can't help being frightened, in spite of your assurances."

"I will be with you again very soon, my darling, and whatever question you may ask, I will answer in full."

Opening the door, he left the apartment, and she heard his uneven footsteps dying away. He sang as he went. "Lavender blue, dilly, dilly—*hic*—dolly, dippy, dandy . . ."

"Oh, Jovian, please take care," she whispered.

When she could hear him no more, she went to the bedroom and closed the door behind her. The room was regal in proportion, and she noted that the elaborate azure-and-gold hangings of the immense Tudor bed were embroidered with the badges and initials of Henry VIII and Anne Boleyn. She extinguished the candles as if going to bed, then went to peep around the drawn curtains into the courtyard.

Twenty-two

*T*orches and lanterns lit the courtyard, revealing about twenty horsemen, among whom Anthea recognized Obed Dennis and some of the faces she'd noticed at the Cross Foxes. Jovian's dapple gray horse was ready and waiting, and Sebbriz was just mounting a powerful bay. The woman from the orangery stood nearby, her face still a mystery because of the lace shawl over her hair. Anthea wished she'd remembered to ask Jovian about her; now, like all her other questions, it would have to wait until he came back.

The window, being hundreds of years old, did not fit all that well in one corner, so that sounds from the courtyard carried clearly to Anthea. She heard the jingle of harness and the occasional murmur of a voice, and then she heard Jovian's singing as he emerged from the main entrance and began to descend the steps. "Lavender stew, dilly, dolly, lavender stew, if I were rich, dully, dally, you'd have some too . . ."

He came into her view, still teetering a little. He made such a fumble of mounting that an irritated Sebbriz was obliged to dismount and manhandle him into the saddle. Jovian's acting was worthy of the new genius of the boards, Edmund Kean, for no one could possibly have guessed that he was probably far more sharp-witted and alert than anyone else.

Suddenly another horseman rode swiftly into the courtyard, scattering gravel as he reined in. Some of the other horsemen tried to make him leave again, but he maneuvered his mount defiantly alongside Jovian, then casually drew a pistol from inside his coat. It was a gauntlet no one was prepared to pick up. He grinned at Jovian, whose discreet answering smile told Anthea he genuinely liked the man. So, she thought, he was Jovian's friend, but not the steward's, and he therefore certainly had *her* approval.

The newcomer's courage impressed Anthea. He was in his fifties, a fine looking man of rather Celtic appearance, with expressively dark eyes and a mop of gray curls that had probably once been coal-black. His horse was a stout cob, and he wore rough clothes, so he was not a gentleman. Nor was he at all welcome as far as Sebbriz and the others were concerned.

The steward scowled, and Anthea heard him shout. "We do not want you here, Huw Gadarn!"

Anthea gasped. Aunt Letty's old love!

"Well, I'm here anyway, and I'm not leaving until I am sure His Grace is safe and well." Huw had a very pronounced but very pleasing Welsh accent.

"I will have my revenge upon you, Welshman!" cried the steward.

"You'll need to be sharper than you have been until now, you damned Greek dog. Your sleight of hand with pomegranate will never deceive me, so like it or not, you have me on your shoulder."

"Sir Erebus will make you wish you had never been born."

Huw grinned at Sebbriz and cheekily waggled the pistol again to indicate that he was ready for them all to set off. "Lethe can go to the Devil, although even Old Nick is a little choosy about the company he keeps. Well, let's get going then and get this barbarism started."

Anthea's lips parted with dismay. Barbarism was a strong word to use and hinted at so much of that which she would rather not think about.

Sebbriz looked fit to strangle Huw, but the Welshman's pistol put paid to such rash notions, so the steward wisely left well enough alone and gave the order to depart. The horsemen rode out in single file, with Jovian and Huw bringing up the rear.

The torchlit cavalcade disappeared beneath the gatehouse and reappeared on the drive, then followed the path by the ha-ha toward the Scotch pines. It passed out of Anthea's sight, so she hurried to the other side of the bedroom and looked from another window. The line of lights bobbed through the trees toward the lavender field, and as she opened the window a little, she heard pipe and tabor music coming from the large wheatfield where the reapers had been.

A pale blue sheen lay over the land, and the horsemen's torches and lanterns passed the abandoned carriage, then continued along the lane for a few hundred yards. Anthea could just see an entrance into the field, in which the last neck of wheat was now surrounded at a respectful distance by what appeared to be the entire population of Cathness.

The music came from morrismen, six dancers and four sword bearers, all wearing black billycock hats, white shirts, and breeches. They carried staves that were struck together as part of the dance, and although Anthea could not hear the morris bells, she knew they would be jingling. Such costumes and dancing were suddenly no longer lighthearted and delightful but possessed of a chilling air that seemed to reach back into the very mists of time.

As Sebbriz's horse entered the field at the vanguard of the procession, so many torches were lit that the night flickered with flames. The morris dancing ended as the cavalcade approached, and the crowd parted to provide a way into the heart of the circle. Silence descended, and Sebbriz and his horsemen encircled the central area, then halted facing the neck of wheat. Jovian and Huw had remained on the edge of the crowd, but now Jovian rode to the neck and dismounted. He brushed against the wheat as he placed himself directly between it and the steward.

Huw, still taking no chances where Jovian's wellbeing was

concerned, rode swiftly up to Sebbriz's side and pressed the
pistol to his temple. It was a clear warning to all the others
that if anything befell His Grace the Duke of Chavanage, the
steward would suffer the consequences. Sebbriz raised his
hands pacifyingly, but the pistol remained where it was.

For a moment time seemed to stop. Then a boy—Anthea
thought it was Billy Dennis—hurried to lead Jovian's horse
away, and Anthea sensed the increasingly expectant air of the
crowd. She waited with bated breath, aware of the pumping of
her heart. There was a slight stir at the far end of the crowd,
which gradually parted again to allow the line of reapers to
enter. They may have been the same men she'd seen earlier,
but all she could be sure of now was that they carried only
sickles, not scythes.

The reapers formed a second ring inside the circle of
horsemen, and the crowd began to chant. Anthea could not
hear their exact words, but the rhythm and an informed guess
suggested they were repeating the prayers to Demeter and the
Harvest Maiden. *Make the earth abundant, give us fruits, and
ears of wheat, and a goodly harvest, O Demeter. . . . Come to
us, O Harvest Maiden. Protect us from the Lavender Lady.
Come to us, O Harvest Maiden. . . .*

The chanting ended abruptly, and in the eerie quiet that followed, Anthea was distraught to see one of the reapers hurl
his sickle at Jovian. The curved tool glinted in the moonlight,
and she pressed terrified hands to her lips as it seemed the
deadly blade must stab the man she loved. Instead it fell a few
inches short of him and quivered in the wheat stubble. An excited gasp rose from the watching crowds, and Anthea could
hardly bear to watch. Had it fallen short by accident . . . or intent?

A second sickle followed the first and again fell exactly the
same distance short. It was deliberate! Anthea breathed again
as one by one the sickles flew through the air and landed by
Jovian's feet, until at last they had completely ringed both
him and the neck of wheat. As the final sickle struck the

ground, Jovian moved outside the ring, and another sickle was taken to Sebbriz, who stood in his stirrups to throw it. Anthea's heart gave a lurch, as she feared Jovian was the steward's target, but instead the deadly blade struck the wheat without felling a single stalk. There were loud cheers, but all Anthea could think was that if Jovian had remained within the ring of sickles, by now he would surely be dead.

The night's rites were clearly not yet done, for the cheering died away, and the chanting resumed. A movement in the lane caught Anthea's attention, and she saw two figures on horseback moving toward the field. One was a man dressed in a hooded black robe, mounted on a very large and dark horse. Sir Erebus, Anthea thought without hesitation. The other rider was a lady whose white pony, or palfrey, he was leading. Anthea stared at the lady, for even at that distance in the strange blue moonlight, she recognized her missing stepsister.

Corinna was wearing a flowing white gown, and her golden hair had been brushed loose. She was seated astride, possibly bareback, and her gown had been carefully draped in an elegant manner. In either hand she carried what appeared to be a bunch of wildflowers, and she gazed directly in front of her, not seeming to display any emotion at all, even when suddenly confronted by the torchlit field.

Sir Erebus led the palfrey through the twin circles of Sebbriz's horsemen and reapers, and the crowd began to chant again. Sir Erebus dismounted and lifted Corinna to the ground. She seemed in a trance as he led her three times around the neck of wheat and ring of sickles, to the continued chanting of the onlookers; then Sir Erebus conducted her back to the palfrey and lifted her on to its back again.

As two women hurried from the crowd to assist with the draping of her gown, Sir Erebus turned and spoke briefly to Jovian, who had remained nearby throughout. Those few words provoked a violent response. Jovian swung his fist at Sir Erebus's chin like a battering ram, and the latter was lifted from his feet, then fell sprawling back on the stubble. The chanting petered out in confusion, and for a second or so no one moved, but as Sir Erebus staggered to his feet again, Seb-briz and his men urged their mounts toward Jovian, intent upon seizing him.

Huw appeared as if from nowhere, his cob going down on its haunches as he reined it in beside Sir Erebus and then leaned down to clamp a strong arm around his neck. The pistol was shoved to Sir Erebus's temple, and Anthea heard the Welshman shout some sort of warning. The steward and others fell back as Sir Erebus struggled in vain in Huw's unbreakable grip. Corinna had remained motionless throughout, seated quietly on her palfrey, staring ahead like a beautiful statue.

Huw shouted again, and Billy Dennis brought Jovian's horse. Jovian remounted, and Huw began to back his cob away, forcing Sir Erebus to go with him by keeping his arm around his neck and the pistol fast against his temple. With Jovian alongside and Sir Erebus unable to escape, Huw forced a way through the reapers and horsemen. Only when they were about ten yards beyond the crowd did Huw thrust Sir Erebus aside and turn with Jovian to gallop from the field. They were leaving without Corinna? Anthea stared in tearful disbelief.

No one attempted to follow the two fleeing horsemen as they returned along the lavender field and through the Scotch pines, but as Anthea watched she suddenly heard the main door of the suite. Running to the bed, she curled up on the coverlet as if fast asleep. Female footsteps tapped across the main chamber toward the bedroom, and then stopped as whoever it was listened carefully. Hearing nothing, the person opened the door as softly as possible. Candlelight flooded into the darkness, and Anthea saw a female shadow fall across the floor. There was a soft rustle of skirts as the woman tiptoed to the bedside.

Anthea lay as if deeply asleep while the woman observed her intently, as if suspecting trickery, but then, clearly satisfied, she withdrew to the main chamber again, leaving the bedroom door open. Anthea dared to open her eyes and saw the other's reflection in a mirror. It was the woman who had been in the orangery, but as she had now discarded the lace shawl, Anthea also recognized her from St. James's and Green parks. It was Abigail Wheatley, who Anthea could now be certain beyond all doubt had also been the unfriendly woman from that bitterly cold Christmas Eve in Berkeley Square.

Shocked, Anthea continued to feign sleep as the woman went out of the suite again and closed the door behind her. Fearing her sudden return, Anthea remained motionless, but as a minute ticked by and then another, it seemed safe to leave the bed again. She saw that Abigail had not come empty-handed but had left a tray of cold supper on a table. There was Single Gloucester cheese, celery and pickle, fresh bread, a little dish of honey cakes, and a jug of kykeon. Anthea was hungry but did not dare eat anything.

Oh, where was Jovian? Surely he and Huw had returned to the castle by now? She looked hopefully at the panel he said opened to the secret passage and for the first time noticed an old engraving fixed upon it. Curious, she went a little closer. It depicted a scene in a harvested field, with morris dancers and a crowd of people watching a black-robed man whose arms were outstretched like some diabolic savior. Sir Erebus, she thought.

Beside him on one side was a young woman with long fair hair and a flowing white gown carrying a bunch of ripe wheat and wildflowers in either hand. Standing by a neck of wheat and surrounded by a ring of sickles, she looked exactly as Corinna had tonight. On the black-robed figure's other side, confined in a large wicker cage, was a dark-haired young woman in a gown of flowers. The engraving was dated 1738, and entitled *Ye Harvest Maiden Offered and Ye Lavender Lady Captured*.

There was no mistaking that Corinna was the Harvest

Maiden. Anthea looked at the wicker cage and the imprisoned woman's gown of flowers. Recalling those mysterious moments on the walk to the castle when her own clothes had seemed to be made of flowers, she could not help wondering if she, Lady Anthea Wintour, was the Lavender Lady?

Suddenly the engraving slid to one side as the panel opened to allow Jovian to step out of the secret passage. "Yes, my darling, Corinna is the Harvest Maiden, and you are the Lavender Lady," he said quietly.

Twenty-three

$\mathcal{A}$nthea went into Jovian's arms, and they clung together before kissing. She could smell the night air in his hair and taste late summer on his lips; then he drew back to take her flushed face in his hands. "My darling, in spite of what is depicted in that old engraving, nothing terrible ever befalls Lavender Lady. She has to be detained and driven away every year, but is never held in captivity for long."

Burning with questions even before seeing the engraving, Anthea was now beset by a hundred more. Jovian saw the look in her eyes and quickly went to pour some of the kykeon Abigail Wheatley had brought. "Drink, for it can do you no harm and will help to calm you," he said, handing Anthea the goblet.

She drank a little. "You always seem to know what I am thinking; yet, I never know what is in your mind."

"Call it my gift . . . or my curse."

She sipped the kykeon again and then took a deep breath. "It was just the shock of the picture. I feel a little better now." She glanced again at the engraving. "What exactly does it depict? I mean, the part concerning the Harvest Maiden is plain enough, because it is what I saw tonight. It is also plain to me that Sir Erebus is the figure in black. But what of the wicker cage and the Lavender Lady? If that is my part in it all, I was certainly not there tonight, nor did I see the cage."

"The cage will be there tomorrow night, and so will you, although not to be imprisoned. Like Corinna tonight, you will just be paraded. It all leads up to the climax of the full moon the night after tomorrow, August 30th. On that night the cycle is set to come to a close, and the new one to begin. But Lethe isn't going to succeed in his purpose, because I have very different notions about what is and isn't going to happen this year."

"Different notions?" she asked.

"It will be tit for tat, my Roland for his Oliver," he said with a smile, "except that this time, if all goes as I pray it will, Roland will vanquish Oliver. Now, I will tell you everything from the beginning, and it is a long story, so we may as well be comfortable." He took her hand and led her to a large, comfortable chair, sat down, and pulled her on to his lap. She settled against him, her head on his shoulder, and he held her tenderly.

"Anthea, I admit to always having known something of the harvest rites in these parts, but they always seemed innocent tradition, so the annual merrymaking never met with my disapproval or troubled my conscience. But then I discovered that every nineteen years, when the cycle is complete, they take a different and horrible form."

"I have never heard of this nineteen-year cycle. What is it?"

"Every nineteen years, the moon, sun, and earth return to the same relative position in the heavens, and there are two full moons in at least one month of the final year. The cycle prior to this one ended in July 1795, so the rites were performed early that year. The new cycle that began in that same month ends on August 30th this year, so the rites will be performed again then."

"1795 is the year Corinna was born."

"Yes," he answered, "and if you count back in nineteens you will come to 1738, the date of the engraving. It is always nineteen. I was eleven in 1795 and was sent away to stay with relatives so I didn't see or hear anything that happened then. Maybe my father was trying to protect me, or maybe he just preferred not to have to deal with my childish questions. I will never know his reason. Suffice it to say that when I became duke, I was ignorant of the cycle and what it entailed. But on those fateful nineteenth years, the Duke of Chavanage has to participate in the rites, so I had to be told the truth."

Anthea looked up at him. "Was that the reason for your sudden recourse to drink?"

"In a way, for the two things are irrevocably connected," he answered. "My unwilling involvement commenced when Lethe bought Wycke Hall a few months after you and I came together. Everything changed with his arrival. He seemed a fine fellow, most amiable and witty, and I was fool enough to like and trust him, until one night he engaged me in conversation about the rites, and I told him what I knew. He feigned surprise that I did not mention what occurred every nineteen years. I said that I knew nothing of any nineteen years, so he explained that the entire population of Cathness and the surrounding area has a primitive belief that if they do not follow the ancient way every nineteenth year, the harvests will fail and there will be famine. I was shocked and left him in no doubt that I regarded it all as superstitious claptrap, and that if I really thought people on my land were indulging in pagan goings-on, I would put a stop to it immediately."

Pagan goings-on? Anthea looked away, for she was beginning to suspect what might be involved, and it was something so terrible that she recoiled from it with every fiber of her being.

Jovian was aware of her dread and so allowed her a little more time by not describing the rites in full just yet. But they would have to be described soon, and she would have to cope with them in all their awfulness. "Anyway," he went on, "my expressed opposition to the nineteenth-year rites was all Lethe needed to know. If I would not be a willing accomplice, I not only had to be forced into it, but my, er . . . powers had to be kept in check as well. He had already managed to give me mistletoe without my realizing it, so I was susceptible to his will anyway, but now he made finally certain of me by slipping pomegranate juice into my glass of wine. From that moment on, I was completely in his clutches."

"What is Sir Erebus? A warlock? A wizard?" The words might have seemed foolish, were not the situation so very serious.

"He is neither, just a very dangerous and persuasive believer in old ways that ought never to have survived into these modern times. He knows about the properties of plants and how to use them, and with the assistance of Abigail Wheatley, who adores him and who certainly *is* possessed of supernatural powers, he manipulates those around him. It is through her that he achieves his sleight of hand with mistletoe."

"Why did you deny Abigail Wheatley's existence?" Anthea asked. "I know she is here in the castle, because I have seen her. She brought that tray." Anthea pointed.

"Yes, she is here, and she is the one who administered pomegranate to me, but Abigail Wheatley is not her real name. Who she is I do not know, except that she is certainly *not* Corinna's kinswoman, and be warned, Anthea, she is no ordinary woman but can shift her shape to become a—"

"—a hare?" Anthea broke in.

"Yes, she is Lethe's familiar. It is her task to be his eyes and ears, and in her four-legged form she can travel many miles without effort. But in common with many witches before her, to change her shape from woman to creature, she must first raise thunder. That is why you hear it whenever the hare appears. She has to spy upon me, and it is far from easy to elude her, but it can be done. I have slipped away to see you on a number of occasions, and right now she is keeping a close watch upon my apartment door without knowing there is a secret passage."

Anthea thought of Corinna. "So my stepsister doesn't have an aunt after all?"

"Not surviving. The only aunt she ever had was her mother's twin sister, Flora Pranton, who . . . er, died the year Corinna was born."

Anthea could not help but notice the hesitation about Flora's death, but she did not press for an explanation; instead she asked another question. "So there aren't Pranton records after all?"

Jovian hesitated. "Not as Corinna was promised, but I know a great deal about the family."

"You do?" She sat up to look at him. "Actually about the Prantons?"

"Yes, and I will tell you in due course."

Again, she saw something in his eyes, a forewarning of things to come that would not be pleasant to know, so she endeavored to postpone the moment. "Why does Sir Erebus use mistletoe? And why pomegranate?" she inquired.

"He uses mistletoe to make someone malleable, but with Abigail's assistance disguises it as another plant so that the act of giving it will not seem odd. He then has to use pomegranate to impose complete servitude. Only pomegranate; nothing else will do. Generally Abigail is the one to administer it."

"How did they disguise the mistletoe for you?"

Jovian smiled in spite of himself. "Do you have visions of Lethe presenting me with a lover's posy?"

She blushed. "Such a thing had not crossed my mind."

"I'm relieved to hear it. Actually, he stirred a mild argument about whether a particular plant was a gray speedwell or a field speedwell."

Now Anthea was the one to smile. "Aunt Letty would say that you surely mean *veronica polita* or *veronica agrestis*?"

"Whatever. He picked the wretched thing and gave it to me to inspect. At least, that's what he seemed to do; in actual fact, he merely handed me a sprig of mistletoe. Anyway, that is by the by, for the fact remains that he brought me into his web and kept me there constantly so I would do what would otherwise have appalled me. So you see, my darling, I could not help but drink too much and alienate everyone I held dear. It broke my heart to know what I was doing to you, but there was absolutely nothing I could do to stop myself. I had no idea that my Achilles' heel was the pomegranate juice continually administered in my food and drink; it was just that, for some reason, I was Lethe's lapdog."

Jovian leaned his head back sadly. "I was such a fool, Anthea. Why didn't I see through his false friendship from the outset? Because of him I lost you, my freedom, and my self-respect, just because he needed my cooperation on one single night, August 30th of this year."

"Oh, Jovian . . ." She linked her arms around his neck and hugged him tightly.

He rested his cheek against her dark hair. "Another effect of that abominable pomegranate juice was that it relaxed my control of my gift; hence the tales of flying up to windows and wine bottles that came to my beckoning. Until then I had always been careful to hide the truth, because people have been branded witches for far less. You were the only person with whom I ever knowingly and willingly tossed caution to the winds."

"That night at Carlton House?" she inquired.

He nodded.

She felt very guilty. "And to think all this had befallen you; yet, I accused you of being a beastly drunkard. Can you ever forgive me?"

Jovian's lips brushed her hair. "My darling, there is nothing to forgive. To all intents and purposes I *was* a beastly drunkard, so how could you be expected to know the truth? All I could pray was that redemption would fall my way, and with it the chance to win your love again. My chance came when at last I discovered how Lethe was manipulating me. I saw Abigail add the juice to the bottle of wine that was placed to my hand every night at dinner. I managed to dispose of the vile concoction without them realizing it had not been consumed, and by the next morning I was very much my own man again. But I pretended to remain Lethe's puppet in order to stand a chance of spiking his damnable guns."

"Jovian, there is something I don't understand. If you are trying to make Sir Erebus think you are still under his control, why on earth did you knock him down tonight?"

He smiled. "You saw that little episode, did you?"

"I watched it all. What did he say that provoked you so much?"

There was a pause. "He . . . insulted my honor. I was rash to fell him, but he taunted me too far. I did it while still pretending to be inebriated, however, so I fancy his suspicions will not be aroused."

"Well, drunkards are often violent, are they not?" she said.

"Maybe, but a cruel tongue and selfishness beyond belief have been the extent of my sins."

"It was enough," Anthea murmured, as the night of the Farnborough ball returned to her memory yet again. *"Oh, go away, my lady, for I have h-had enough of your whining complaints. I'm s-sick of your face, your voice, your person, and—hic—your prissy standards. I vow you will be as comfortless as a prayer b-book between the sheets! A man can drink as he pl-pleases and should not be expected to do otherwise, simply because a damned w-woman doesn't like it!"*

Again he knew her thoughts and closed his eyes ashamedly, but she stretched up to kiss his cheek. "Now I know that it wasn't the real you, those awful days do not matter any more," she whispered.

Being together like this made it only too easy to want to forget everything else. Desire had burned between them for so long that this present intimacy was almost too much for him to endure. He wanted to carry her to the bed and make sweet love until the dawn, but now was not the moment to let passion rule. "We must talk while we have the chance," he said, gently but firmly, "because I have so much more to tell, and a plan to divulge that involves you. You will need all your courage if you are to help me end Lethe's odious reign." Unexpectedly he smiled. "And you may need that courage all over again if another of Lethe's plans is to be halted as well."

"Another plan? What do you mean?"

"Simply that the pretense that your aunt has brought you here for me to negotiate a match for you with Lethe is not, I fear, a pretense at all. Lethe really does intend to marry you."

With a gasp, she straightened and looked at him. "Tell me you jest!"

"Would that it were so, but I fear it is fact. He lusts after your person and your inheritance, for both are irresistible to him. Not that he will succeed if Abigail has her way, for she is very jealous and, I suspect, hates the very sight of you. She will assist him with the rites but not in his desire for you."

Anthea recalled Christmas Eve, and Abigail's look of absolute loathing. So it was jealousy that lay behind it. . . .

Jovian drew her close once more. "Lethe isn't going to have you if *I* have anything to do with it either, because you are mine. At least, I hope you are."

"Of course I am," she replied, and raised her lips to his. They kissed lovingly, and then he looked into her soft eyes. "We were always meant for each other, Anthea," he breathed, "and having lost you once, I do not intend to let you slip through my fingers again."

Talk of love slipping through fingers reminded her of her aunt and Huw Gadarn. "Jovian, the man who was with you tonight, the one you called Huw . . . ?"

"Huw Gadarn? He is my head gardener, and my one staunch ally since I decided to set myself against these savage rituals." He raised a curious eyebrow. "Why do you ask?"

"Well, I . . ." She wasn't sure whether to say anything more, for the secret wasn't hers to tell.

Jovian studied her face and read her thoughts. "So Huw and Lady Letitia were once more than they should have been, and she now wonders if he is married with a family? Well, he isn't, nor have I ever known him to court anyone."

"Aunt Letty loves him still and deeply regrets allowing herself to be separated from him all those years ago."

"Maybe all is not yet lost. Now, where was I in the tale?"

"You had discovered how the pomegranate was being administered and become your own man again," she said.

"Ah, yes. Well, the obvious way to pit myself against Lethe was to prevent you and Corinna from leaving London."

"Corinna would not hear of staying in Berkeley Square, no matter how I tried."

"He knew she would be desperate to learn more of her family, so he chose well when he sent Abigail to pose as her aunt."

Anthea's thoughts returned to the harvest rites. "Jovian, how can Sir Erebus possibly think he will get away with all this?"

"The same way his predecessors have perpetuated the rites throughout history—subjugation through supernatural assistance and the imposition of forgetfulness. If he succeeds in his purposes, Lady Letitia will not remember anything of her stay here except that it resulted in your betrothal to him, and if you had been as beguiled as your aunt, you would be very happy with the match. You will both believe Corinna stayed behind in London, so it will not be until your return to Berkeley Square that her disappearance will be discovered. The servants will say she accompanied you to Gloucestershire, but you will both insist she didn't. You will suspect them of knowing what happened and covering up to protect themselves. The authorities will be called in, and it will soon be revealed—through the ever helpful Lethe, of course—that Corinna took passage back to Ireland. It will be assumed that she was unhappy here and simply returned to the land in which she had lived most of her life. That will be the end of it. Her true fate will never be discovered." He looked deep into her eyes in the candlelight. "And it will have been a terrible fate indeed," he added softly.

She knew the moment had come to face up to the truth. "What is that fate, Jovian?" she asked in a small voice, then hid her face against his shoulder as she awaited his answer.

"I think you already know," he said gently.

"She . . . will die?"

"Yes, my darling. Corinna is the Harvest Maiden, and in this year of 1814, when the nineteen-year cycle closes, she is to be sacrificed."

Twenty-four

*S*acrificed. Anthea's blood ran cold, for Jovian's answer was what she had dreaded in her heart of hearts, but she fought against it. "No! I won't accept it! If you were able to escape the effects of pomegranate, then Corinna can too. *Surely* we can do something to free her? Can't we go to wherever it is she is being kept and—?"

"We can do nothing until the rites begin on the night of the full moon, because I have no idea where she is. It might be at Wycke Hall, or the Cross Foxes, or any other of a hundred places in and around Cathness. The entire population has fallen to Lethe because the people hereabouts have a primitive belief in the rites. They are convinced that if they do not follow the ancient way every nineteenth year, then the harvests will fail, and there will be famine."

"But—"

"Listen to me, Anthea. All this is what Lethe *intends* to do, but he can only achieve it if the rites proceed without error. That is where we come in, for I mean him to fail abysmally."

"Meaning something and actually managing it are worlds apart, Jovian!" she cried accusingly. "Oh, *why* did you leave Corinna in the field tonight? Why did you allow her to be taken away again?" She started up from his lap, but he caught her hand to hold her back.

"Anthea, you must hear me in full!"

"Let me go this instant!" she cried, struggling against him.

He tightened his grip and clamped a hand over her mouth. "Be quiet! Do you want to bring them running?" But still she squirmed furiously to break free, so he shook her. "Damn it all, Anthea, be sensible! Do you honestly imagine I'd have left her with him if there were any other way?"

For an angry moment her lavender eyes blazed at him, but then common sense rushed back, and she stopped fighting him. "Tell me the rest, then. Tell me why you and Huw Gadarn saved yourselves tonight but left my stepsister behind." She knew she was being unfair but was too frightened for Corinna to be reasonable.

He relaxed his hold upon her but did not answer, and she knew how much her accusations had hurt him. Then he made himself go on.

"I have already mentioned that everything is connected with the myth of Demeter, Persephone, and Hades, which story you are bound to know already but which I will outline again anyway, so there is no misunderstanding. Hades, god of the nether world — signifying barrenness and death, the part played by Lethe — falls in love with Persephone, goddess of young crops, spring and new growth, who is now Corinna. By handing her mistletoe in the form of a narcissus, he renders her helpless to protest as he takes her down into the nether world to be his bride. Her grieving mother, Demeter, goddess of the ripe crops and fruitful earth — also identified as the Lavender Lady and you, my darling — sorrowfully creates perpetual winter. Mankind suffers dreadfully and implores Zeus — me, I fear — to force his brother Hades to give up Persephone. Zeus fears that mankind will starve and become extinct, leaving no one to serve the gods, so he makes Hades surrender his bride. Before letting Persephone go, however, Hades gives her pomegranate in some form or other, some say the seeds, others the juice. This binds her to the nether world and her husband, but she is allowed to return to Demeter for six months of the year. In return for this concession, Demeter relents and permits the resumption of the four seasons. To this day many believe that, at the end of every harvest, Persephone returns to the bowels of the earth to be with Hades, and rites are performed annually that imitate this, but every nineteenth year it ceases to be a pretense. Persephone, in the form of a Harvest Maiden, is really sacrificed. That is the truth, Anthea, and on your journey to Cathness, you witnessed at least one other instance of the same rites that take place here."

Anthea responded slowly. "Yes, in the field when Sir Erebus halted our carriage, and . . . he tried to give Aunt Letty some mistletoe disguised as honeysuckle."

Jovian nodded. "To discover if she, like you, was protected by my—drunken, of course—interference. But that is of no consequence, merely an idle investigation on his part that has no bearing upon the reenactment of the myth, which is what these rites really are."

"So Sir Erebus is Hades, and you are Zeus. Corinna, the Harvest Maiden, and Persephone are all one and the same, and Demeter, the Lavender Lady, and I are too?"

"Yes," he replied.

Anthea was close to tears. "But why Corinna? What is there about her that makes her their choice?"

Jovian breathed out and leaned his head back again. "Corinna has been chosen because in this part of Gloucestershire, the Pranton family has always provided the Harvest Maiden. The name Pranton is nothing more than a corruption of *printemps,* the French word for spring. The Harvest Maiden is always nineteen at the right time, has golden hair in recognition of the ripe harvest, and green eyes for the lush grass." He paused. "And Zeus is her father."

Startled, Anthea pulled away to look at him. "What are you saying?"

"Not that *I* am Corinna's sire, for I was only eleven when she was born. What I'm saying is that my father and Corinna's are one and the same. She is your stepsister but my halfsister."

Anthea was so thunderstruck she took a moment to recover. All sorts of things began to fall into place. "So Corinna's mother, Chloe Pranton, was the unsuitable woman with whom your father was in love in 1795? Aunt Letty told me about her. She also said that this woman was suspected of having his child?"

"Yes. The year of Corinna's birth was also the year that her aunt, Chloe's twin sister Flora, was the Harvest Maiden. By the way, the hair in Corinna's locket doesn't belong to her grandmother, as Abigail told her, nor indeed to her mother, but to her aunt, Flora Pranton. A lock of hair from one Harvest Maiden is always given to the next, although for some reason at the rites it is the Lavender Lady who wears it to the field, then it is given back to the Harvest Maiden."

Anthea shivered. "I must wear it?"

"Yes. Anyway, we digress. I know now, from a letter he left in Huw's keeping, to be given to me only when it was clear I would not follow in the ritual footsteps of previous dukes of Chavanage, that my father had come to realize how very wrong the ceremonies were. When he fell in love with Chloe, the only way he could help her and his unborn child, who was almost certain to be a girl and therefore the next Harvest Maiden, was to conceal her somewhere safe. He confided in his brother-in-law, my uncle Lisnerne, who had nothing whatsoever to do with the rites. My uncle agreed to take her to his estate in County Fermanagh. Thus, Chloe Pranton and the child disappeared. Everything possible was done to make sure Corinna would not suffer Flora's fate when the nineteen years came around again, but Lethe found her anyway."

"Did his finding of her have something to do with Chloe's sudden death?" Anthea asked.

"Yes. Lethe had her poisoned. She was designated the next Lavender Lady, a true mother Demeter to her child Persephone, but she was too wily for him, avoiding every attempt to administer either mistletoe or pomegranate. Lethe soon realized she was expendable because you could take her place, so he had her done away with."

Salt stung Anthea's eyes. "Poor Papa, he was ecstatic to have her in his life and so grief-stricken to lose her again." She loved her father very much and hated to think of his sorrow.

Jovian drew a long breath. "And now Lethe is set to bring the cycle to a close once more, and in spite of her parents' efforts, Corinna has become the Harvest Maiden."

"Who was the Lavender Lady in 1795?" Anthea asked, curious about her predecessor.

"A young woman by the name of Jocasta Frost, who now lives in Scotland, I believe. She has no recollection of what went on here, and the only thing—apart from the locket— that is passed from Lavender Lady to Lavender Lady is the gown of flowers, which is now two hundred years old."

"That is a venerable age," Anthea observed.

"And the garment is becoming rather fragile, but it is assiduously repaired and stored each time it is worn. The belief is that something must be preserved from cycle to cycle, the gown for the Lavender Lady, a lock of hair in a locket for the Harvest Maiden. By the same token corn dollies are made from the last of the harvest and kept in houses until the following year. Such things do not apply only to harvest beliefs, for at Christmas there is a strong tradition of keeping a fragment of yule log each year to burn upon its successor, and so on."

"I can understand that, but what I cannot understand is how I can become Lavender Lady in Chloe's place. Clearly the same family does not always have to be involved, for as far as I know the Wintours have nothing to do with the Prantons or Frosts, yet it seems the Lavender Lady can come from all three. Or aren't they three separate families after all?" An awful thought occurred to her. "I-I mean, if your father was Corinna's father . . . ?"

He knew what she was thinking before she spoke. "Please

do not fear that you and I are half siblings too, for I assure you, we are not," he said with a quick laugh.

"It's not funny, Jovian!"

"Forgive me." He made himself become serious again.

"So, how *have* I been chosen?" she asked.

"Well, as a general rule, the same few families are always involved, but not always, although the Harvest Maiden *always* comes from the Prantons. What really matters is the first name but not necessarily the surname too. In my case the name Jovian, which is always given to the males of my family, is a tradition based upon the rites. Jovian is another term for the Roman god Jove, more usually known as Jupiter, and whom the Greeks knew as—"

"Surely you aren't telling me that you really are Zeus? Because if so—"

"—you will rightly think me fit for bedlam," he finished for her. "No, Anthea, I am merely the latest Duke of Chavanage to be cast in the role of Zeus in the myth, which is rather different than being Zeus himself. Supernatural powers and the name Jovian have always been in my family, but that does not make me Jove, Jupiter, or Zeus, any more than calling you Regina would make you royal and place you upon a throne. As it happens you are called Anthea, which means 'lady of the flowers,' and you were given that name because my father was induced by the then Hades—a distant cousin of Lethe's surnamed Acheron, after the River of Woe—to badger your father until he gave in."

Anthea was dismayed anew. "Please don't tell me Papa condones any of this . . ."

"Have no fear of that, although in the past there *were* members of your family caught up in it, but no one who is alive now and certainly no one you have ever known. Your surname, Wintour, indicates the barren season that Demeter brought to the land until Persephone's fate was resolved. Thus the Lavender Lady—Demeter—has sometimes come from your family and sometimes from others whose name denotes some aspect of the goddess, as in the case of Jocasta Frost."

"So it is simply a matter of chance?" Anthea asked.

"For you, yes, but not for Corinna. She was destined for the role of Harvest Maiden. The name Corinna is one of Persephone's titles; her mother's name, Chloe, refers to Demeter."

"Perhaps *that* is why I have been chosen!" Anthea broke in. "I am Anthea *Chloe* Wintour!"

"Then in all likelihood that is indeed the reason. Flora Pranton was named for the Roman goddess of springtime and flowers. Cathness is a corruption of Chthonysis, which is Zeus's title in his capacity as god of earth and fertility. Obed Dennis means servant of Dionysis, which befits an innkeeper. Jocasta Frost is easy enough to understand, for the surname equates with winter, but Jocasta means shining moon. Sebbriz is Cerberus, guardian of Hades. The two maids you encountered on arriving here, Phoebe and Cynthia, are named for the moon. Abigail Wheatley is—"

"The servant of the wheat field," Anthea interposed, for he had already explained. "What of Huw Gadarn?"

"Ah. Well, the first Huw Gadarn was a Celtic leader, probably mythical, who brought his people safely to Britain and taught them how to grow crops without resorting to magical means. The present Huw Gadarn is a fine gardener too, the finest I have ever come across, and he abhors these bloodthirsty harvest ceremonies. He and I both know the crops flourish hereabouts in spite of the rites, rather than because of them." Jovian looked at her. "Have I frightened you too much with all this?" he inquired gently.

"Only a fool would not be frightened," she replied, "but I have no choice but to do what is necessary to stop all this and save Corinna."

"Is there anything I've said so far that you do not understand?"

She nodded. "I have never heard of a Lavender Lady before, although there are all sorts of other ladies, ghostly gray, white, and black ones, and so on."

He smiled. "Most harvest traditions have a White Lady, to represent the snow and frost caused by Demeter, and there was a White Lady here too until one strange year about two hundred years ago when the seasons were confused by an unusual period of very warm, wet weather. The White Lady always walks to the rites through the lavender field, which bloomed very late that year, and on impulse, she picked some and tucked it into her bodice before continuing to the ceremonies. The following summer was the most bounteous the area had ever known, and the people believed the lavender had added some potency to their rituals. From then on lavender was pinned all over the White Lady's gown, until eventually it was so covered with flowers that it seemed made of them. Naturally enough the White Lady was called the Lavender Lady after that, and it so happens that the lavender here has flowered late ever since. Every nineteenth year it is in bloom for the whole twelve months. That is a mystery I cannot explain."

"There is another mystery I think you *can* explain," Anthea said after a moment, the glaring question at last springing into her mind.

"Name it."

"If your father and Corinna's are the same, will the Harvest Maiden of"—Anthea counted—"1833 be *your* daughter? If so, for her to be nineteen in that year she must already have been born or at least conceived. Therefore, I presume you must know who she is, or at least who the mother is?"

Jovian seemed a little disturbed and made her get up from his lap. Then he got up as well and ran his hand agitatedly over his hair.

Anthea watched him. "Jovian, surely you know whether or not you have—?"

"No, I don't! A healthy virile man cannot be a monk all the time, and you must understand that when I really was continuously intoxicated, there were periods I could not recollect afterward. Corinna cannot possibly be the only surviving member of the Pranton family, which at one time was known to be very large and scattered across the kingdom. If I fell by the wayside, I have no idea what the woman concerned looked like, let alone whether she was named Pranton or had Pranton blood in her veins. Fondness does not have to enter into the union, you know. My father and Chloe Pranton happened to be lovers, too, but my grandfather certainly went about it as a means to an end. So did most of the other dukes before him. If I am guilty of fathering the next Harvest Maiden after Corinna, it was while I was too drunk to know what I was doing."

Anthea did not know what to say. She could not bear to think of him with anyone else, and the fact that he pleaded drunkenness did not lessen the pain that ran through her now. Unreasonable as it was, she felt as if he had been deliberately unfaithful.

He turned to her again. "Please believe me, Anthea, for I would not—could not—willingly betray my love for you."

"I believe you," she whispered, and it was the truth. Looking into his eyes now and hearing the unhappiness in his voice, she could not possibly blame him for something that might or might not have happened. Her hand stretched out and his fingers curled strongly around hers.

He pulled her close. "Lethe knows the truth of it and taunted me tonight. That was why I struck him."

"Oh, Jovian . . ." She clung to him. "Jovian, if something did happen, and somewhere there is an unfortunate baby girl destined to be Harvest Maiden in 1833, we must more than ever do everything in our power to stop this horrible thing now."

"You will need all your courage and initiative," he warned.

"I have both in plenty," she replied.

"I know," he said tenderly, then began to tell her how he hoped to overthrow Sir Erebus Lethe and the gruesome harvest ceremonies that were the bane of Cathness's beautiful countryside.

At first the plan seemed too audacious by far, and Anthea doubted its feasibility, but by the time Jovian had explained in full, she knew it might—just might—succeed. They spent much of the night going over and over the details, trying to think of anything and everything that could possibly go wrong. Outside, clouds began to obscure the moon, banishing the ominous blue and returning the night to some semblance of normality.

As dawn approached, and a breeze rustled the trees in the park, Jovian returned to his own apartment by way of the secret passage. The plan had been laid, and they both knew exactly what to do. All that was needed now was luck.

Twenty-five

*D*awn had broken and the birds were singing when Anthea at last managed to fall asleep. She was exhausted and slept very soundly, so that it was midafternoon when Cynthia roused her to say she must get up, because Sir Erebus was soon to visit the castle. The maid evidently knew of that gentleman's marital aspirations and assumed that his intended bride would hasten to please him. It did not seem to occur to her that the groom might be the only one who desired the marriage.

Very mindful of Jovian's instruction to appear submissive, Anthea did not show the maid the utter abhorrence with which she regarded the prospect of Sir Erebus Lethe as her husband. Nor did she display her nervousness that in a short time now the first part of Jovian's plan would be put into practice. Sir Erebus's visit was prearranged and would be put to good use, but come the evening, when he had departed again, Anthea would be put to the test in her first public appearance as the Lavender Lady. She did not know which of the two ordeals alarmed her more.

The carriage had been brought to the castle during the morning, and while she was asleep, her luggage had been carried up to her rooms, unpacked, and put away. She permitted Cynthia to select a yellow gingham gown and dress her, and was agreeably surprised with the way the maid combed and pinned her hair, but it was not really possible to take pleasure in anything. For all her brave smiles, Anthea's true mood was one of fear and trepidation.

Cynthia brought a light breakfast of tea, toast, butter, and marmalade, but hungry as she was, Anthea feared to touch anything because it might contain pomegranate. Jovian's voice soon put her right. *"Everything is all right except the tea, which has been tampered with. Ask for the milk on its own."*

So she waved the tea away. "Just the milk, if you please."

Cynthia was put out. "Oh, but—"

Anthea gave the maid an innocuous smile. "I have no fancy for tea because I fear I drank too much of the kykeon that was brought last night."

Reassured, Cynthia poured the milk into the cup and then busied herself with little tasks around the rooms, singing softly as she worked. *"Lavender blue, dilly, dilly . . ."* She had a pleasant voice, and under other circumstances Anthea would have appreciated her singing, but here at Cathness the old song was eerie.

The maid was looping the curtains neatly back into place when she remembered something and broke off from her singing. "Oh, Lady Anthea, Lady Letitia begs to inform you that when you go down, you will find her in the library."

"I will see her directly."

"You must finish your breakfast quickly, so you'll be ready and waiting when Sir Erebus arrives."

A sharp retort burned on Anthea's tongue, but she managed to overcome it and remain complaisant. "Of course, for it is my earnest wish to be with him."

Cynthia nodded as if this were not only understandable but fully expected.

When the maid had gone, Anthea waited a few minutes before going down to seek Aunt Letty in the library. The yellow gingham gown was very bright and fresh, and the castle was quiet as she descended the grand staircase, but halfway down she came face-to-face with Sebbriz.

The steward paused watchfully, having heard from Cynthia about the declined tea. "Good afternoon, my lady."

"Sebbriz."

"I trust you slept well?"

"Excellently, thank you. I believe Sir Erebus will be calling soon?" She was all eagerness as she gazed innocently into his uncannily canine eyes.

"Yes, my lady."

"I trust I will be informed the very moment he arrives?"

He gave a faint smile. "Of course, my lady."

She smiled as if the reassurance made her very happy, then she glanced down the staircase. "My maid told me Lady Letitia is in the library . . . ?"

"Yes, my lady. It is the door on the left at the foot of the stairs."

She inclined her head and continued down the steps, conscious of his gaze following her. He was still there when she reached the library door, and she was relieved to go inside, where Aunt Letty was not alone but had Jovian with her. They were seated at a table, poring over a priceless first edition of Culpeper's *Complete Herbal*.

The library was filled with rare books, maps, and papers, and its walls almost completely sheathed in bookcases. Maroon brocade draperies hung at the windows, and an ancient pendulum clock ticked slowly in a corner. Beyond the open windows there was a beautiful knot garden where Anthea noticed Huw Gadarn instructing two undergardeners. Even from that distance, it was possible to see that he had a pistol thrust into his belt; evidently the previous night was not an isolated instance.

The Welshman was aware of Lady Letitia's presence in the library and kept glancing toward her, but Anthea wasn't quite sure if her aunt was equally conscious of him. Lady Letitia looked fetching in a deep shade of apricot and beamed at

Anthea as if today were all that was delightful and to be appreciated. "Ah, there you are at last, my dear. I was beginning to fear you would never awaken. I trust you are fully refreshed?"

"Oh, yes, thank you, Aunt Letty." Anthea gave her a warm hug.

Jovian had risen to his feet the moment Anthea entered. He was dressed for riding, she noticed, although his coat was old gold in color rather than pine green, and he, too, smiled at Anthea. "Good morning," he said, but then his smile faded as a slight roll of thunder announced the arrival of the hare on one of the neat gravel paths in the knot garden. The open window meant that it—or rather Abigail—could hear every word said in the library, so Jovian's reaction was swift, smooth, and faultless. A slight unsteadiness immediately marked his gait as he came around the table to Anthea. Lurching just a little, he took her hand to raise it to his lips. "You are l-looking delight—*hic*—ful, Anthea."

"Thank you," she replied, then took her hand away a little reproachfully. "Jovian, you seem ever so slightly tipsy again. I will be most displeased if you cause any problems in my alliance with dear Sir Erebus." The words almost choked her, but somehow she managed to sound as if she meant them.

"Such sentiments must turn your stomach, for they certainly turn mine," came the reply in her head, but aloud he said, "Don't you worry y-your pretty h-head. I'll negotiate a handsome little c-contract for you."

He conducted her to the table and drew out a chair for her. As she sat down, Lady Letitia reached across to tap her hand fondly. "I'm *so* glad about this match, my dear. Sir Erebus is quite perfect for you, and my only regret is that dear Corinna did not accompany us on this visit. Still, I suppose I can well understand her desire to remain in London to be with her new aunt. Miss Wheatley was so very charming when she called upon us that I was quite taken with her."

"Yes, Aunt Letty," Anthea replied, catching Jovian's fleeting glance.

Lady Letitia leaned closer. "Anthea, do you see that fine fellow outside? The one giving orders to those two gardeners?" she whispered, "Well, it is Huw! And what's more, Jovian tells me he isn't married and doesn't have a sweetheart!"

"Oh, I—I'm so glad he is still here, Aunt Letty. He certainly is very handsome."

"Isn't he just? I knew him the very moment I saw him." Lady Letitia gave a wistful sigh, then continued, "Jovian has informed me that in a short while now Huw will be meeting him in the old orangery to discuss what must be done to make it presentable again. I am to go too, but, for appearance's sake, I think you should come as well."

"Of course, if that is what you wish." Anthea already knew about the meeting in the orangery, for it was part of Jovian's plan. "Sir Erebus will be conducted to us there, I trust, Jovian?" she asked, looking the picture of innocence.

"Of course." *"Unless Dame Fortune has obliged us by tipping him from his horse and breaking his odious neck! By the way, his purpose today is to give you the Harvest Maiden's locket, which now contains Corinna's hair, not Flora's. You will allow him to place it around your neck, to conform to the act of giving and receiving. Neither you nor your aunt will know you have seen it before."*

Huw left the knot garden by way of a postern in the high wall, and Lady Letitia immediately got up from her seat. She was flustered and her hands shook as she carefully closed the volume of Culpeper. Jovian and Anthea rose too, and he offered them both an arm to leave the library. From the doorway Anthea glanced back. The watchful hare was still there.

Huw had still to come to the orangery when they arrived, so Anthea looked around as they waited. The first thing she noticed was the tree from which Abigail had been gathering fruit the night before. It grew directly out of a circular bed that had been cut into the otherwise stone-tiled floor and was about twelve feet tall, with thick, glossy, almost evergreen leaves, and pinkish gold fruit about the size of apples. These were the pomegranates from which was extracted the vital juice with which Sir Erebus enmeshed his victims.

Anthea also knew from Jovian that the mistletoe growing secretly among the foliage could be used against Sir Erebus as well as by him. According to the Greek myth of Aeneas, the golden bough provided a certain means of entering the nether world. If presented to the Harvest Maiden tomorrow night it would ensure her a way *out* of that same nether world. It was therefore part of Jovian's plan that the Lavender Lady should carry it to the rites and present it to Corinna in order to lay waste to Sir Erebus's wicked ceremony.

Once a sprig of the mistletoe had been cut, both the pomegranate tree and its golden-leafed guest would be destroyed in Sir Erebus's presence without him realizing it. As they withered away, so would his power to hold sway over others. His ignorance of what was being done was very important, and the carrying out of the deed was the real reason for the meeting in the orangery; Aunt Letty's reunion with Huw Gadarn was serendipity.

Anthea surveyed the other plants, but they were all beyond redemption, either completely dead or too far gone in neglect for there to be any hope of reviving them. It seemed odd, she thought, when Huw was such a dedicated and skillful head gardener.

"Huw refuses to tend anything in here because of the pomegranate tree, which Abigail has to care for," Jovian explained.

The rest of the orangery had become a makeshift storeroom for a pile of old trunks, a dilapidated harpsichord, a stack of oil paintings in elaborate frames, and a large, rather ugly wine cooler, as well as all sorts of gardening tools and terracotta pots. On a row of hooks directly by the door there hung coils of twine, a string of withered onions, two rustic walking sticks, fishing rods, and a rather battered but particularly elaborate fan fashioned from ripe wheat ears and stalks. This last was called a corn dolly, even though they might be of various shapes and made of wheat, barley, oats, rye, or any other crop as well as corn.

This one was the work of someone very skilled in the craft, and how old it was Anthea could not guess, but its rather battered condition suggested it had come from a harvest twenty or more years ago. Nineteen years ago, she thought then, guessing that this one had been made from the harvest of 1795.

"You are right, my love."

Lady Letitia noticed the corn dolly too. "Good heavens, I cannot believe it . . . !" she gasped.

"Believe what, Aunt Letty?"

"That fan is exactly like one that was made when I was here in '95. Huw said it would be used for the harvest home, and I was looking forward to watching all the festivities, but my disapproving parents hauled me home before then."

She, too, looked around the orangery, and like Anthea her glance happened upon the pomegranate tree. "Why, *punica granatum!*" she cried in surprise, for such trees were far from common in England, even under glass. She went closer and then drew back in surprise on noticing the mistletoe almost hidden beneath the foliage. "Oh, dear, I wonder if Huw is aware it has an invasion of *viscum album?*" she murmured.

Anthea suddenly felt the hare's presence by the entrance to the orangery. The creature was trying to keep out of sight behind the curtains that flanked the doorway, but the end of a drooping brown ear gave the game away. Abigail Wheatley was nothing if not dedicated when it came to eavesdropping for Sir Erebus.

The sound of hooves and wheels approached along the drive outside, and Anthea recognized the black traveling carriage she had last seen outside Green Park. The coachman drove the horses along at a rattling pace, and gravel was tossed up as it passed the orangery. Its blinds were lowered, but there was no doubt that Sir Erebus Lethe was inside.

A man walking along the drive in the opposite direction had to step hastily aside as the vehicle swept by, and when it had gone, Anthea saw that the man was Huw Gadarn. He gazed sourly after the carriage, then approached the orangery by way of a glazed door Anthea had not noticed before because it was in a corner and partly obscured by the stacked trunks. Snatching off his hat, he rapped respectfully at the glass, and Jovian nodded to him. The door creaked as it was opened, and then the gardener's boots clumped on the stone floor as he came toward them and then bowed. He smiled in that almost roguish Welsh way that was so very attractive, and Anthea understood more and more how as a young man he had swept Lady Letitia Wintour from her feet.

"Au, Huw," Jovian drawled, "I'm thinking about p-pulling the whole—*hic*—damned orangery down but will hear your opinion f-first."

"It may come to that, your grace, but I will see what can be done," Huw replied, unable to prevent his gaze moving to Lady Letitia, whose face was very pink indeed and who could not stop smoothing her gown like a self-conscious miss in her teens. "Do you remember me, Lady Letitia?" he asked. "It was a long time ago, I know, but—"

"Of course I remember you," she replied quickly. "How could I not? It is *very* good to see you again."

"I am honored, my lady," he answered, his brown eyes dark and shining as they lingered on her. The years of separation ceased to matter, for she was still his beloved, still his *cariad.* Nothing would ever change that.

Sebbriz spoke from the doorway. "Sir Erebus Lethe, your grace," he announced, and the jingle of spurs sounded as Sir Erebus came into the orangery.

Twenty-six

Sir Erebus was dressed in a gray coat and cream breeches, his dark hair was perfectly combed, and there were costly rings on his fingers. The bunch of seals dangling from his fob would have pleased Mr. Brummell himself, and he looked ready for a leisurely lounge down fashionable Bond Street, rather than a social call at a country house. The only thing to spoil the effect, Anthea noted with satisfaction, was the black eye he sported as a result of his encounter with Jovian's fist.

The owner of said fist was all smiles as he went to greet his loathed caller. "Ah, Lethe. *Hic.* Good G-God, whatever happened to your eye?"

Sir Erebus's nostrils flared a little. "Are you implying my injury is new to you?"

Jovian's puzzled frown was exquisite. "Of course it's n-new to me. What happened?"

"I fell from my horse."

"Nasty brute that h-hunter of yours. You really ought to get something more r-reliable. *Hic.*"

Anthea had to fix her eyes on the floor to stop a smile, because Sir Erebus really had no idea how deftly he was being twitted.

Everyone—except Lady Letty, of course, because she had no idea that anything was afoot—was relieved when Sebbriz and the hare withdrew, leaving Sir Erebus alone with his victims and foes. The continued presence of his supporters would have made the first part of Jovian's plan difficult, if not impossible. As it was, the conspirators found themselves with a perfect opportunity to perform their deed.

Jovian nodded discreetly at Huw, and the gardener moved away toward the pomegranate tree, pretending to commence a general inspection of the orangery. He made much of examining a wall and part of the floor, then shifted some pots to look behind them. His movements were slow and methodical and did not attract any undue attention from Sir Erebus, who now found himself the object of Lady Letitia's gushing greetings.

"Why, Sir Erebus, how delightful to see you again! And how *splendid* you look! I vow your togs put the duke to shame!" There was nothing forced about her delight, for she had drunk the kykeon the night before and this morning had taken tea laced with pomegranate. She meant what she said.

"Lady Letitia." Sir Erebus sketched a bow, but his dark eyes fixed upon Anthea. "We meet again, Lady Anthea," he said softly.

But Anthea was so preoccupied with whether or not Huw would succeed that she quite forgot what was expected of her. Jovian issued a sharp reminder. *"Anthea!"*

She gave a guilty start and hastily mustered what she hoped was a warm and welcoming smile. "Forgive my distraction, Sir Erebus, but I fear I am rather overwhelmed by the honor you do me."

"Honor?"

"In wishing me to be your wife."

"Ah, yes. But how could I *not* wish to marry you, Lady Anthea? You are all that is perfect, and you have charmed these eyes from the moment they saw you."

It is my inheritance that charms you, you monster, she thought, but all he saw was the false and foolish smile on her soft lips as she answered, "I—I cannot believe that I am to know such happiness."

"You are the delight of my heart, Lady Anthea," he replied smoothly.

"I'm flattered, sir."

"I have brought a small token of my esteem," he said, and took the locket from inside his coat.

She evinced pleasure. "Why, how beautiful it is!"

Lady Letitia was in full agreement. "A most exquisite trinket, Sir Erebus. You are clearly a man of superb taste."

"I am when it comes to my choice of bride," he replied smoothly, then addressed Anthea. "May I place it around your neck, my lady?"

"Yes . . . of course." Anthea hated the touch of his fingers against her skin, and all she could think was that the locket now contained a lock of poor Corinna's hair. They shouldn't be standing around in polite conversation with Hades; they should be forcing him to surrender Persephone!

The locket rested coldly against her throat as she smiled again. "It is truly lovely, Sir Erebus. I will be sure to treasure it always. My only regret . . ."

"Regret?" he said quickly.

"Yes. I wish my stepsister were here too."

"Ah, yes."

"Corinna and I may not have known each other for very long, but we have become very close."

"A family tie can overcome all else," he murmured.

"Indeed so."

Jovian spoke silently to her. *"Suggest a little perambulation to the end of the orangery and back."*

She smiled at Sir Erebus. "Shall we stroll a little?"

"Why, of course." He offered her his arm, and they walked slowly toward the far end of the orangery, away from the pomegranate tree.

Lady Letitia turned to Jovian. "Do you think I should tell Huw about the *viscum album* in the *punica*—?"

Jovian interrupted quickly. "He already knows, Lady Letitia," he said quietly, hoping Sir Erebus had not heard anything.

"Really? Oh, well . . ." Lady Letitia thought no more of it.

Anthea strove to engage Sir Erebus's complete attention. Afterward she would not remember anything she said but would learn from Jovian that it had concerned everything from fashionable bonnets and how best to wear ribbons to how Wycke Hall might be refurbished after their marriage. She behaved exactly as an adoring, rather empty-headed bride should and carried it off with considerable panache. Sir Erebus, it seemed, did not care how empty her head was, provided her purse could not be similarly described.

Jovian kept Lady Letitia busy by asking her about various trees in the park, and no one actually saw Huw take a sharp knife and bend swiftly beneath the pomegranate tree. In a few seconds he had deftly cut out a ring of bark a quarter of an inch wide all around the trunk, then he straightened hastily. So nimble and quick had he been that the branches of the trees had barely moved at all. Now the tree would gradually die, and with it the mistletoe that relied upon it for sustenance, but first a sprig of the mistletoe had to be removed while Sir Erebus was present in the orangery.

Anthea and Jovian maintained their diversionary measures, and a moment later the mistletoe had been cut and the sprigs stuffed safely inside Huw's coat. All had been achieved, and under the most perfect of circumstances.

It is said that necessity is the mother of invention, and for Anthea that was very true indeed for the duration of Sir Erebus's visit. She did not know how she managed to behave as if he had completely beguiled her, but when he eventually left, she was satisfied that her counterfeit smiles had been almost as impressive as Jovian's supposed drunkenness.

Just prior to Sir Erebus's departure, they all partook of a goblet of kykeon in the great hall. Sebbriz brought it to them, and Abigail Wheatley stood to one side, her face very cold and still as she looked at Anthea. It was a gaze that left the lat-

ter in no doubt at all that she felt immense jealousy over Sir
Erebus. However, Abigail's deep resentment was the least of
Anthea's problems, her day of testing being far from over.
Next she had to play the Lavender Lady for several hours
under the watchful gaze of the people of Cathness, and she
was very apprehensive indeed about her ability to carry it off.

First, however, Sir Erebus sent Lady Letitia to her bed. He
waited until she had drunk the kykeon, then quietly told her
she was very tired and should sleep. Without demur she went
up to her rooms. Then he turned to Anthea. "Lady Anthea,
your task begins now. You know you are the Lavender Lady?"

"Answer truthfully," Jovian instructed watchfully, knowing how anxious she was.

"Yes, Sir Erebus, I know."

"Well, you must be seen all over the neighborhood, so that
everyone knows you are here again to pose the ancient threat
to the harvest. Your gown of lavender has been laid out in
readiness, and your mount will be brought to the courtyard.
The duke will escort you on the ride."

*"It's all right, my darling, just show your consent. It is only
a sort of royal progress, so you do not need to be as nervous
as I know you are."*

She nodded at Sir Erebus. "Very well."

"Go and put on your gown."

Turning, she went to where Cynthia waited in the staircase
hall.

She returned a few minutes later, clad in the décolleté
white silk gown that was entirely covered with artificial silk
lavender flowers. Lavender oil had been stroked on her skin,
her loose dark hair was adorned with a coronet of fresh lavender, there were satin slippers on her feet, and the gold locket
shone at her throat.

Jovian gazed at her. *"You look breathtaking, my darling."*

Sir Erebus's dark eyes were intense. "I believe you are the
most beautiful Lavender Lady of all," he breathed, his eyes so
ardent that for a moment she thought he was going to force a

kiss upon her, but to her relief, he merely inclined his head, then went out to his waiting carriage. The moment it pulled away, Anthea saw two saddled horses waiting, Jovian's dappled gray thoroughbred and a cream palfrey like Corinna's for her. Maybe it was even the same palfrey.

Sebbriz brought Jovian's top hat and gloves, and as he put them on, Jovian continued to silently instruct her. *"We ride a predetermined route around Cathness, and everyone will stand by the wayside to watch. They will not touch you in any way, except perhaps to toss lavender in your path, and the only thing they will say is one of the chants connected with the rituals. There is no need at all to be nervous, for I will guide you throughout."* He nodded at the steward to dismiss him, then held out a gloved hand to her.

Her fingers slid over his, and he led her out into the courtyard, where most of the servants had gathered. As he lifted her on to the sidesaddled palfrey, the only sound was the breeze playing in the battlements. She was thankful for the saddle, not having relished the prospect of riding astride as Corinna had done the night before.

Jovian mounted as well, and they began to ride slowly out of the courtyard. Maids scattered lavender before them, and the chanting commenced. *"Come to us, O Harvest Maiden. Protect us from the Lavender Lady. Come to us, O Harvest Maiden . . ."*

As the two riders passed beneath the gatehouse, Anthea saw Huw Gadarn waiting outside on his cob. He took up a respectful position behind them, and as Anthea glanced around at him, he gave her an enormous wink. Heartened, she was able to respond with a little smile. She would carry this off successfully. She *would!*

Twenty-seven

*F*ollowed by Huw, Jovian and Anthea rode along the drive toward the lodge. People stood in the churchyard, where the long grass waved in the breeze, and she heard them joining in the chanting. More onlookers waited on the little cottage-edged green by the bend in the road and from place to place along the way up into the town. Lavender was frequently strewn before the horses, and when crushed by the hooves, it released its invigorating scent into the warm air of the early evening.

As the horses reached the town, Anthea was startled to see what appeared to be every man, woman, and child lining the way. The hooves echoed between the buildings of the High Street, and the chanting was loud, monotonous, and very daunting to Anthea as she looked straight ahead, pretending that the Lavender Lady—Demeter—cared nothing for their prayers.

Jovian was ready as always to bolster her confidence. *"You're doing famously, my darling, and I agree with one thing Lethe said, for you are indeed the most beautiful Lavender Lady."*

"I don't feel beautiful. This is all too horrible to warrant such an adjective," she replied silently.

"But if all goes well for us, my darling, you will also be the very last Lavender Lady."

"I take comfort from that." She gave him a quick smile.

Obed Dennis stood, arms folded, outside the Cross Foxes, his lips moving as he too chanted. Anthea could not help a glance at him, and her dislike hardened as she saw the cold light in his eyes. Intuition told her that the innkeeper was as dangerous as Sir Erebus himself and might prove a stumbling block to their ultimate success.

"He will not stop us, my darling," Jovian said reassuringly, but she could not share his confidence.

If Anthea hoped to leave the crowds behind as they rode out of Cathness into the surrounding lanes, she was gravely disappointed, for the chanting populace followed. They progressed for mile after mile, passing farms and tiny hamlets, where more and more people joined the great concourse. Evening shadows were beginning to lengthen, and the sky was turning to gold as at last Anthea recognized ahead the harvested field where the neck of wheat stood in readiness for the following night's rituals. The morrismen were waiting, and the crowd's chanting stopped as the pipe and tabor music began. The morris bells jingled sweetly, the staves clacked together in perfect rhythm, but Anthea would never again be able to enjoy England's traditional and much loved dance.

Sir Erebus had led Corinna around the neck of wheat the night before, and now Jovian helped Anthea down from the palfrey to do the same. Their shadows fell darkly across the stubble, and the rays of the setting sun were dazzling as suddenly a brightly-skirted hobbyhorse cavorted out of the gathering. Jaws snapping loudly, ribbons and streamers fluttering, it leapt and danced toward Anthea as if to attack. She flinched fearfully, but Jovian steadied her. *"Remember it is only a pretense at driving you away from the crops. Show no fear."*

Show no fear? Such advice was more easily issued than achieved, for there was something very intimidating indeed about such a primitive, almost savage figure. To her relief, the hobbyhorse withdrew again, but then Obed Dennis and some of the men from the Cross Foxes brought the wicker cage. It was exactly as it had appeared in the engraving and looked too sturdy for comfort as they placed it on the stubble in front of her.

The innkeeper faced her and shouted for all to hear. *"Threaten our rites at your peril, O Demeter, O Lavender Lady, for we will capture you and deny you your victory."*

At this she took an anticipated step backward, as if daunted, and a great cheer went up around the field. She then turned away completely, and Jovian conducted her back to the palfrey and lifted her gently on to the saddle. Now came her vocal response, just three defiant words. "I will return!"

She was greeted with booing and general derision, but she did not care, because at last Jovian was leading her out of the field again, and this time Huw was the only one to follow. They rode back to the castle by way of the lavender field, which was very strongly scented in the evening air. The sinking sun enriched the color of the flowers, and a tingle ran through Anthea as she thought of tomorrow night, when she would walk through the bushes to the rites. She glanced up and saw that the first isolated stars had begun to twinkle in the deepening azure sky, although there was as yet no moon.

Jovian quoted a line from a poem. *"Before the starry threshold of Jove's court / My mansion is . . ."* She looked at the castle, which tonight could really make her think of Jove's court; then she looked around at Jovian, wondering about the quotation. He explained, "Milton's *Comus,* 1634."

A roll of thunder rumbled across the starry sky, and a second later there came a rustling in the lavender as the hare bounded past them and disappeared toward the castle. Huw gave a snort of disgust. *"Diawl!"* he breathed in Welsh.

"A devil indeed," Jovian observed.

"Lethe's imp is always on the prowl," Huw muttered. "Doesn't she *ever* let him down?"

"She will tomorrow night," Jovian replied.

Huw laughed. "So she will, for if luck is on the side of

right, the full moon will find both witch and dog hoist with
their own drug-laced petard!"

Anthea knew what he meant, because the myth of Aeneas
told that he had been able to pass the dog Cerberus by dis-
abling him with drugged honey cakes. Jovian was certain that
not only could Sebbriz be similarly eliminated, but Abigail
Wheatley too.

They rode on out of the lavender field and through the
Scotch pines toward the castle, which stood out more and
more against the setting sun as the minutes passed. They followed the ha-ha toward the drive, where Anthea suddenly
reined in.

"What is it?" Jovian asked.

"I — don't know. I just feel I must walk in the churchyard."

"Well, I see no reason why not." He led the way out into
the lane to the lych-gate, where he dismounted and helped
Anthea down as well. They left Huw with the horses as they
passed through the lych-gate and up the steps to the raised
churchyard. A light breeze rustled the trees, and her heavy
skirts brushed behind her as they left the stone path to walk
through the long waving grass.

Anthea really had no idea why she felt compelled to walk
here, but the feeling was so strong that it could not be denied.
She wished she and Jovian could hold each other properly, for
she needed the comfort of his arms around her, but eyes were
watching, brown eyes set beneath long brown ears. . . .

The sound of an approaching vehicle drifted toward them,
and Sir Erebus's black traveling carriage came into view from
the direction of the town. As it turned the corner by the church
and swept past Huw and the horses, Anthea saw that the
blinds were lowered, except — the corner of one was raised
suddenly, and a pale little face framed by golden curls peeped
out. It was Corinna.

Forgetting everything, Anthea caught up her flowery skirts
and ran through the grass toward the drop of the churchyard
wall. Corinna's eyes met hers without any sign of recognition;

then the blind was lowered again, and the carriage drove smartly on into the maze of country lanes where the horizon was beginning to be streaked blue by the rising moon.

Jovian's voice was urgent in her head. *"That was foolish! Abigail is watching and will now be suspicious!"*

Anthea was dismayed and sought some way of undoing the damage. She found inspiration, or at least what she hoped was inspiration. "You will never guess, Jovian, but I could have *sworn* that was my stepsister! How very silly of me, for I know she is in London with her aunt."

Jovian smiled at such quick thinking. "I s-suppose the lady in the c-carriage was indeed similar," he said, satisfied that Abigail would not only hear but accept the explanation at face value. Then he added silently, *"Corinna is safe as yet, I promise."*

Anthea returned to him and whispered, "She didn't even recognize me, Jovian."

"Lethe is the River of Forgetfulness," he reminded her gently. "Be strong, my darling, for she needs you."

"Well, at least I know why I felt I had to come here. Perhaps my bond with her is even stronger than I thought." She looked curiously at him. "She is only related to me through marriage, yet you and she share a father. You haven't said how that makes you feel."

He hesitated. "To be truthful, I do not know how I feel. At the moment, I think of her as a maiden in distress for whom I must be St. George. When she is safe again, and this is behind us all, then maybe my feelings toward her will clarify into something more—something warm and brotherly, I suppose. . . . It is a very strange feeling to discover so late in life that one has a blood sibling." He smiled at her. "I do not suppose you found it easy to accept you suddenly had a stepsister."

"It was a great shock," Anthea admitted, "but now I love her very much. As I am sure you will, too, when you know her properly."

There was a furtive movement in the long grass nearby, and a glimpse of long eavesdropping brown ears, so Jovian drew Anthea's hand quickly over his arm. "Well," he said briskly, "ye g-gods, I think I am becoming almost s-sober. Enough of this f-fresh air, let's—*hic*—to the nearest decanter."

He conducted her back to the horses, and soon they had returned to the castle, where Abigail Wheatley waited in the great hall. "Good evening, your grace, my lady." Her voice was cool, low, and mellifluous, and she was coolly elegant in a long-sleeved, nut brown gown, with a cream shawl over her arms and diamonds in her ears. It was hard to credit that a few moments ago she had been a hare in the long churchyard grass, though it was very tempting to imagine she had a white scut beneath her skirts.

"I trust you enjoyed your ride, my lady," Abigail said then, making the inquiry sound as if she hoped to learn of a very nasty fall.

"It was . . . memorable," Anthea answered, matching tone for tone. "Where is Lady Letitia?"

Abigail's gaze rested on the locket around Anthea's neck. "Still asleep, my lady . . . as no doubt you will be shortly, too."

It was an impertinent reply, and one to which Jovian responded. "Madam, it is not f-for you to comment upon what Lady Anthea will or will not d-do."

Even when aping the drunkard, Jovian was every inch the duke and master, and Abigail almost recoiled but managed to overcome any display of weakness. "As you wish, your grace," she replied levelly and held his gaze in a most brazen way. "Do you wish dinner to be served?" she inquired then.

Dinner? Anthea had no appetite, yet she knew she must eat something if she were to remain equal to tomorrow's tasks. Jovian read her mind. "We would both like a light meal in our separate suites," he said, for once forgetting to sound influenced by alcohol.

The woman's clever eyes rested thoughtfully upon him. "As you wish, your grace," she murmured, and walked away.

Jovian escorted Anthea up to her suite, and paused at the door. "Abigail was not jesting about sleep, for there will be something in your supper to bring that about. If it is kykeon, then you may eat and drink without fear, but if there is red wine, then you must only eat, I fear," he whispered, glancing back into the passage to see if anyone was there, but it seemed deserted.

"Sleep again? But I didn't get up until this afternoon. And must I really wear this disgusting locket?"

"I fear so, for to remove it will certainly arouse suspicion. Bear with it, my darling, and discard it with pleasure when the time comes."

"Then I can throw it away as I walk through the lavender field?"

"Quite so." He took the stolen mistletoe sprig from his coat, Huw having slipped it to him earlier. "Keep this safe now, and remember to hide it in your gown bodice tomorrow night. Only with the golden bough will you be able to successfully breach the hold Lethe has upon Corinna. Put it somewhere secure now, for it will not do for it to be found before we can use it."

"I will."

"And take this too." He produced a small vial of laudanum. "You know what to do with it?"

"Add it to the honey cakes."

"Yes." He smiled and glanced around to see if anyone was there, then risked taking Anthea in his arms to kiss her passionately on the lips. A moment later he had gone to his own apartment.

The supper that was brought to Anthea consisted of a cold chicken salad and, thankfully, a jug of kykeon, so she was able to eat and drink what she needed. She had not expected to have any appetite, even though she had eaten very little all day, but to her surprise she was quite hungry. To her further surprise, she felt very tired afterward, perhaps because of all the stress and strain of the past hours. Whatever the reason, she fell asleep quite quickly and enjoyed a restorative slumber filled with gentle dreams of pleasing things. She would awaken in the morning feeling refreshed and well able to find the courage to face what was to come.

Outside the blue moon sailed its course across the night sky. When next it appeared, the time would have come.

Twenty-eight

*T*he next morning was spent in fashionable idleness, talking in the library, strolling in the grounds, inspecting the gardens, and taking a leisurely luncheon in a summerhouse by a delightful lily pond. It was hard to appear so nonchalant and unconcerned, but it had to be done . . . and done well. As the hours ticked relentlessly away, Anthea's resolve faltered now and then, but Jovian's support was always to hand, his words of encouragement and love renewing her strength.

Late in the afternoon, the Lavender Lady made another progress through the lanes, this time culminating in a sham attempt by Obed Dennis to force her into the wicker cage. The crowds shouted encouragement to him and then aped great wrath when he was forced to let her go again. But her second escape was what the rites demanded, and it would only be on her third appearance that she would actually be shut in the cage. If all went as Sir Erebus intended, she would walk alone to the rites across the lavender field as the full moon rose and be taken as she approached the neck of wheat. On the other hand, if all went as Jovian planned, it would be Sir Erebus himself in the cage.

They returned to the castle as the evening's shadows grew long and the sky golden, but Jovian parted from her in the courtyard because he and Huw had matters to attend to. As far as any listening ears were concerned, the matters in question pertained to estate business, but in fact they concerned the plan to bring down Sir Erebus Lethe and his accursed rites.

Anthea entered the castle alone to prepare for her final and most important appearance as the Lavender Lady. She found Abigail waiting in the great hall, where candles were being lit.

"Good evening, my lady," the woman said, although through gritted teeth, Anthea thought.

"Good evening. I wish some honey cakes to be brought to my rooms directly."

"Honey cakes, my lady?" Abigail looked surprised, to say the least.

"Yes, the ones of which the duke tells me he is so fond. I understand he requested some to be baked today?"

"I . . . believe so, my lady."

"Don't you know?" Anthea looked inquiringly. "You *are* aware of the cakes I'm referring to, aren't you?"

Abigail recovered. "Yes, my lady, and if His Grace requested them, then they will have been prepared."

"Good. He wishes them to be taken to his rooms directly, and I would like some as well."

"Yes, my lady."

"And some kykeon, if you please," Anthea prompted.

"My lady."

"Now, if you please."

"My lady." Pure loathing shaded Abigail's brown eyes as she inclined her head, then walked away to attend to the honey cakes. The swish of her brown gown made the candles flicker.

Anthea gazed after her and murmured, "Believe me, my dear, you are more than welcome to Sir Erebus Lethe."

Cynthia was waiting in the King Hal suite and immediately began to attend Anthea. A warm bath scented with a little lavender oil had been prepared, and as soon as Anthea had undressed, another maid took the gown of flowers away to be refreshed in readiness for the evening ceremony. A little later, her dark hair tumbling loose about the shoulders of her robe, Anthea sat on a window seat to enjoy the cakes and kykeon Abigail brought. She was careful to show approval of the honeyed delicacies, which she declared to be the most exceptional she had ever tasted.

Outside it was now getting quite dark. The sunset was fading, and the fiery shades had turned to deep azure. Occasionally she heard music drifting from the green by the church, and the jingle of bells as morrismen danced. Once, much nearer, maybe even down in the torchlit courtyard, she heard a girl singing "Lavender Blue." The atmosphere was so intense that the air seemed to crackle with danger and suppressed excitement. She was conscious of the last sands of the great nineteen-year cycle draining away. Soon the full moon would rise. Anthea gazed past the old gatehouse at the shadowy, suddenly mysterious park. *Please* let them rescue poor Corinna and consign Sir Erebus Lethe to perdition!

Abigail remained in the suite to make certain Cynthia understood the important details that must not be overlooked if everything were to proceed smoothly. Certain herbs had to be applied to Anthea's forehead, the locket must be worn in an exact position around her neck, and her hair had to be brushed a set number of times, then combed very precisely. Lastly, the coronet of fresh lavender had to be placed on the Lady's head at the proper time, neither too soon nor too late. The rules had been laid down over the centuries, and nothing must be overlooked or changed.

Anthea appeared to be preoccupied with the honey cakes and kykeon while all this was being discussed, but in fact she was waiting for an opportune moment to empty the contents of the laudanum vial over the cakes she had not eaten. She pretended not to be taking any notice of what was going on around her, but the moment Abigail and Cynthia were diverted by the return of the other maid with the gown of flowers, she applied the laudanum. No one saw, and the trap was set.

With a satisfied sigh, Anthea licked her fingers and got up from the window seat. "Those cakes are absolutely exquisite," she declared, as she washed her hands in a silver bowl of aromatic water. "Why don't you finish them?" she said to the three others in the room.

Abigail hesitated, but then went to take one. Cynthia and the other maid followed her example, and Anthea took great pleasure in watching them eat every last crumb. They began to dress her but were soon stifling yawns. They all succumbed to sleep at the same time. Abigail had just put the last touch to the Lavender Lady's hair when she sank to the floor, and Anthea was intrigued to note that the laudanum appeared to have had an unfortunate side effect. The woman's ears grew long and brown, and two long buckteeth protruded over her lower lip; it was almost certain that she now had a scut as well, but Anthea had no intention of looking to see. The two maids collapsed into chairs, arms dangling, mouths open.

Anthea was relieved that the stratagem had worked well and prayed that Jovian's similar sleight of hand with Sebbriz had been as successful.

"It has indeed, my darling, for the old dog now snores fit to raise the castle roof. But take no chances with your three graces. Tie them up with ribbons, and put handkerchiefs in their mouths. That will keep them completely out of mischief until it is all over and done with."

Over and done with? Oh, *please* let that be the outcome.

"It will, sweeting, it will."

Following his advice about the ribbons and handkerchiefs, Anthea soon made certain her three victims would not be able to move or raise the alarm if they awakened. Then, looking as the Lavender Lady should, but with the sprig of mistletoe pushed into the tight bodice of her gown, she left her suite.

Before going down to the great hall, where Jovian would now be waiting for her, she went first to Lady Letitia's rooms.

Her aunt was sleeping comfortably, a faint smile of content-
ment on her lips. Reassured, Anthea withdrew again and then
went down to Jovian. There were servants in attendance in the
great hall, but they were now as Anthea had never seen them
before, wearing masks and antlers, animal skins, and primitive costumes. Such things she had seen at May Day festivities, when all had been lighthearted and enjoyable; like this,
they were frightening.

Her mouth had gone dry as she embarked upon the brief
conversation she and Jovian had practiced during their night
of conspiracy. "Where is Sebbriz, Jovian? I thought he would
be here to be sure we left on time."

"Oh, he h-had things to do—*hic*—so I told him I would
not need him again t-tonight."

"What a coincidence," Anthea replied, "for I have just said
the selfsame thing to Abigail, and I told the maids their duties
were at an end for today as well. They worked so hard to prepare me and dress my hair that I thought it was the least I
could do."

"My—*hic*—thoughts exactly." *"Have you remembered the
mistletoe?"*

She nodded, and he offered her his arm to go out into the
torchlit courtyard, where the remaining servants waited, all
garbed like those in the great hall. As soon as the Lavender
Lady appeared, the courtyard erupted into shouts, whistles,
and animal noises, and the servants streamed out of the castle
to run noisily across the park toward the Scotch pines.

Anthea's heart pounded as Jovian conducted her beneath
the gatehouse and along the drive to the ha-ha. The servants'
racket could now be heard from the lavender field and was
suddenly joined by a great roar from the wheat field, where
the people of Cathness had assembled.

"Courage, my darling," Jovian said quietly, as they followed the path that led to the pines.

"I'm so afraid that we may have overlooked something, a
tiny detail that will make all the difference."

"We haven't overlooked anything, and in a short while now we will be victorious."

Huw was waiting at the edge of the lavender field with two horses, having hidden in the trees until the castle servants had passed. The moon was about to peep above the horizon, and already there was a touch of blue across the far-off clouds of night. By now Anthea's heart was pounding so hard that she felt almost faint. Her skin felt cold, even though the night was warm, and she trembled visibly. She was painfully aware that Corinna's very life now depended upon her.

Jovian led her past the Scotch pines until they were halfway along the lavender field, then he drew her warmly into his arms, and kissed her passionately on the lips. "You can do it, my love, and Huw and I will be ready to do what is necessary."

"But if I fail . . ."

"You won't," he said firmly, taking her by the shoulders and looking urgently into her eyes. "You have all the strength that is needed, and you have my unending love. We are doing this together, Anthea, and as one we are invincible."

A timid smile crept to her lips. "Invincible?"

"Of course," he whispered, then drew her close to kiss her again. "Huw and I will be near you throughout, so do not be afraid. Soon it will all be over, and we will have Corinna safely with us again."

As the moon's rim appeared at last, the bell of Cathness parish church sounded once, to signal that the time was exactly twenty-five past ten. As the full moon's uncanny blue light began to slant over the countryside, Anthea heard a rustle of anticipation from the wheat field. Jovian kissed her forehead. "Go now, it is the moment to begin your walk," he said softly.

Almost in a dream, she turned and stepped into the lavender. The scent of the blooms filled her nostrils, and she was aware that she was not in contact with the ground as she walked slowly toward the scene of the rites. Her gown felt more and more like real flowers, cool and gentle against her legs as the train dragged behind her. This was the vision of herself that she had seen when first going to the castle. When she was halfway across the field, she ripped the locket from around her neck and tossed it away. It fell somewhere with a slight chinking sound, but she neither knew nor cared where. Almost immediately, she felt as if a great weight had been lifted and replaced by a new strength. She could do this; she really could!

The crowds in the wheat field waited expectantly as the moon's light fingered further and further above the horizon, the ghostly blue beams stretching until at last they touched the neck of wheat. A sigh went up, and almost immediately the slow clip-clop of hooves carried from along the lane. Two riders came into view, Hades and his Persephone.

Sir Erebus, unaware that things had begun to go very wrong, was again dressed in his black robes. He had no idea that Abigail, his eyes and—literally—ears, was tied up and insensible, as was his guard dog, Sebbriz. The fact that they had not come to him assured him that all was well as he led Corinna's palfrey. The Harvest Maiden was in her flowing white gown, her golden hair, so completely the opposite of Anthea's raven curls, cascaded loose over her shoulders, and she again carried the bunches of wheat and wildflowers.

Anthea reached the edge of the lane and halted to watch her lovely stepsister. "We'll save you, Corinna, I promise," she breathed.

As Persephone and her dark lord entered the suddenly silent field, Anthea stepped into the lane to approach the field entrance. Suddenly Obed Dennis barred her way. The burly innkeeper stood arms akimbo, and for a terrible moment, Anthea thought she had been found out, but then she remembered that he was *supposed* to be here like this, in order to succumb to Demeter's will. The only things that might go wrong at this point were that he might perceive that Jovian and Huw were following at a distance on their horses, or that she was not wearing the locket. She met his eyes squarely, challengingly almost, and after a moment he stepped aside and bowed low to let her pass. His heavy tread was just behind as he followed her into the wheat field. Further behind still, unheard but there all the same, were Jovian and Huw.

Twenty-nine

*T*he chanting commenced immediately as Anthea appeared in the field. *"Come to us, O Harvest Maiden. Protect us from the Lavender Lady. Come to us, O Harvest Maiden!"*

Everything was as it had been the evening before, with the crowd gathered respectfully around the neck of wheat, in front of which the Harvest Maiden now stood awaiting her destiny. The wicker cage was in readiness nearby, and the reapers were prepared, their polished sickles shining in the blue moonlight. This time the deadly blades would not be thrown to form a circle in the ground but would be hurled directly at Corinna.

Anthea walked steadily toward the dreadful scene, and with each step, it seemed the chanting grew louder. The blue moon was now almost completely above the horizon; the moment it was, the Harvest Maiden would be sacrificed. Obed Dennis now kept pace at the Lavender Lady's side, and Anthea bowed her head slightly so that her long dark hair cast a shadow where the locket should have been. The crowd parted for her to reach the edge of the inner circle, and as she did so, Obed Dennis suddenly outpaced her and again stood to bar her way.

A ringing silence ensued, as everyone expected her to submit to capture and imprisonment in the cage. Instead she walked around the startled innkeeper and continued toward

Corinna. For a moment no one seemed to realize what was happening. They thought it was a misunderstanding, that she had not been properly prepared. Sir Erebus realized nothing, for he was too intent upon Corinna, fearing some last minute awareness that might prompt her to run for her life.

Using his preoccupation, Anthea quickened her pace toward her stepsister, just as Obed recovered from his confusion and raised the alarm. Anthea caught up her flowing skirts to run the final yards to Corinna; then she halted triumphantly and took the mistletoe from her bodice, holding it up for everyone to see.

There were horrified cries, and she was aware of the crowd falling back slightly, as if merely being close to golden bough that had obviously been stolen was anathema to them all. She was later to discover that it was the moment when most people began to realize they had been taken in by Sir Erebus's silken words and persuasive practices.

Sir Erebus froze where he was, but his eyes flashed angrily. "Hand that to me," he breathed, but she shook her head.

"Oh, no, for while I have the golden bough, and while I stand here, Persephone is safe from Hades. If Demeter is present the neck cannot be cut, and while it stands, Persephone cannot be taken. That is how it must be, Sir Erebus, and nothing you say or do can change that. And do not think that your disgusting rites can proceed in any case, for I am not wearing the locket. Without it around her neck, Persephone cannot be sacrificed."

Her voice carried to the watching crowd, arousing a stir of whispers. A nerve twitched at Sir Erebus's temple, and he glanced sharply around, evidently wondering why the faithful Abigail had not warned him something was wrong.

Anthea smiled. "You look in vain for your monstrous hare, Sir Erebus, for she has unwittingly taken laudanum—a dose of her own medicine, I fancy. The same goes for Sebbriz, who has taken the same sop. How little you really know your Greek myths, for they were far more vulnerable than you realized." This last was said for the benefit of the onlookers, and it did not fall upon stony ground.

Sir Erebus's thin lips curled with bitter fury. "I should have guessed that Chavanage was deceiving me!"

Jovian himself answered as he and Huw rode into the circle, pistols drawn and ready. "Yes, you should indeed, Lethe," he shouted, and the uneasy crowd fell back still more. Anthea saw that some people were already beginning to skulk away, but unfortunately the reapers were not among them. The sickles were still ready and waiting. Corinna had not moved, and she gazed ahead without knowing or seeing anything around her.

Sir Erebus looked at the full orb of the moon as it floated clear of the horizon to sail among the first stars. Anthea could see how his mind raced, and her breath caught as he whirled about to the reapers. "Kill the Harvest Maiden!" he cried. "Kill her now!"

"No!" Anthea screamed, and ran to stand in front of her stepsister. But the reapers were too far under Sir Erebus's control to disobey him, and one by one they threw their deadly sickles.

Jovian fixed his gaze upon each one, and his face twisted with effort as he pitted his gifts against the flying weapons. One by one he halted their flight so they fell harmlessly to the stubble at Corinna's feet. As the last sickle fell to the ground, something quite wonderful happened. The moon ceased to be blue and instead cast its true silvery glow once more. Gasps arose from the crowd of onlookers, the vast majority of whom still remained.

Huw grinned and drew his pistol, then waggled it at Sir Erebus. "Come on, *tomen dali*, to the cage with you," he commanded.

Before Anthea could even wonder what the Welsh words meant, Jovian explained aloud. "That means dung heap."

"How very suitable," she replied, then went in consternation to embrace Corinna, who still remained in a trance.

Sir Erebus had no intention of bowing to a gardener's command, even a gardener with a loaded pistol, but as Jovian fired a single shot that raised dust from the ground within an inch of his ungodly feet, Hades hastened to obey. His abominable rule over Cathness was at an end.

Huw took great delight in ordering Obed Dennis to lock the cage. As it happened, it was a mistake not to force the innkeeper into captivity as well, for it was an error of judgment they would later regret.

Now, however, Jovian stood in his stirrups to look around at the great crowd of local people. "Behold, an honest moon above and Sir Erebus Lethe in all his ridiculousness below. What price now his promises and lies? Go back to your homes, for you will see no sacrifice tonight or any other night. Our harvests do not need blood to ensure their bounty; they just need hard work and good weather, both of which Cathness can provide in plenty."

For a moment no one moved, but then the exodus began, everyone deeply ashamed that they had taken part in such savage and primitive rituals. As Obed Dennis left with them, he did not share their shame, for he had as little conscience as Sir Erebus and meant to help his defeated master all he could.

Within minutes the field was empty, leaving only Anthea, Corinna, Jovian, and Huw. And Sir Erebus, of course, although within moments Huw had tied the cage to his horse and ridden away with it bumping and bouncing behind him. He was taking Hades to a dungeon beneath the castle, there to await arrest by men from the nearest army barracks.

Corinna remained in a trance until Jovian gave her some rosemary he had picked earlier in the castle's kitchen garden, together with some lavender flowers he had taken as Anthea left his arms to commence her walk to the field. At last Persephone was liberated from Hades' influence, and she stared around in consternation as she found herself in a moonlit field. For a moment she was frightened, but then she saw Anthea. "Anthea! Where are we? What's happened? I remember being lost in the lane trying to find my aunt's house, but then . . ."

Anthea hugged her tightly. "It's a very long story, Corinna, and I will tell you when we reach the castle."

"The castle?" Then Corinna noticed Jovian. "Your grace?"

He smiled. "Jovian will do, for after all this I feel I know you well enough to dispense with the formality of Miss Pranton." His glance caught Anthea's, then he added, "In fact I am bound to know you much better before long, for we are more closely associated than you know."

"We are?" Corinna looked puzzled. "What do you mean?"

"We are half brother and sister," he replied.

Corinna's green eyes became very round. "We . . . are?" Her gaze flew to Anthea for confirmation. "Is it really so?"

"Yes. You do not have an aunt called Abigail Wheatley, but you do have a brother called Jovian, who is surely the finest, most perfect man in all the world." Anthea smiled at Jovian.

They returned to the castle, Corinna on her palfrey and Anthea riding before Jovian. Many lights were on at the castle, and the servants waiting uneasily in the great hall, unsure what would happen to them now the rites had been halted and exposed as false. Abigail Wheatley had escaped, having awoken and been able to turn herself into a hare in order to slip free of the ribbons with which Anthea had bound her. After releasing Sebbriz, she had escaped in her four-legged form and disappearing into the countryside, never to be seen in Cathness again. Sebbriz also decided it was wise to leave and slipped out of the castle kitchens while everyone else nervously awaited Jovian's return.

Although they probably did not deserve his generosity, Jovian was prepared to let his staff keep their positions. He promised to forgive and forget, provided they were completely loyal to him in the future—and provided there was no more dabbling in dark things of any nature. If someone was to whisper so much as a charm to get rid of warts, he would know and dismissal would be instant. Everyone, including Cynthia and Phoebe, swore to abide by his terms.

It was as he finished addressing the servants that Lady Letitia came sleepily down the grand staircase. She paused in delight on seeing Corinna, all false thoughts of her having remained in London now vanished. "My dear, you've been found!" she cried, and hastened to hug her. Then she drew back and surveyed the white robe and wheat crown. "Hmm. Well, I do not know that I care to discover what has been going on, but if you will just assure me that you are safe and well?"

Corinna laughed. "Oh, yes, Lady Letitia! I most certainly am."

"Call me Aunt Letty, my dear, for your disappearance made me realize how very much part of the family you have become.

"What happened in the lane?" Lady Letitia asked then. "One moment you were there, the next you had vanished."

"To be honest, Lady—I mean, Aunt Letty—I don't know what happened to me. I was by the oak tree, feeling terribly ill, then suddenly I was dressed like this and standing in the middle of a moonlit wheat field."

Jovian took charge of the conversation. "Anthea and I will explain everything, but I think we will be more comfortable in the library." He turned to a footman hovering nervously nearby. "Some Turkish coffee, if you please, and if I detect so much as a *sniff* of that damned pomegranate juice, I will separate your head from the rest of you. Do I make myself clear?"

"Yes, your grace." The man scurried away as if wildfire lit his coattails.

Explanations went on into the small hours as they all sat in the library, and Lady Letitia and Corinna became more and more astonished as the amazing tale unfolded. No one in the castle was aware of it when Obed Dennis entered the castle and released Sir Erebus from the dungeon. Under cover of darkness — and the black traveling carriage — Hades and the innkeeper drove away from Cathness and escaped the dire punishment to which the law would otherwise have sentenced them. The escapes were discovered soon enough, but without Abigail or Cerberus either, Jovian realized there was little point in sending for the army. Everyone in Cathness had been drawn into Sir Erebus's web, so the army would have had to arrest every man, woman, and child, which was hardly sensible. Better to leave things to calm down, Jovian decided, and Anthea, Lady Letitia, and Corinna were in full agreement.

Sebbriz had seen to it that the unfortunate coachman, Longton, had been locked up in a stable since arriving at the castle, so the latter did not think much of Cathness Castle at all. In fact, he was impatient when Lady Letitia and Corinna delayed their return to London by several weeks. Lady Letitia had resumed her great affair with Huw, and they planned to leave the country so they could be together without anyone questioning their vastly differing backgrounds. However, Lady Letitia was certain of one thing: wherever they went, it would *not* be the Amazon!

On the two ladies' arrival back in Berkeley Square, the first person to call was none other than Viscount Heversham, who was agreeably surprised by the delight with which Corinna received him. Lady Letitia was soon busy with her matchmaking again, and her industry paid dividends.

There was no need for matchmaking between Anthea and Jovian, because it was on their account that Lady Letitia and Corinna had delayed their departure from Cathness. One warm and sunny day in late September, with the local population once again gathered to watch, the Duke of Chavanage and Lady Anthea Chloe Wintour became husband and wife in the beautiful parish church. What should have been a grand Society wedding in St. George's, Hanover Square, or in the Mayfair house, was instead a country affair at which the only people of consequence, apart from the bride and groom, were Lady Letitia and Corinna.

It was a beautiful wedding, one which the Earl of Daneway would always wish he had been in England to see. The local people were very happy for their duke and his new duchess. The recent past might never have been, and all trace of Sir Erebus Lethe had been removed from the landscape, even Wycke Hall, which was pulled down brick by brick.

On their wedding night in the bed once occupied by Henry VIII and Anne Boleyn, Anthea and Jovian lay in each other's arms watching the moon. It was a very ordinary moon, not even full, but it was very lovely. Anthea snuggled more deeply against her adored new husband. "I think that if I ever, *ever* hear that song again . . ."

"What song?"

"*Lavender Blue.*"

"Ah," he breathed, and kissed her neck, where her dark hair was warm and sensuous.

She closed her eyes and shivered deliciously. "If I ever hear it again, I shall be very uneasy indeed."

He raised his head from kissing her. "Why?"

"Because it was when that wretched ditty suddenly came into my head from nowhere that it all began for me."

"It's only an old song," he whispered, and leaned over her. "It occurs to me that there is another old tradition that I must attend to if all is to be well."

"Old tradition?" She looked up at him.

He smiled. "That of making absolutely certain, beyond all shadow of doubt, that this marriage is properly consummated."

"But we have already—twice."

"I know, I know," he replied teasingly, "but to be on the safe side . . ." He bent his lips to hers, and she slipped her arms eagerly around him again.

The moon sailed serenely against the stars as the Duke of Chavanage and his bride made passionate love again. A gen-

tle breeze whispered through the Scotch pines, and a faint
echo carried through the night.

> *Lavender blue, dilly, dilly,*
> *Lavender green.*
> *When I am king, dilly, dilly,*
> *You shall be queen. . . .*